RULE NUMBER THREE

RULE BREAKERS SERIES
BOOK 3

NICKY SHANKS

LIMITLESS PUBLISHING, LLC

Rule Number Three

Copyright © 2018 by Nicky Shanks.

All rights reserved.

First Print Edition: July 2018

Limitless Publishing, LLC

Kailua, HI 96734

www.limitlesspublishing.com

Formatting: Limitless Publishing

ISBN-13: 978-1-64034-405-1

ISBN-10: 1-64034-405-5

ONE
VERONICA

THE WORST THING about not having any family left isn't the emptiness you feel when holidays come and go without a second thought; it's not the look people give you when you get lost in a daydream while staring at *their* beautiful family as they eat at the table next to you in a diner. That always happens to me— anywhere I go where I see a mother with two sons, I instantly get sharp pains in the bottom of my stomach. I think about what could have been—how Oliver might have turned out if I chose to give everything up and stay with him.

But, *no*...the worst thing about not having a family is knowing that they couldn't care less about you.

In my perfect life daydreams, the older son would always taunt the younger son when the mother isn't looking. The boys aren't too far apart in age, maybe just a few years, but they both look so different that it always makes me sad each time I dream about it. I often wonder if anyone had ever found out—I ran away

1

when I started to show with Casey—but Colin would've said something if he'd known. Especially when I came crawling back after having Casey, or whenever I'd slump back onto his cold, rainy doorstep for more money to inject into my veins.

Or snort through my nose.

That's my life. *That's me.*

Cliché poor girl turned rich-girl drug addict.

But I was more than poor before Colin and I met at the Lake Reed Inn over twenty-six years ago. He whisked me away into an entirely new world full of opportunities, choices, and money. I just grew so very tired of having nothing, so when Colin handed me *something*, I took too much and took it too far. I know I screwed it up a little more each time I showed up in his life, but Mac just kept me feeling so damn good all the time that I kept finding it harder and harder to resist what he was offering me:

Freedom.

When I found out I was pregnant with Oliver, there was no doubt in my mind that I would stop doing whatever I wanted. I wanted to actually *try* to be a perfect mother—something my own mother tried her hardest to be too. In turn, I stressed out so much that my weakness to the freedom got the best of me, and to this day, *I swear*, I thought Oliver would have died the moment he came out of me.

I had nightmares about him coming out soaked in heroin and coughing up cocaine, but it was never enough to scare me straight. Despite my efforts to not have him at all, he came out screaming and just addicted to drugs a *little*. The first few weeks were pretty scary, though—I honestly thought he wasn't going to make it. Of course, I *wanted* him to make it—that wasn't even a question—but I knew it was going to be my fault if he didn't. Once Colin took over and showered him with love and his ability to make everything feel painless and like it would all be okay, Oliver started to recover and get stronger.

Strong and handsome like his father.

He looks almost *exactly* like Colin. I think about that as I close my eyes in the front seat of the van where Mac parked down the road from the bar where we spied on them. The van is hidden by some thick brush and trees, but I still had a perfect view of the place where people all gathered like moths for the aftermath of Oliver and Casey's bar brawl. The darkness surrounds me like it always does, tight and suffocating. I take a few hits of a cigarette that Mac has left in the ashtray, trying to calm myself enough to go through with our plan.

I'm going to kidnap my son's girlfriend.

I keep repeating it over and over in my mind. The chill that makes me shiver isn't from the outside air—it comes from a dark place deep inside of me that wonders if I'm going too far. Mac—the man who helped me destroy everything good I ever had—snores next to me, jolting me back to the present and my decision. It's gonna have to happen if Oliver won't give me any money; his father, grandfather, and I all had an understanding. It's too bad they both died before they could fill him in on it, but that isn't my concern.

I do wonder what I would've said differently to my son in the hospital a little while ago if I'd been a different person, though.

3

Would I have cared more about his injuries?

Would I have cried?

A different me would've been fucking worried to the point where my nails were bitten down and my eyes were red and puffy from crying. I would cry with Colin and we would tend to his bedside like worry-wart parents. That's what a damn-near-perfect mother would do.

But that ain't me.

I was never meant for something like that.

I'm a shitty mother…No, I'm just a shitty person all around.

So, for now, I'll pretend our conversation went in a different direction. In my perfect-life daydream, I'd go out to lunch and get my nails done with my son's girl-friend. I wouldn't have to slink around town and offer favors to people to find out her full name, either.

Julie Remington.

Perfect little blonde girl with her porcelain skin and rosy cheeks is going to steal my money from me. Once she gets her hooks all the way into him, I *know* I won't see another dime. My anger flares again but I keep my eyes closed, breathing steadily and imagining my perfect life again, this time *without* Julie in it; both of my sons are together again instead. I knew Colin hadn't told Oliver about his half-brother because my ex hadn't even known himself, and that's the way I'd wanted it. Mac and I skipped town for four months after I started to show with Casey and didn't even bother going to a hospital once I began labor.

After we dropped the baby off on a fire station's front doorstep and ran, Mac and I promised each other we would never speak of it again, and we haven't.

Until now.

"That's gotta be him, Mac." I sigh, and Mac stops snoring. He groans and kicks the dashboard as hard as he can to get me to shut up. He doesn't care, and *I* don't care that he doesn't care. "You *know* that's him—did you see his brown eyes and olive skin like yours, and his long nose like mine and those broad shoulders? That's *gotta* be him."

Mac hisses at me, half-asleep. "That little jerk-off ain't mine. I told you we ain't talking about this anymore, and I mean just that. Are you *trying* to piss me off?"

I ignore him and go back to my daydream where my two sons love and adore me because of how perfect I am. I wonder how they met and how they became friends—if they love each other like brothers would and care for each other now that Colin's gone. They both seemed to grow up with money and silver spoons, so at least I did something good for the both of them. I gave them a life of luxury instead of a life of them sleeping in bags in the back of Mac's van while watching him and me blow through money like it was endless. I won't have to endure my humiliation getting worse and worse year after year.

If I'm right and he *is* the one I dropped off so long ago, it's too odd of a coincidence that they ended up being best friends. Colin's father must've had something to do with this—he hated me with a thousand fires burning down under from the moment I left for good. I think about the way the boys look at Julie—her little sweet and innocent self completely unaware of the effect she has on men, which I have to say I like a little. She reminds me of my old self, the person I was before Mac got ahold of my insides and burned me up. Still, she has Oliver and Casey drooling all over the floor for her, and if she asked them to lick it up, I'm sure they wouldn't even hesitate.

I could use that to lure her in…try and expose a secret relationship that may or may not be there. My bones feel like stone; I don't even know what these kids are like or how to exploit them, but that isn't going to stop me from getting what I need.

Maybe she'll just go with me knowing that Oliver will pay.

The snoring fills the van so I flick my eyes open and step outside. The October air whips against my skin— my fragile and paper-thin skin—making it feel like it's on fire. I think about the photo I sent earlier to a few of Mac's friends. I managed to snap a picture of Julie and find out her name and all kinds of useful information about her. I know I still need more to make this entire thing come crashing down and get her out of the way… so the more they dug, the more they found.

I got her last address—some condo on the east side of Rockford, where her name is on the lease with someone else, Brandon Whitehouse. I rub my chin and breathe out, watching my breath disappear into the night air. They also found their marriage license, and I have a copy of that shit tucked into my back pocket for safe keeping. That's something Mac doesn't fucking know about, and the less he knows, the better. So, sweet little Princess Julie is already married and fucking my oldest son.

I have to pay this Brandon kid a visit and see what he can tell me about Julie before I make my next move. I have to be smart about this, though—I don't need or *want* any more jail time.

But Mac won't wake up now, so I have to wait until morning, and that pisses me off. He sure likes helping me snort and blow the money, but he doesn't want any part of helping me get it.

Maybe it's time to leave ol' Mac behind.

I wish I could.

I really *wish I could.*

TWO
OLIVER

LEMONADE.

That's all I can think about right now as I watch Julie's pale, milky white skin squirm, begging for me to touch her. She puts up a thick brick wall between us just to make me work harder for it. I don't care. This woman has twisted all my insides into knots—*miles and miles of endless knots*—that I would miss if they ever went away. I never, *ever* want to leave her side again.

She makes me feel alive.

She makes me think of lemonade.

Sugary and sweet with a twinge of tart if you do it right.

And she does it right.

Her sexy, pouty lips beckon me, calling out my name to come closer and attach myself to the flesh underneath her jeans. I love this woman more than anything I've ever loved in my entire fucking life; the hope that grows for us makes my heart beat every second of every damn day. I can't think of anything else to do to know for sure that she's mine other than ask her to marry me for real.

I shiver.

Do I *want* to even go there?

Her smile tugs at my heartstrings and my mouth opens before I can even think of what's going to spill from it.

"Marry me, Julie," I whisper into the air between us. Her body quivers at the feel of mine so near, and she knows she will give into me.

I can feel it.

"Julie?" I wait for her to answer me, letting myself have more time to look her over. My eyes rest on her thick lips again, but they don't give me any indication of what's going through her mind. I know she *wants* to say yes; she *wants* to be mine forever, but time is always the enemy to her. I can see the gears turning in her eyes, frantically searching for the way out. "Is something wrong?"

She shakes her head and my entire body melts onto the floor.

She's saying no.

I open my mouth to protest immediately after I start to panic in my head, but she holds up her palm to my chest and my skin burns even to her touch over my shirt. Her honey blonde hair smells like her familiar aroma of strawberries. I want to know what flavor her lips taste like today as I draw closer to her body and smell the mint on her breath from the gum she just finished chewing.

"Oliver—"

I shake my head violently. My dark hair falls into

my face, but I don't bother with it because I'm so focused on her and her deep blue eyes. "Don't think. Just answer."

"We've only known each other a few—"

I let a growl escape my throat. I don't mean to, but she's always letting time get stuck in her mind. This isn't a game to me…I want her by my side, and if putting a ring on her finger prevents her from leaving me again, then so be it. I know how to appeal to the woman I want to wake up to for the rest of my life. "We can have a long engagement. I know you're scared about everything that's happened around us and between us. We don't have to get married right away, Julie."

"Yes," she whispers, looking surprised at her own words. My eyes widen—even *I* find myself surprised at her answer, but I'm not going to ask her if she's sure and let her dwell on it.

"You mean…you said yes, right?" My mouth is dry and I blink a few times, hoping that I'm not seeing or hearing things that could make me look like a fool. "Like, as in you'll marry me…*yes*?"

Julie giggles and bites her index fingernail. "Yes, I'll marry you."

The world explodes around me—it's better than anything I've ever felt in my entire life, including any intimate moment I've ever shared with Julie besides this one right now. I pull her against my chest and attempt to pick her up, managing to hold her in the air for a few minutes before she starts scolding me to put her down and rest my knee.

"I don't care about my knee…are you serious?"

There's wonder and amazement in my voice, and her eyebrows rise with intrigue. "Julie, I literally don't care about anything else in this entire fucking universe right now except for you—you get that, right?" My mouth devours hers and I know I have to part from her or else I won't be able to stop, and it's too soon to try and get her to let me break my promise.

Now she's laughing at me. Okay, I can handle that. "Come on, let's celebrate," she says.

"I have to let Harley know you said yes. Let's call him," I say. Her face turns a little green as I stand up and steady myself, wincing in pain. She tends to me, but I can feel her reluctance to call and tell him the good news. I want the whole fucking world to know that Julie is mine and no one is going to take her away from me this time. "Maybe he'll tell Casey and I won't have to."

"I thought you didn't care about Casey anymore." She frowns, and I don't like the way it makes me feel. "Have you forgotten what a lost cause he just turned out to be?"

I take the image of her frowning and tuck it in the back of my mind; I don't like upsetting her. Casey and I are best friends—and apparently brothers—but I can't turn my back on her over something like this.

He tried to steal the love of your life.

Then he punched her in the eye…okay, on accident, but still.

I look at Julie's bruised eye—it's turning different shades of green and black and my stomach sinks so far down in my abdomen that it might never feel whole again. She hasn't spoken about the incident for a few days, and I'm okay with that. I don't want to be reminded that my best friend cold-cocked my girl-friend, either.

Oh, and not to mention his little *crush* on her.

I put my arm around her and she snuggles into my body. I like tucking her underneath my arms; she fits perfectly next to me like a puzzle piece. I smell the new lilac perfume she's using and the scent wafts around my nose, driving me wild.

"Did Casey know you were asking me to marry you before all of this?" Her fingers move around in a small circle in front of us. "Is *that* why you aren't speaking?"

"No, it's just because of what he told me about my —*our*—mother." I narrow my eyes. "Do you know how Casey feels about you? I want to rub it in his face that you're going to be Mrs. Oliver Jackson."

She doesn't want to say yes.

But I know her better than that.

It's nearly midnight and we sit on the edge of my bed in our apartment. I know she has no clue what she does to men, but something's not right here. I want to pull her down into this bed with me and I don't give a shit what that doctor said about it. It's a risk I'm more than willing to take, but something's bothering her…I can feel it. I try not to draw attention to the negative as she sighs and loops her arms around my neck. The way she gazes deep into my soul is terrifying…and completely unraveling.

"I wonder if Lucy is okay after all of that earlier." Julie's voice is small. "She can't be thrilled that her new boyfriend was brawling outside of a bar like that."

Shit. I forgot about Lucy.

Julie will *never* marry me if she finds out I brought Lucy home with me—even if I didn't sleep with her.

Her honey blonde hair tickles my nose as I turn and pull her tighter against me. "To be honest, I couldn't care less about her or Casey right now. I'm not going to dwell on the fact that he's a dick, and I'm sure as hell not going to sit here and pretend that he's my real brother. You can spank me later for it if you want." I wink and she slaps my shoulder playfully; her smile matches mine and it makes my heart melt.

My mind wanders and I think about her in the kitchen, wearing nothing but an apron.

This "not having sex" thing isn't going to work for me. She smells so fucking good…I have to violently shake my head to bring myself back to reality.

I don't care about anything but her.

My Julie.

I remember the naïve Julie who I could hardly be within a few feet of. The Julie that had absolutely no idea what she was doing to my insides.

What she *still* does to me.

She takes my fucking breath away.

She smiles and squeezes my leg as it brushes against her. I make sure when we're near each other that we're touching at all times. Since I woke up from my accident, all I can think about is how her skin feels against mine and how lucky I am to be able to touch her in the first place. Being with Julie makes life bearable again, and without her…well, what *else* is there to really live for?

"What are you going to do on Monday when my classes start?" Her long eyelashes look like strands of silk caressing the tops of her blushed cheeks. "I'd hate for you to sit in the apartment all alone while I'm at school all day…maybe you *should* make amends with Casey."

I snort. "What the hell for? You're right, he's a lost cause. He wants you and I'm not letting him within a hundred feet of this place."

Her fingers twist around my hair and it drives me fucking wild. "Oliver Frankford Jackson, you are frustrating and stubborn." I lick my lips and press them onto hers. My lust for her grows so fast inside of my sweatpants that I have to force myself to stop touching her.

Because the doctor is right…now my side hurts from the blood rushing down south.

My face heats instantly. "I can't wait to marry you, sunshine. I can't think of anything in life I want more than to see you walking down the aisle to me. It's going to be perfect—just like you." I kiss the tips of her fingers and see tears form in the corners of her eyes.

"Is this real?" Her whisper reaches my ears. "Sometimes this is all so crazy that I have to remind myself that it's not a dream."

I inhale deeply and pull her down onto the bed with me. As she snuggles into her space at my side, my chest is about to explode.

"Baby, you gotta believe me when I say this to you: You're *my* dream. I dreamed about you before I even knew you. You're everything I've wanted without even knowing I wanted it. That's why I want you to be my wife someday, Julie. You make me into a person I never even dreamed about being, and now that I know that person, I can't ever let you go."

It will always be her.

It feels like I've waited for her forever, like I've been just living life by a script until she burned it down to show me what real love can do to someone. Real love makes you weak; it strips you down until you surrender to it. It can be dark and emotional…and amazing and beautiful.

"Hey, are you okay?" Her fingertips find my jawline and blood rushes to my lower half like a waterfall. "How do you know the right things to say to me all the time?"

My laugh is colorful and echoes in the darkening room. "Not *all* of the time, baby." I reach over and turn the bedside lamp off, but I can still see her in the darkness. She fiddles with her left ring finger and a deep hole burns inside my stomach. "I'm sorry I don't have a ring for you yet."

Her smile lights up her face. "I don't care about that."

"But I do." I bring her fingers to my lips and playfully nibble on them. "I want to give you everything, Julie. You deserve everything in life."

I'll always do anything in my power for her.

Or die trying.

I chased her and fought for her for so long, and look what happened.

I finally have her. I finally have what I want.

No one is going to take her from me.

There isn't a set of rules that will keep me from getting my heart smashed by her, either.

All I can do is hold onto rule number three…and keep the secrets from her that will make her leave. Even though the rules haven't helped me with Julie at all since I've met her.

I broke my first rule: Don't let your guard down. I broke that fucking rule so hard that it knocked me on my ass and flipped my entire life around...and upside down.

The second rule—don't take anything for granted—I shattered right through, and it's not something I like to remember this soon. I nearly died after I let loose and allowed myself to put my guard down; I built that brick wall Julie smashed through over years and years of hurt and betrayal. Still, I walked away with my life back in my own hands and the light in my darkness still by my side.

Now, here we are.

Smashing these rules down one by one like bricks.

I can't let the other two fall—it's all I have left to hold onto.

One man's secret is another man's ammunition.

I have to make amends with Casey before he tries to shoot me down.

THREE
JULIE

WHATEVER KIND of person I've become in the last few months, it isn't someone I recognize. I'm smarter in the choices I make, sure, but in the department where Oliver Jackson is concerned—I make the worst decisions most of the time.

How can I do this to him?

I can't marry him. I really wanted to say no. I wanted to plead with him and shake his muscular body hoping that some sense would get knocked into it somewhere. What is he *thinking*? I just started to get my life back together from the wrath of Brandon, and he goes and does something like this. It isn't without surprise, of course, and he plays on that like a silky-smooth violin chord.

He knows Casey has some sort of weird feelings for me.

I frown as Oliver breathes deeply against my bare shoulder. This time, he doesn't take his usual place behind me, breathing into my hair. Something's changed since he woke up in the hospital, like there's an aroma to my skin that he can't get enough of. Regardless of whatever's going on with Oliver, the few college courses I signed up for start in three days, and my stomach is churning. I'm *nervous*—I haven't been in a classroom in over four years.

The moonlight dances on the naked skin peeking out from the sheet that barely covers his ass. He's been sleeping naked for the past few nights because the pain meds make his skin feel like he's on fire. I smile and blush, knowing he isn't awake to catch me trying to examine whichever parts of his body I can in the glow of the moon. A dog howls outside the apartment building and all of my thoughts scatter, zipping too fast for me to catch them all again and focus.

Oliver sighs into my shoulder and tightens his grip on the hand he's holding. The pressure of his arm snaking around my body to pull me on top of him with little effort surprises me, but he manages to steady me on his hips and his bright teeth glimmer in the glow of the moonlight. The beautiful rhythm of his lungs expanding against my thighs excites me, and I'm only three seconds from letting him swallow me whole and not looking back.

"You know we can't," I whisper. The dry air puffing from my lungs makes me cough. "The doctor was adamant about *no* physical activity, Oliver."

His smooth laugh tickles my burning skin. "Come *on*, sunshine. Please don't do this to me."

I bite my lips so I can't smile at his fake pout. "I need water—do you want some?" I quickly shift my body away from his and glare back at him. "I know you won't last the whole five weeks, so I'll compromise with you. Just...be a big boy about it, okay?"

I know he wants to argue. "Fine. What's your proposition?"

"Two weeks. Maybe you'll be healed enough where —if we're careful—I won't hurt you."

His laugh returns to echo in my mind. "You're *not* going to hurt me. You weigh like—"

I glare at him and his voice trails off. There are times when he sticks his foot so far into his mouth that it's hard to believe he's twenty-five and not fifteen. Still, that's a thing I love about him. He's not afraid to bare himself, and most of the time it's too goofy to be mad at for very long.

"Okay, two weeks," he agrees.

I slide back into my spot next to him, forgetting that I actually *do* want a glass of water. He leans up and kisses my forehead before he stands, bare naked ass and all. I don't bother looking away because if I do, he'll get offended and wonder why I'm so shy looking at his godlike frame so...*up close and personal*.

Oliver disappears into the bathroom, returning with a small glass of tap water from the sink. Before handing me the glass, he puckers his lips comically and leans in for me to kiss him. I smack my lips against his cheek and he chuckles, finally handing me the glass so I can gulp the cold liquid. I don't know if *I'm* going to last an entire two weeks, either. I'm definitely not going to last the five weeks, and I'm glad I could blame it on him and not expose myself.

"So, what time are your classes on Monday? Do you need me to drive you?" I know it's coming from a good place, but I don't need him dropping me off at school on my first day. It's going to be rough and awkward enough without my rich fiancé making a scene.

Wait.

I feel *gross* calling him that.

"Oh, my first class is at eight, but I can drive myself. You can't drive yet, remember?" I giggle and hope he snuggles into me and goes back to sleep. I angle my body like it was before, but he senses that something isn't right.

"Julie, I'm not incapable of living—I can drive. But, I get it—you don't want your *fiancé* dropping you off." He smiles and pulls me down onto his chest. "I get butterflies in my stomach when I say that out loud."

I *really* want to stop talking about this.

That damn piece of paper is still in the pocket of my jeans on the floor.

I can't marry Oliver until I know what to do about it.

"I know that feeling." I yawn against his chest and he tightens his grip. "Oliver? If you don't mind, maybe I can go to lunch with Staci and Nora tomorrow? I haven't seen them lately."

I feel him nod his head. "You aren't my slave, baby. You can do whatever you want. You don't need permission. I do appreciate the heads-up, though—I like knowing where you are in the event of whatever crazy shit seems to happen around us." He laughs and his body shakes, making my ear vibrate and tickling my skin. "I love you, Julie. You're my person."

"Your *person*? What does that mean?"

His yawn electrifies my body. "It means that you're everything to me."

I don't answer and let him drift back off to sleep, holding my body against his and caging me enough where it's too irresistible not to fall asleep on his warm chest.

———

"Good morning, sunshine," Oliver breathes against my neck and kisses the curve of my shoulder. The strap of my tank top has fallen down and he's able to nibble at my collarbone freely. "My beautiful and *insanely* sexy future wife." My heart skips a few beats when his breathy, sleepy voice penetrates my dream and pops it like a bubble. I snake my arm around his neck and meet his lips with mine; I don't even care that I could have morning breath or think about running into the bathroom to brush my teeth.

I don't know what I was dreaming about, but it sure put me into a good mood waking up.

Of course, I wake up next to Oliver, and that's something to be in a good mood about.

His boyish grin slays me. "What time are you meeting Nora and Staci?"

"I don't know, I have to text them." I ignore the fact that he's eyeballing me; he hates that I do everything at the last minute. But he always forgets one thing: If we hadn't been smashed together at the last minute, we probably wouldn't be where we are right now.

"Okay, baby. I'm going to get up; I have some business I need to take care of this morning. Are you going to be okay without my full attention?" There's laughter in his voice, but I know he's halfway being serious.

I nod and stay silent as he stands up naked again, this time with the daylight breaking into the room and illuminating his already-perfect skin. He doesn't say anything to direct attention to his rock-hard morning wood, but my eyes can't escape it.

He faces me full-frontal and walks out of the room backward, grabbing a pair of boxers on his way out. I know he's toying with me, but there isn't much he can do—including being naked—that won't get my attention.

I find my phone on the bedside table and text Nora first. She replies instantly with confirmation that she can meet me for lunch at noon. Staci takes a bit longer—I think she's hesitating for some reason, because every time I try to talk to her about Oliver…her voice tenses and she quickly changes the subject.

Once she agrees to meet with us, I pull on one of Oliver's t-shirts over my tank top and my bare legs underneath my shorts shiver when the chill of the morning air in the apartment reaches them. The sound of the shower running echoes in the hallway, and when I see his naked silhouette through the steamy shower curtain, heat rushes through my entire body…I'm frozen where I stand, gawking at him.

"Come in here." His deep voice startles me. "I know you want to."

I blush and shake my head, even knowing that he can't see me. "I'm going to brush my teeth. I'm meeting Staci and Nora at noon."

He laughs and shakes his shaggy, wet hair. "You have time for a shower with me, then."

My breath catches as the shower curtain opens and his naked, wet body is on full display for me. Steam billows around his bare legs and I find myself in a trance. The water drips off his thick lips as he smiles knowingly at me.

"Julie." His serious voice breaks through my fuzzy head. "You *know* you want to."

"I-I want to," I choke out and swallow so hard it feels like a baseball is in my throat. He opens the curtain wider and laughs because I'm *still* gawking. "Just give me a minute, okay?" The panic in my voice must be bleeding through, because he nods and closes the curtain again.

Okay, crunch time.

I'm getting in that shower.

The chilly air hits my naked skin when I slip the last piece of clothing off my body. I lay my panties on the floor next to his boxers and try to shake the goose-bumps off my skin. This isn't like me—I'm not that comfortable being naked in the first place, and when I open that curtain, he's going to see more of me than I want. It's not like he hasn't seen me naked before, but the shower…it's such a *personal* place.

Oliver's long arm reaches out and the heat from the shower radiates to my skin. Without saying a word, he pulls me into the stall with him and turns my body so the water hits my skin, wetting the hair around my face.

My gaze trails down his torso and rests on the deep stitches on his abdomen. I frown and reach out to touch them, but quickly pull my fingers back carefully so I don't hurt him.

"Baby, it's okay." His silky voice caresses my cheek. "You can touch me; I'm not going to break."

A laugh escapes the back of my throat. "I just don't want to put you through any extra pain. I want you to heal so we can get back to normal."

"What the hell is even normal around here?" His laugh billows through the steam and he doesn't hesitate to grab my body tightly and press himself against me. "I *want* you to touch me." His fingers find mine and he places them on his chest; his heart is beating so hard that it feels like it's going to burst from his hard, wet chest. His erection is pressing against my hip and I don't know if it's the hot water or some break from sanity, but my feet rise onto tiptoes and my tongue enters his mouth without me even thinking about it first.

He moans and locks his lips around mine, pushing me against the cool wall of the shower. I don't have any more defenses, and I knew this would happen if I got in here with him. He deepens our kiss and his hands explore my lower back before finding the curve of my ass and squeezing gently.

"I'm so fucking in love with you." He breathes into my neck before picking me up despite my swatting hands. He seems to be in control of his pain and swings my legs around his body so I clutch my thighs around his back. "I don't know what you've done to me, Julie."

I giggle and tug on his hair, his eyes filled with wild-fire. "All I did was need a ride."

He sucks in air and devours my lips, crushing our

tongues together. "Oh, you're about to get a ride, baby." I'm surprised at how little effort it takes on his part to ease inside of me before I can fully protest; it feels too good to make him stop. I don't even care that we aren't using protection…*again*.

We feed off of each other's moans until the shower starts to shake. I can feel Oliver's body tense and then lose a little momentum like he's losing strength. Underneath his ragged breath, he chuckles and kisses my jawline before releasing my legs.

"Bend over," he demands, taking a small chunk of my hair and tugging. I hear his teeth grinding so loudly that it's almost distracting. "You don't know how fucking beautiful you are, Julie. Your skin is soft and smooth…" His rough fingers tickle the backs of my thighs before he nips at the back of my neck and gently bends me over. "I think about all the things I want to do to you every second of every day."

I don't have time to respond as he bucks into me so hard that I nearly fall over. His grip on my hair steadies me and I close my eyes, because if I open them, then the world will explode. Sparks of electricity zip up my spine as I feel his fingers tug on my hair, and he brings my body closer to his, snaking his fingertips toward my breasts. Once he has my nipples in between his fingers, he tugs at them and makes the electricity more intense.

I'm losing control.

I scream his name somewhere in between his hard grip on my breasts and his nails raking down my back once he couldn't hold on anymore. The water has gotten so cold that our bodies are the only things giving off heat in the bathroom, but that doesn't stop him from gripping the round flesh of my ass and finishing so brilliantly that chaos erupts in my mind.

I can't catch my breath.

I dry heave beneath him as he tries to compose himself enough to pull out of me. I feel him leave the space and he pulls me upward, clutching his arms around my shivering frame.

"Jesus, baby." His voice is strained and low. "I guess we didn't wait two weeks."

I cough when I try to laugh. "What a little sneak."

He looks down at me and I swear I see tears in his eyes, but there may be a slight chance it's water from the now-freezing shower. He releases me and grumbles something before turning off the water. He tries to hide it, but I can see the blush in his cheeks. I know him better than that. I like when Oliver is vulnerable because it means that he's letting me in to see sides of him no one else gets to see.

"Are you feeling okay? How are your stitches?" I fumble around in the steam to find the side of his body. A little blood trickles down his hard stomach. *"Oliver! We ripped one of your stitches!"*

He laughs, and it makes me angry. "It's a little scratch, come on. Don't worry about me."

I wave him off and let him help me from the slippery shower. I don't even care that I'm naked and cold; the way he picks me up and places me on the shaggy bath mat seems so effortless. I know I've been basically stress eating lately, but the wobbly bits on my body don't seem to matter to me as much as his chilled lips pressed against mine without warning. His rough fingers grip the flesh on my ass and squeeze; the electric jolts start pulsating again, and I know I have to stop him or we'll never leave this bathroom.

"I have to get dressed." I laugh as he tries to keep his grip on my elusive body. "I thought you had things to work on while I'm gone?"

"I do." The sound of sandpaper fills the air as he scratches his jawline. "I need to shave and then it's all business for me. Which reminds me…" He brings down a towel and wraps me inside of it. "I know you start classes on Monday, but we still have to move into the new house."

Oh. I forgot about that.

Let's just focus on one problem before we add another, shall we? Like that piece of paper that's simmering inside my brain.

I have to find out what to do about it, and Staci and Nora are going to help me.

This is just like Brandon to stake a claim on me when he has absolutely no right.

Oliver won't be happy when he finds out I'm keeping this from him, but it's *his* rules that I'm following, after all. He wants to keep his own secrets safe, so I only feel it's fair for me to do the same. I hardly think he'll find solace in knowing I'm keeping this kind of secret from him. Not when something this big is going to blow his mind into oblivion.

He's never going to trust me again.

I frown. "Can we put a pin in the house? I want to get things settled before we dive into something else, okay?"

I hold out my toothbrush for Oliver to squeeze paste onto. "I get it, sunshine—I really do. Are you sure you want to put a pin in that? This place isn't five minutes from campus like the new house is. You'll have a longer commute."

"I don't mind a drive." I hardly want him to see me spit the used toothpaste into the sink, but I have no option but to hold my hand next to my lips and quickly wash it out.

His eyes are hooded and he doesn't even seem to notice. "How long do you want to wait?"

I don't have an answer for him.

"Oliver, let's just talk about it later." He notices the chill in my voice—this conversation will always be looming over us, tapping on our shoulders and making a mockery of me until I give in. "I don't want to fight before I go to meet Staci and Nora."

"We aren't fighting." He turns my body to face him and takes my hand into his. "I just don't want you to start being afraid to live life again because of some bumps in the road."

"You nearly *died*!" I fight back angry tears. "That's hardly just a bump in the road! Why can't you take this seriously?" The shrillness wrapped inside my fearful voice startles him. Oliver knows me—he knows that I let things build inside of me until I explode. He knows how to push those buttons just right, but I know he means well.

He still has a very funny way of showing it.

His teeth sink into his bottom lip. "Okay, just calm down. I'll do it your way, don't worry."

"Are you just saying that to make me happy?"

Oliver blushes and smirks, looking down at his feet. It takes him a few seconds to have the courage to look back into my eyes. The fire has settled between us and he's giving me the space I need to think about things before I end up spewing word vomit everywhere only to regret it later.

Score one for Oliver.

"I'm not telling you what you want to hear, Julie. We're fighting for no reason, so I'm letting it go so we can move on and not let this ruin our day."

Score two for Oliver.

My mouth feels like it's super-glued shut. I force my heavy lips to move, making some awkward sound before choosing my words carefully. I'm still so surprised that I'm afraid of opening my mouth and erasing every good thing that's just happened.

"Thank you." I blow out so much air that his hair moves a little. "And I'll give you an answer tonight about moving, okay?" I squint my eyes playfully to lighten the mood. "Since we've already broken the no-sex rule from the doctor way, *way* too early…"

His laugh crashes into my sentence. "I told you that I'm fine. Look…" He bares his side and I'm looking more at his rippled, wet stomach than his broken stitches. "There's no more blood and it was only one stitch, see?" He points to the top of the wound and smiles. "I'm okay…you're going to have to let me be a normal person and do things. That's how I'm going to heal and be as strong as I was before."

"You *are* a strong person." I wink at him and smile.

"That's such a Julie thing to say." He laughs and twirls me around, the towel spinning like a ribbon around my body. "Okay, so…tonight. You'll have my answer?"

I cross my fingers over my heart in an X-pattern. "I promise."

"I trust you." The words he says before he walks into the bedroom to dress bounce off of the walls inside my head.

I trust you.

I should have asked him to repeat that so when he finds out I'm betraying him and lying...*giving into his rules again*...maybe he'll choose to forgive me.

I have to get rid of this problem before he finds out.

FOUR
CASEY

I EXPECTED tears to fall down my cheeks when Julie squealed the car from the parking lot; she's trying to get as far away from me as possible, and right now...I feel like shit just enough to understand.

I just screwed everything up.

I told Oliver a deep Jackson family secret that I was fine with keeping.

I showed my cards and somehow Oliver knows I have a thing for Julie.

I hit Julie in the eye—on accident. But still. I hit her. There's no coming back from that. I just lost a brother, a best friend and someone who genuinely cares for me over nothing. Over a stupid crush that I know, deep down, is a lie because I'm so fucking lonely.

Lucy.

Shit.

She's storming off through the crowd and I come out of my fantasy just in time to catch her before she gets into a waiting cab. The feel of her hot skin on my palm as I grab her arm excites me.

"Lucy, wait," I plead, but she glares directly into my eyes.

"I'm not stupid, Casey. I know when it's time to get out, and this was a huge indicator." She rolls her eyes before she slams the door in my face. She doesn't bother looking back at me as the cab rolls through the now-thinning crowd. I've watched *two* women drive away from me in the last five minutes.

There's nothing I can do now but go home.

Alone.

Oliver got in some good punches to my jaw; I rub it as I walk past the doors of the bar and toward my car that's parked down the street. A woman steps out of a raggedy-ass van parked damn near in the bushes and I think she's going to pass me on the sidewalk, but her lanky body stops a few feet in front of me. Her green eyes peer knowingly into mine, and I freeze.

I *know* this woman.

"You're the nurse from the hospital." I allow myself to wave. "Thanks for the snacks. My friend woke up—"

She cuts me off. "I don't give a shit about Oliver Jackson."

"Well, then. That makes two of us." I shake my head and snicker. "See you later."

Her bony fingers grab my wrist when I walk past her. "I'm here to talk about *you*, Casey."

I snatch my wrist from her and jump back a few steps; I don't remember telling her my name when she handed me all those snacks. Julie must have told her or something…there's a logical explanation for this, I'm sure, and I'm just messed up.

"I have a proposition for you."

"A…*what*? Oh, I see." I start to nod and chuckle, nervously looking around to see if anyone is watching. "Look, I may not be able to keep a girlfriend—or get the one I want, for that matter—but I sure as fuck don't need a prostitute."

The woman slaps me in the face so hard it stings. "Don't talk to your mother that way." I hold my face and she shakes her head back and forth, frustrated. "I hear you know a little something about my secret." She moves closer but doesn't dare come within slapping distance again. "And I hear that you also told Oliver about that little secret."

"What the fuck, lady?" My voice is hoarse. "I don't know what you're talking about!"

She growls and gets into my face. "My name is Veronica Newson, and my son is Oliver Jackson. You're aware of him, right? The kid you just fought in the damn parking lot of a bar? Yeah, you know him… you're in love with his little gold-digging bitch."

I nearly lunge at her for speaking about Julie that way. "Listen, I don't know what you want from me, but FYI, Oliver wants nothing to do with me right now."

"Because you two are fucking idiots." She scowls. "You were both raised like guppies, not piranhas."

This is fucking weird.

"Okay, I have to go. It was nice…*no*, it was *weird* meeting you." I scoff and jerk from her grasp again. I've had enough shit today—I don't need my supposed birth mother verbally attacking me in the middle of the street.

Although I'm not surprised.

I hear her call to me from where I left her. "I can help you take Julie from him."

This makes me stop dead in my tracks.

Why do I want Julie? She does bring sunshine to a dark mind—Oliver is right about that. There's something just so...warm and *comforting* about her that I lose myself whenever she's around me.

Oliver doesn't deserve someone like her.

I find myself walking back to the woman and looking down at her rubbery, pale skin. This is not what I pictured my birth mother to look like at all. I know she's a drug addict, but come on, she's literally a walking poster for an anti-heroin campaign. Her stringy, bleach blonde hair washes out her already pale skin, and her lips are so cracked that it's hard to look at them.

"I'm listening."

Her lips lift into a smile and it hurts to look at the gaps from the teeth that she's missing. "I knew that would getcha." She laughs and pats me on the shoulder. "I'm going to help you win your little shared girlfriend. You're just gonna have to trust me."

"Trust you?" I yell, and it echoes through the street. "That's rich coming from you."

"Calm down, you little heathen. I just want the money that's promised to me, and Oliver is holding out. If I help you take her from him, maybe I can convince him to pay me to help win her back. I won't, of course..."

My throat feels like it's bleeding. "So this is all about *money*?"

She nods like it's nothing.

"There's *no* fucking way it's going to work."

She releases a deep sigh, and I can hear the rattling of her chemically tainted organs crying for some sort of freedom. "It's a good thing you're good-looking," she snarls, "because your fucking brains sure as hell aren't what's keeping you out of trouble."

"And if I say no? What's stopping me from telling Oliver right now?"

Her hand stops me from dialing my phone. "I saw the way you two fought back there. You're jealous of him always getting everything: Money. Girls. Popularity. I *know* you, Casey. I've watched you over the years just like I've watched Oliver. You grew up with a silver spoon in your mouth too, but it's not enough for you anymore. I can help you get what you want."

I lick my lips and stall before I make a stupid decision. She's playing my emotions like a fucking fiddle.

"I don't want to do this," I whisper into the wind. "I can't *let* you do this."

"I just want the money, boy."

I can't believe I'm even considering this.

"What am I supposed to do? Julie won't talk to me —she told me she never wants to see me again. Oliver won't let me near her after what happened, for sure."

Veronica laughs and it sounds like smoke will puff out any second. "You let *me* worry about that. You start by getting your brother back on your side; just be ready to save her when she needs saving, you hear me?"

Before I can ask her what she means by that, she gets

into the van and smacks the side with a few loud bangs. A man drives her away but doesn't bother looking at me as they pass like she does.

So much crazy shit has happened in the past hour that I just want to go home, take a hot shower, and drink an entire bottle of tequila while I drown in my sorrows. Cliché, sure. Do I care? No. Honestly, I could use a little downtime to relax and think about where I went wrong. I had everything with Nora I could possibly want, and I crushed it by sleeping with Heather.

Or rather—letting Heather sleep with *me.*

I didn't say no, though.

I could have—*should have*—pushed her off of me.

The echo of my real mother's voice bounces inside of my head. I've known about my adoption since I turned eleven, but my parents asked me to keep it a secret in public. I never questioned why they'd want that, but judging from the meeting I just had with the real woman I originated from…I can see why. I wonder if they even knew she was—and still is—a money-hungry shell of a person.

It's *always* about money.

I relax on the sofa in my apartment once I get there and kick my shoes off, putting my feet onto the coffee table. I sigh; I can't get Julie off my mind. I can't put my finger on it, but there's something about her that makes me feel…*good.*

I'm not a fucking unicorn!

Her voice pulsates in my ears.

She fucking hates me. Of course she does, after what I did. I didn't mean to, but I punched her in the eye. Not that anyone will believe me, but I was aiming for Oliver and he dodged my swing just as Julie tried to get in between us. Then Lucy realized that I'm a bigger fucking mess than I initially told her about and ran away.

Maybe I can get *her* back, at least.

My thoughts sicken me. I've never treated women like objects before now.

I grab my phone from the table and stare at it blankly. What am I going to say to her? Should I lie and keep my feelings for Julie a secret? Oliver always told me to keep my secrets safe—at least, the ones that would only cause me personal harm. He's good at that, keeping secrets.

At the funeral, I tried to tell Oliver about everything I knew, but he acted like I was a stranger. To be fair, I was the most drunk I'd ever been. I mean, Oliver is my brother and I was trying to tell him. Once I found out about it, I stole Oliver's toothbrush and used a mail-in DNA test to confirm that Oliver and I are actually blood related, and I know who my father is—that's the part that no one would know except me and Veronica, our mother. But hell, I'm not sure *she* even knows who my real father is.

That's *my* secret. No one is going to squeeze that one from me.

Oliver doesn't deserve Julie and he doesn't deserve the money that Vic left him, but he *does* deserve to have good memories...not of someone who's been his best friend for twenty years destroying his entire life with one large swoop. I mean, I already want his girlfriend.

Lucy's name pops up on the screen and I hesitate to text her.

Hey, can we talk?

I wait for an hour before she responds at all.

I'm five minutes away. I'll come to you.

I jolt up from the sofa and race around, picking up the apartment before she arrives. She'd just been here hours before, so I'm not exactly sure what nonexistent mess I'm trying to clean up, but when she knocks on the door, my palms start to sweat and I can't focus.

"Casey, come on…let me in." Lucy's voice is muffled from the other side of the door. I have to force myself to open it and see her disappointed face staring straight at mine. "Okay, talk."

I scoff. "Well, at least come inside."

She rolls her eyes and steps a few feet pass the threshold, carefully watching me like I'm going to pounce on her any minute. I keep a safe distance and linger next to the sofa. The air between us has gotten so awkward that I regret asking her to speak to me.

I clear my throat and go for it. "I *do* have feelings for Julie."

She snorts. "Yeah, no shit."

"Let me explain. I can never have Julie—she belongs to Oliver and she's never going to leave him. Trust me, there's been shit she should've ran away screaming about, but for whatever reason, she's still with him. I don't even want to break them up—it's a little weird crush that developed and won't go away. She's never kissed me, I've never touched her, and we sure as hell haven't slept together. So, I'm not really sure why I have feelings for her, honestly."

"She seems to have that effect on people." Her sigh fills the room and she sits on a bar stool nearby. "I know Oliver. I mean, before I just met him."

My eyes grow wide. "How?"

Lucy licks her lips and stalls—trying to come up with something to lie about, probably. "We met at a bar not long ago—the bar we were just in, actually. I went home with him, and well…" Her eyes search mine for confirmation that I'm a little jealous and intrigued. "The rest is the rest, I guess."

"Wait, wait." I hold up my hands to stop her. "Julie and Oliver have been together for like almost six months, how can that be—oh, *shit. You're* the girl he picked up in the bar that Harley told me about!"

She crosses her arms over her chest. "Don't judge me for doing something that everyone else does."

"I'm not." I wave my arms in front of her. "I'm not judging you. Did you know about Julie then?"

I can tell she doesn't want to say any more, but this is going to crush Oliver's soul when Julie finds out that he cheated on her. Fuck what I said before: I'm going to use this to my advantage.

Look out, Oliver Jackson. I have the smoking gun that's going to pry Julie from you forever.

Your rules aren't going to save you now.

FIVE
JULIE

STACI AND NORA wait for me at a small table in Rosseau's Café; I take my time driving so I can think about what I'm going to say to them. It has to come off the right way because I honestly can't remember doing something like this. I know it's safely tucked in my pocket, but it feels like it's bulging out so far that someone's going to notice. When I reach them, both of their gazes darken and Staci smacks her lips because she knows something isn't right.

"So, how *is* Oliver?" Her snide attitude oozes from her question. I know she doesn't really care. Nora glances at Staci and back at me, her nose twitching with curiosity.

"Oliver is much better, thanks for asking." I throw Staci's attitude right back at her and sit down in the empty seat in front of me. "Have you ordered?"

Nora nods, her questions still lurking around us. "Yeah, we ordered you that big, greasy double bacon cheeseburger monstrosity you love so much."

My tongue darts from between my lips like I can taste the goodness already. "That works perfectly, thanks Nora." I smile at her and a lightbulb shines above her head. She definitely knows that there's tension between Staci and me about Oliver, but even *I'm* a little confused on what her problem is. Oliver hasn't done anything to her—that I know of—and even when I told her how he nearly died coming to find me before reading the test results…she didn't blink an eye.

Nora waves the waitress over to our table. "I think we could definitely use some mimosas over here." Her eyes burn as she looks at Staci and smirks. "Maybe make hers a double."

Staci scoffs. "How about we just keep those mimosas coming, huh?"

The waitress blushes and nods before scurrying off to complete their request.

"Okay." I clap my hands to get their attention. "I need your help."

Staci leans in closer, just waiting for me to drop the bombshell on them. But *this* particular bombshell isn't worth sitting on the edge of your seat for. No…I hardly want to even speak the words I need to say to them because of how it's going to make me feel inside.

Nauseated.

Disgusted.

Confused.

A dozen other weird feelings twisting inside of me.

"Well, spit it out." Staci takes the drinks from the waitress and hands me my own, now that she knows I'm not pregnant and I can partake in day drinking with her. "I hope this isn't going to make me homicidal and want to kill Oliver, because right now—" She takes a big gulp of the orange liquid and swallows it easily down. "—I'm not exactly his biggest fan."

Nora snorts. "We've noticed. Why *is* that?" Her signature gold hoops are the smallest ones I've ever seen on her ears since I've known her. Nora's leg has almost completely healed, but she still carries her crutches around to milk the last of her injury sympathy looks and well wishes. The hoops are almost completely covered by her bouncy, soft black curly hair that I've always been envious of.

"I'm just not, okay?" Staci's light eyes dart to Nora and she hisses. "I think he's lying about something and I don't want Julie to get hurt."

"You haven't even spent any time with him!" Hurt falls from my lips. "How can you *possibly* know anything about him if you're not interested in asking?"

"I know all I need to." She pouts. "Can we just drop it? What do you need our help with?"

I glare at her because I'm not done defending Oliver. I'll *never* stop defending him from people who like to judge him by his past actions and not by what's inside of his heart *now*. I see Oliver for who he really is— someone he *wants* to be but is afraid to show to people— and I don't intend to lose his trust by talking shit behind his back…or letting anyone else get away with doing it.

I know I have to bite the bullet.

"Oliver asked me to marry him."

They both gasp so loudly that I feel the air being sucked even from my own lungs. I want to say I thought they'd both be happy for me, but the look on

Nora's face is so heartwarming while Staci's expression of horror stares at me.

"You didn't say yes, right?" Staci asks.

Nora holds up her hands. "Let her finish. Oliver asked you to marry him, and you said…"

I down the mimosa in my hand and put the empty glass on the table. "I said yes."

Nora squeals with glee and starts naming off everything that we've put on our wedding wish lists in our minds since we've met. Staci downs her second mimosa once the waitress brings another round and looks so green in the face that I ignore Nora's planning and focus on her.

"What is the matter with you? Why aren't you happy for me? Is this about Oliver's actions before the accident? Because I've forgiven him—"

"—It's nothing. Just forget it, I'll try harder to get to know him better, okay?" Staci waves me off. "Forget I said anything, I'm just in a bad mood. I *am* happy for you. When are you setting a date?"

I don't believe her, but I don't want to sit at this table and fight with her, either. I let her lie to me because I have more to my story that I haven't told them yet. I started with the easiest part because I'm too much of a chicken to even admit the second part to myself. The paper crinkles as I reach into my pocket and pull it out. Both sets of eyes are locked on it as I unfold it and hand it to Nora.

Her eyes scan the words and she's speechless; she hands it to Staci and looks at me with so much sadness in her eyes that it's blinding. "Is that true?" she whispers, allowing Staci to finish reading it before she folds it back up and hands it to me in silence.

I shrug. "I don't know. I don't remember it, but the document is real."

Nora starts to laugh and snorts it back down when she realizes that I'm not kidding around. "You don't *remember* it? How does that even happen? You'd remember something like this—this isn't a small thing you've done."

"I know."

Staci hisses and looks around nervously. "*Do* you? Oliver won't like this." Her lips quiver. "You haven't told him, have you?"

"No, of course not. I can't tell him I'm married to Brandon when I'm supposed to be marrying him." The words slip from my mouth and just like I thought, I feel so sick that the world starts to spin underneath me. I haven't told anyone about the contents of this piece of paper until now, and it feels good to share it with people I trust. "I *can't* be married. Randy would have known, right? He would have found it during one of his weird background checks on Brandon."

Nora taps the table with her long, baby pink fingernail. "Not unless he was looking for this in particular, I guess. So, let's think about this. Brandon is a psychopath and nearly kidnapped you at the cabin...he tried to beat Oliver's ass and failed...and came to me screaming when he couldn't find you again...he's *crazy*, Julie. He probably fabricated that thing so you'd have no chance at happiness."

Staci grunts. "Or it's real and he drugged you."

Something about her statement clicks in my mind.

"He kept asking me to marry him a year into our relationship and I kept denying it because it never felt like the right time. I don't think he would drug me into marrying him, though…that's *crazy*."

Nora giggles and her stacks of bangled bracelets against her tanned skin sound like metal wind chimes with each deep breath she inhales. "*Life* is crazy, Julie. Brandon is definitely nutso. I think Staci could be onto something. Why *else* wouldn't you be able to remember?"

"Not to mention your signature is all weird and sloppy." Staci takes the paper from my hands and unfolds it, examining the signature lines. "It's possible you were just too drunk or something to remember. Unless it's fake, and then we're talking about nothing."

"That's the first thing we need to do." Nora takes the paper from her and starts looking over every square inch of it with her concerned eyes. "Make sure it's even real. I can talk to my cousin Barney—remember he's a lawyer in Albany? He can tell me if it's real or not faster than we could find out; I can email him a picture of it." She pulls out her phone, snaps a picture, and takes a few seconds to compose a quick explaining email, her fingernails clicking on the screen so fast it's distracting.

I shake my head. "I already know it's real. It doesn't take but three minutes and an internet search to know the truth. I just need him to help me understand my options and what to do about it."

Staci howls with laughter. "Remember that time when Barney wanted to skinny dip with me so bad at the Hamptons and I tricked him into getting into Old Lady Werth's hot tub and left him there for like two hours?" Nora tries hard not to laugh, but Staci's booming howls are too contagious for even me to resist. My lips lift into a smile and within seconds, Nora and I are both joining in her laughter like it's our very own tale to tell. "And then she came outside to find him naked in her hot tub and called his mom!" The three of us are uncontrollable now, and the other patrons start glaring at us to keep it quiet.

Someone clears their throat behind me and Nora instantly stops her laughter. "What the hell are *you* doing here? In what universe would it even be okay for you to come over here and say *anything* to me?" There's a fire brewing in her eyes. "You can just turn right back around and walk the fuck back to wherever you spawned from."

"I just wanted to come and talk to Julie." Casey's voice rips my laughter from my throat. I whirl around and glare up at him. "Hey, can we just talk for a minute? Just sixty seconds." He holds his hands up in surrender, and I want to punch him in the face so badly that I have to ball my hands up at my sides to keep from smacking him a second time.

"I have nothing to say to you." My voice is cold. Nora and Staci look at me confused again—this time Nora is the more pissed-off one. I decide I have to tell her something before she blows her top and we get kicked out of the restaurant for good. "Oliver and Casey got into a fight and Casey accidentally punched me in the eye." I point toward my eye; it hurts a lot more than it looks. The bruise was light enough that I could cover it with makeup for the most part, so I wipe a smudge of the foundation off and they both gasp.

Nora gets to me first. "He did *that* to you?" The fire in her eyes is raging now, and if we didn't have dozens of people watching us already, she very well could jump from her seat and tackle Casey to the ground.

"She said it was an accident," Casey defends himself. "Julie, *come on*. One minute."

I groan out loud on purpose. "Fine, *one* minute." I turn back to Nora and shrug before standing up and following Casey to a secluded part of the patio out of earshot from anyone. Sadness radiates from his body; it wraps me up like a thick, itchy blanket, and if I stop making myself breathe through this…I'm not sure that I won't suffocate.

"I'm going to tell you something, but you have to *promise* to listen. After I say what I have to say, then you can tell me to fuck off."

I cross my arms over my chest. "I already want to tell you to fuck off."

He doesn't like it, but he accepts my attitude. "I just want you to really think about what's happened. Do you think I'd really hurt you on purpose? You are one of the only people left in my life that I can trust with the real me. I'd never let anything happen to you if I could help it."

My patience is wearing thin. I already hear these things from Oliver, and with him they actually *mean* something. "Forty seconds left."

His eyes darken. "I just want to be your friend again. I don't need you to love me or to even care about me, but I just need you…*there*."

"That's a pretty big request."

Casey nods and scratches his chin. "Yeah, I know. It

feels good to have someone like you believe in me, that's all."

I close my eyes and try to process what he's even saying. "I don't think you can help yourself, Casey."

"Oliver is putting you in danger by not giving his mother what she wants."

"How so?" I snap. "So far, *you're* the only one that's put me in danger."

He swallows a ball in his throat, the information he was about to share so freely crawling back into his dark mind. "Julie, come on. You know I didn't mean to hit you. I have feelings for you—why would I do that? It's killing me inside knowing that you hate me, but I can't do anything about that now except help keep you safe."

"So…what? You think Veronica is going to hurt me to get Oliver to pay her?" My sneaker taps against the hardwood floor beneath our feet. "Well, thank you for the warning, but I think I can handle myself. I have nothing to do with Oliver's money, anyway."

Casey grabs my arm to keep me from walking away. "They aren't the kind of people who are going to give a shit about that. Oliver loves you, therefore you're a liability."

This is insane.

I've had enough of all this drama that isn't even mine.

"Let's get some things straight right here. I told you: You *don't* have feelings for me. *I* don't have feelings for *you*, so you have to get over that. I'll talk to Oliver about what you've told me—that's all I can promise you. As for his—*your*—mother, I hardly think that woman can lift a cigarette anymore, let alone hurt me."

His grip lessens on my skin. "Don't underestimate her, Julie. You don't know her—"

I allow myself to look into his eyes, matching his grim stare. "And you do?"

Casey's gaze lifts to the ceiling as he tries to figure out a lie to push past his teeth. "I don't know her, but I know *about* her. My parents have told me things."

I sigh loudly. His sixty seconds are long gone. "Oliver isn't going to like what you're telling me."

"I don't give a shit about Oliver."

I've struck a chord on purpose, and I'll admit...it feels *good*.

But I still want to scream.

"God, Casey...don't you get it? I don't want to see you ever again, okay? You're borderline stalking me, it's getting out of hand. Yes, I'll admit...I miss talking to you...but Oliver is everything to me. You're—"

His lip quivers. "Don't say it."

I look at the ground and close my eyes before making the decision to say what needs to be said.

"You're nothing to me."

He's gone before I open my eyes. I feel the breeze of his body rushing past me before I dare to look. Nora and Staci are watching with such wide eyes that it's going to be hard for me to lie my way out of this one. I sit down and explain the entire story to them from the beginning, and I leave nothing out. By the time I'm finished, Staci looks exhausted and Nora looks pissed.

"Casey is such a jerk." Nora shakes her head.

Staci laughs. "I can't believe this is your life."

I fold the paper back up and shove it into my pocket. The food they ordered has arrived and I want to sink my teeth into that ultra-greasy cheeseburger more than anything else right now.

Casey obviously doesn't want to play by my rules and stay away.

Still, a part of me deep down feels weird about being so cold to him.

"Okay, I'll let you know what Barney says about that...*bullshit*." Nora waves her bangled hands around my body. "I love you, Julie...we're going to help you with this."

Staci gives me a comforting pat on the back. "Yeah, you deserve to be married to someone like Oliver."

Someone like Oliver.

What does that mean?

Someone smart and headstrong, willing to do anything to keep me safe and happy?

Casey is wrong.

Oliver wouldn't put me in danger—he'd never let his mother put me in danger, either.

I'm sure *that's* one rule he wouldn't break.

SIX
HEATHER

THE SUN IS SHINING and birds are chirping as I step out of the passenger side of Brandon's car. He lowers his sunglasses and winks at me like he's from a cheesy eighties movie. I owe him a lot—these past few weeks have been extremely hands-on and crazy wonderful. All of his attention has been on me instead of Julie, and it's honestly like he's forgotten that she ever existed. In return, I've tried my best to leave Oliver behind too.

Brandon even paid for my tuition at the community college in Rockford so I can start making something of myself instead of living off of other people for the rest of my life—or rather, *men*. Living off of men.

I strut on my long legs around the front of the car and he smiles, maybe even blushes a little. I know I've gained a little weight since we started fully dating—he's made sure that I don't throw up when I get nervous anymore, and I can even eat bacon in front of him without feeling disgusting.

Things.

Are.

Amazing.

I lean my head into his window and peck his lips. My body turns from his and I feel his hand grip the thick part of my thighs beneath my ass and squeeze before I walk away. I don't look behind me as he speeds off; he has work to get to, and I have my very first class of the day in fifteen minutes.

The small campus isn't exactly NYU, but that's no surprise. I mean, we *are* in downtown Rockford, where we're smack dab in the middle between Rochester and Albany. Nothing happens in between the major cities and surely no one is just itching to go to school here, either. But I have no choice. I have to go to school here if I want to be close to Brandon, and plus, it's not like I can just pick up where I left off so many years ago at NYU.

I have to do this.

The campus is pretty—the perfectly planned and manicured trees make me feel good about myself and more studious as I explore the grounds before finding the building I need. It's not a large campus, but it's still confusing when you skipped orientation and have no idea where you're going. I look at the paper in my hand and then back up at the building to make sure the names match in both places.

"Garrett Building, Room 312," I say out loud, putting the paper into my pocket. There isn't anything more annoying to me than being late to something— well, maybe except for perfect little Julie Remington with her heart of gold and locks of hair to match—so I jog up the stairs and enter the building to find the room where my first class of my new life takes place.

Economics 101.

When I reach the open door of the classroom, I start to panic. I don't know what I was thinking, coming here and enrolling in classes. I barely passed the classes I took at NYU. I turn around to run, but someone bumps into me, nearly knocking me over.

"God, could you watch where you're going?" I snarl without looking at the person.

"Sorry," a familiar voice says.

Lucy.

"What are *you* doing here?" I'm gaping at the woman standing in front of me. She doesn't look jazzed up like she did before: Her long, red hair is tied behind her head and there isn't any makeup flushing her face at all. She looks...*normal.*

Lucy scoffs. "Nice to see you too." Her nose sticks into the air as she passes me, and I know it's for good reason. She went to lunch with me as a courtesy, to see if I'm the same person I've always been. I follow her into the room and look around quickly—she's positioned herself in the middle of everyone, so I sit in the back of the class to keep an eye on her. She acts like she doesn't know me when only a few days ago she was chomping at the bit just to see me.

A few minutes roll by and I think I'm going to die of boredom until a glimpse of something catches my eye and my mouth drops open again.

No.

It can't be.

It's Julie fucking Remington. Here, in my class.

"Lucy?" I hear Julie squeal as she sees my former friend. "I didn't know you were taking classes! It's nice to see you." Her bright smile actually does light up the room, and that pisses me off. It's hard knowing what men see in her, even if she has no idea. "Do you mind if I sit with you?" she asks, and Lucy nods and opens her hand for Julie to sit down at her side.

Are you kidding me?

How do they know each other?

A smile spreads across my face as I glare at the two of them. Julie puts her things down onto the table in front of the empty chair, and as she turns to sit down, she notices me and frowns. Our eyes lock for a few minutes, both of us unable to really process what we feel in this very moment.

Run, Julie.

Run back home to Oliver.

This is *my* new beginning, and *you're* not a part of it.

Okay, so maybe—deep down—I have to admit it would be nice to have Julie as a friend. If I wasn't so put-off by her existence, I mean.

Her head shakes and she sits down in the chair without looking at me again throughout the entire class. As the professor drones on and it comes closer to time to leave, I'm only halfway listening to what he's saying. Instead, I'm seething at the fact that Julie has ruined my new beginning. I'm supposed to be free of my old life and everyone in it...*especially* Oliver and Julie. When the professor announces that we'll be teaming up in groups of four for a start of semester project, I see Lucy and Julie giggle amongst themselves as the two guys in front of them turn around and lay on the charm so thick that it hurts my teeth from four rows back.

No one around me asks me to be in their group.

"Okay, so...who doesn't have partners?" the professor says loudly through the excited chatter. A few frizzy-haired girls in the front row hold up their hands. My face flushes because I know I have to hold mine up too. I dart it proudly into the air and puff out my chest; Julie's look of amusement at me isn't going to bring my mood down anymore. "Okay, so you four—" He points to each of us and makes some weird slurping noise. "—can work together. Exchange phone numbers and emails, guys. I'll email you the directions for the project tonight. It's been a great first class; see you on Wednesday."

People jump from their seats and rush from the room, forming a clog at the door. I take my time and pack my things with ease because I don't want to get caught anywhere near Lucy or Julie right now. It was bad enough having her here, and now she's seen how pathetic my life has become.

The last kid in class to be picked.

"God, are you five?" I whisper to myself and swing my bag over my shoulder. The three unkempt, brace-faced girls linger to exchange phone numbers, but I try to dodge them without success. The tallest one, her strawberry-blonde frizzy hair going in every direction but down, flags me down and grabs my arm before I shoot her a hard look for her to let the hell go of me.

"Sorry," she whispers. "I'm Isabel, and this is—"

I snort. "I don't even care. See you."

"But we have to exchange numbers and emails! How else are we going to do the project?"

In the periphery of my hearing, Julie's annoying laugh seeps into my eardrums; she's standing in a small group with Lucy and the two guys that had sat in front of them, laughing and passing all their phones around until everyone's number is inside.

That should be me.

I'm the popular one.

I wonder how Oliver will feel knowing what she's doing right now.

I don't know if steam is coming from my ears but I don't care, either. The three girls in my group stare at me with surprise, like they can't believe they're standing so close to someone like me. In this moment, I could decide to be a horrible person and just storm off, but I think about Brandon and how disappointed in me he'll be if he finds out I've turned back into my old self. It doesn't really matter who Julie has in her group or who is in mine—none of that affects me as a person.

I smile at the high road I take and turn back to my group. "I'm sorry." I clear my throat and force myself not to look back at Julie and Lucy. "I'm just a little tired. My name is Heather Michaels...you said your name is Isabel?"

She nods and blinks several times. "Yeah, and this is Willow and Evelyn."

I force a little wave and keep smiling. There's no reason I can't be friends with these girls. Well, maybe the fact that they aren't gorgeous will put me at ease with trying so hard to be something I wasn't meant to be in the first place.

I can do this.

I can take this high road and make it my bitch.

"Nice to meet you guys. Here's my phone." Fishing my phone from my pocket, I hand it to Isabel and she blushes. "Go ahead and put your numbers in and I'll just make a group text for everyone so we don't have to pass phones around like dummies." I say this loud enough for Julie to hear, but I don't look at her for confirmation.

"Do you know that girl?" Willow points to Julie. The waves of her short, black hair that match mine in color bounce as she brings her arm back to her side. "I know her too. Her brother works with my dad."

I feel like I'm smiling like the Cheshire Cat. "Oh? Where?"

"Rockford PD—my dad is a detective just like Randy, her brother. Her name is Julie, right?"

"Yeah, that's perfect little Julie," I mutter, but Isabel hears me anyway.

"I never did like her. She never spoke to me at any police functions. I've seen her with her new boyfriend, though, and he's pretty—"

I hold up my hand for her to stop. "Don't even say it."

Isabel blushes. "Oh, sorry. Do you know him?"

This is my chance to take that *superior* high road.

I'm ready.

"Yeah, I know him. He used to be a friend of mine until she snatched him up."

Dammit.

So much for the high road.

Isabel blushes again and glares at Julie like *she's* the

scorned one. I like that about her already; she's willing to have the same enemies as me just after knowing me for five minutes. I shouldn't have said that about Julie, but I couldn't help myself. I want someone to see Julie like I do.

Without rose-colored glasses.

I clear my throat. "Well, Oliver and I were broken up before she came along, but it feels like the same thing." I quickly smile at the girls. "I'm trying to be a better person and not be the selfish, petty little thing I have been lately."

Willow nods her head, making her short hair bounce again. "That's a good thing! It's always nice to see bullies redeem themselves and be better people."

I open my mouth and close it again. She's right. I *was* a bully…not just lately, but in high school and college I was the biggest bully around. I don't know why I did it. But I *do* know that making other people feel less than human made me feel more…*me.*

"Heather." Julie's cold voice sounds next to my group. "Can we talk?"

I wave goodbye to the girls and tell them I'll send the group text later. When Julie pulls me to a quiet corner of the room, I feel like I could pounce on her and no one would know. Okay, so maybe *Lucy* would know since she's lurking around the classroom door and watching us.

"What?" I snarl at her and cross my arms over my chest. "What could you possibly want?"

"I want us to be able to be in a class together without any drama happening."

I laugh and Lucy takes a few steps toward us. "I can't even believe how this turned out. This was supposed to be my new beginning, and here *you* are, taking that away from me like you took *Oliver* away from me." I blush, but my mouth won't stop. "Now I'm going to have to drop this class and Brandon already paid for it."

Julie smiles. "He's helping you with classes?"

I don't smile back. "Of *course* he is. He's given me anything I've wanted."

"That's really great. I'm really happy for you two."

Why isn't she jealous?

I smirk and tap my foot on the floor. I know Isabel, Willow, and Evelyn are still watching me, and I don't want them to see me in that light. They might not be my usual standard of friend, but these days, I need all the friendship I can get from people who've never met me. I can be whoever I want to be with these girls. I don't have to be labeled like I have been for the past four years.

Heather: Oliver's girlfriend.

Heather: Oliver's ex-girlfriend.

Heather: the vindictive and backstabbing friend.

I can just be…*Heather.*

"There isn't going to be any drama from me, Julie. I'm past all of that. I don't care about you, Oliver, Nora, or Casey, okay? I'm just here to get through this class so I can move on."

Julie smiles and it's the first time I've ever seen her acceptance of me. In another world, in another life…we could have been friends. Lucy shuffles her feet behind Julie and it distracts me from our conversation enough to remember that Lucy has a little secret about where she came from.

I'm going to put it into my pocket and save it for later.

Lucy eyeballs me as a warning that she's no longer impressed by my presence. There's nothing I would love more than to out her to her newfound friend, but this is the new me...taking the high road. My gaze goes back to Julie, who is still beaming at me for being the better person.

"Heather, would you like to—"

"—I have to go." I look at my group. "I'll text you guys later."

The three of them nod and look between Julie, Lucy, and me to see who's going to throw the first verbal punch. I guess it was obvious that there's tension here, but I don't give it a second thought as I wave at them and brush past Julie and then Lucy to head out of the building and to my next class of the day. When I step outside, a firm hand grabs me and I make a small, startled squeak.

"Hey there, gorgeous," Brandon whispers in my ear. "College girls are so...*hot*."

I laugh nervously and look at the doors of the building, hoping that Julie doesn't waltz out of them and whatever lures men to her doesn't waft out with her perfect body. I'm dwelling on things that don't matter—that's one of the things Brandon and I talked about that we would change in ourselves when he finally decided to leave Julie behind and start over with me.

"What are you doing here?" I fake a giggle and meet

his eyes. "It was only an hour-long class; did you wait out here the whole time?"

Brandon's face lights up and I look around for Julie. When I realize it's me that he's looking at, it's almost too hard to believe. "I waited around for you. I wanted to make sure your first class was everything you've been talking about for the last week or so. How was it?"

My lips meet his cheek and I stay there for a long minute or so, trying to find the words to tell him that Julie is in my class. I don't know if I even should, to be honest. I know Brandon likes me—maybe he even loves me—but she can be my entire undoing if I let her.

And I'm not going to let her.

"It was great." I cock my head and sweetly smile. "Thanks for checking up on me. Can you walk me to my next class?"

Brandon notices my reservation, but he puts his arm around my waist anyway and I direct him to the next building, Dr. Carver Building of Science. He kisses me goodbye before leaving me at the steps leading to my next class. Julie isn't anywhere around and I'm thankful for that.

I'm going to start playing by my *own* rules now.

SEVEN
JULIE

THE MOMENT that Heather steps foot outside the classroom door, I tell myself I'll give her the space she so desperately seeks. It shows through her effort to take the high road and I can appreciate that since I'm trying to live a different life too. We aren't so different after all; we both just want to move on with our lives the best that we possibly can.

"Hey, what's your next class?" Lucy stands next to me. I almost forgot that she's even here, not to mention how weird it is that she—and Heather—are both in my very first college class ever. I already felt like an outsider because mostly everyone attending here during the day is a lot younger than me than I'd like to admit. There's nothing worse than feeling like you're too old to be somewhere at the age of twenty-three. Like Heather, I'm choosing to make the best of this and go home to Oliver.

Okay, so maybe only *slightly* like Heather.

My eyebrows crinkle at Lucy, who's staring at me,

waiting for me to answer her. "Oh." I clear my throat and take a piece of paper from my pocket. "English Lit, across the campus."

Her face darkens. "Well, I'm in the Theatre building. Some lame general requirement I wanted to push out of the way before getting back to the good stuff." The vibrant red of her hair shimmers as she leads me outside and the daylight hits us. Sometimes, I forget to look people in the eye unless it's Oliver. There's nothing I can get past him anyway, so looking him in the eye doesn't put me at a disadvantage like it does with other people.

"Lucy…" She's a few inches taller than me, but it's nice to have someone roughly on my height level for once. "I didn't know you were thinking about taking classes here. I mean, we didn't really have a chance to really talk before…you know." She catches my eye and I find it easy to look at her—there's something soothing about the way she holds herself.

Lucy laughs. "I went to state college back home, but by the time my senior year rolled around…I felt trapped and suffocated. So, I left home and moved here without looking back. I figured I might as well try to snag as many classes as I can to help me graduate."

"Is that going to work?"

She shrugs her slim shoulders. "What I can't get here, I'll do online. I'm not going to live in Boxwood for the rest of my life, that's for sure." Her snort is comical, so I let a small giggle slip from my lips. She realizes what she's said and blushes, clapping her hand over her mouth. "I'm sorry, I wasn't trying to invade your personal space or anything."

"Oh, please. Around here, personal space means nothing to anyone." I laugh and throw my bag over my shoulder. "I'll see you on Wednesday, okay?"

Before she can capture me in a conversation about Casey—because I haven't forgotten what he's done or what he's said—I wave to her and skip off toward the English building. The questions in the front of my mind are banging at the walls to get out—questions that I wish I would have asked Casey before he ran off from me the other day.

What happened after Oliver and I left the bar?

Did Casey talk to Lucy about me?

Did she break up with him?

Is she okay?

This entire scenario has gotten so out of hand that I just wish something—*anything*—could pull me back into a normal, real life.

That's why I'm here.

The English department is in a three-story brick building near the main road, and by the time I get there, I'm gasping for air and looking behind me to make sure Lucy hasn't followed me. That's too crazy—how can it be possible that Lucy *and* Heather are in my Economics class? I don't trust that Heather didn't have something to do with this just to mess with people's emotions again.

I don't trust her with anything.

A sinking feeling attacks the bottom of my stomach when I remember the piece of paper that Brandon handed me in that bedroom. It's tucked away in my tampon drawer—somewhere I know Oliver won't go snooping around—until I can figure out what I'm going to do about it. I can't go to Randy about it, even though he would be the logical first person to run to. Randy isn't exactly a friend to me these days. His text messages since I left his house started off robotic and now they're just too overly nice.

Nora keeps me up to date about her cousin, Barney, and she hasn't heard back from him yet. So, all night last night I spent with Oliver like a sitting duck. The wait for him to see right through me was agonizing, so I opted to sit with him on the sofa, watching several action movies and reading through more of Colin's last journal as he held me close. That's all we want…peace.

My phone rings before I enter the building and Nora's name flashes across the screen. My stomach sinks so far down into my body that it's hard for me to answer the call.

"Did you find anything?" I answer without saying hello; I have no patience for formalities.

Nora breathes heavily into the phone. "Well, I heard from Barney."

"*And?*"

She sighs and carefully chooses her words. She knows it's my first day of classes and she doesn't want to disrupt my focus. "So, unfortunately, the license is real, Julie. There's different options you can go through if you want to get divorced or whatever from Brandon. Barney can't help you because he's booked solid or something, but he suggested you find an attorney here to help you."

"I can't afford an attorney without Oliver knowing." I have to sit down on the steps of the building. The heartbeats that are pumping through my chest are so loud and heavy that I dare myself to look down and see it trying to beat right out of my chest. I guess I knew, deep down inside my heart, that no one would let me believe the paper wasn't real…that's just the story of my life. I don't get to have a sweet little romance with a man who sweeps me off my feet so wholeheartedly that it lasts forever without any obstacles.

That only happens in the movies.

"This is bad…this is so, so bad…"

"Hey, we'll figure this out, okay?" Nora tries to comfort me. "I'm sure we can scrape up enough cash to get you a decent lawyer. I'll talk to Staci and see what we can do to make this go away without Oliver knowing."

That makes me want to throw up.

I don't want to keep secrets from Oliver anymore—it never works out well. Even if the secret will hurt him for knowing it, and even if I'm following his own rules by keeping secrets in the first place. How can I get through this? How can I make him see that I had no idea about what Brandon had done?

"I have to get to class," I tell Nora and immediately hang up the phone. I wait for her to call me back and yell at me for hanging up on her, but she doesn't.

Even *she* knows I'm in trouble.

I get through my English Lit class without seeing or speaking to anyone I know, and it gives me the space I need to calm down and think about things. I finally decide that I need to talk to Brandon himself and figure out how this whole thing happened. I'm sure I can get the truth out of him now that he's focused his obsessions on someone else.

Heather.

Does she know about this?

No, she would have said something by now...right?

I don't have another class to go to today, so I head to the parking lot where I parked the rental car and let the silence fill my head once I shut the door behind me. I'm in an overbearing loop where things just won't stop flittering about inside my mind, but that doesn't stop me from pressing the start call button when I reach Brandon's number in my phone.

"Julie?" He answers on the third ring.

I hadn't thought about what I'm going to say to him, so when I open my mouth to speak, words just flow past my teeth like darts on a dartboard. "I need to know why I don't remember getting married and I really, *really* need to know how to make it go away."

He sighs. "This is probably a conversation we need to have in person, don't you think?"

"I'm not meeting you anywhere, just tell me."

I hear people talking in the background and he covers the phone for a few seconds to get them to quiet down. I've disturbed him during his workday, but I couldn't care less in this steam-filled moment. He walks from the noisy room and shuts a door before uncovering the phone, and even his slightly elevated breath in my ear is pissing me off.

"You have to understand, Julie. I was in *love* with you. You were everything to me and I took it too far, okay? I'd been asking you to marry me for a year and you kept saying no. I didn't know what else to do. I wanted you so bad that I did something stupid." His heated voice vibrates in my head. "I was a different person back then…childish and unfair. I can't take back what I've done to you. All I can do is apologize."

A lump forms inside my throat; I want to scream and cuss at him, but he just gets deep inside my heart with that statement. I wanted that with him too, but something changed inside of him when he realized that he had to share me with the outside world. He became hostile and mean, keeping me locked up inside our apartment with no one to talk to besides him…when he finally chose to come back home to me, that is.

"Remember that night when we shared the tequila my boss gave me? Right after you found out about my affair with Rachel?"

"Yes." I play that night over in my mind a few times quickly, trying to piece together what he could possibly have done… "You didn't."

Brandon's voice shakes. "I got you drunk and took you to a twenty-four-hour chapel in Worthstrom, that city that they call 'Little Vegas.' We got married and went home so you could sleep it off."

Oliver is beeping through my phone call with Brandon, but I hit the ignore button, hoping he'll just think I'm still lurking around the classroom having a good time. In fact, I'm *not* having a good time. I'm having a horrible time figuring out how someone could do this and how I'm going to get out of it.

"So, we've been married for two years and I didn't even know?"

"Yeah, I guess so. Actually, October twelfth was our anniversary, so a little over two…"

His voice drifts off and my entire body floods with so much heat that I have to roll the window down. I'm steaming up the car with my hot, exasperated breath and I'm about three seconds away from a panic attack when his voice comes back into play.

"If I could take it back, I would. I'll get the paperwork drawn up to get divorced, okay? Don't worry about a thing, I'll take care of it all. I'll get a lawyer in my office to do it or something."

I lick my dry lips. "What exactly were you hoping to gain from this? Just another thing you had control over, right? You wanted to control me so fucking bad that you stooped to tricking me into marrying you? I'm only *twenty-three*, Brandon! We were too young to make that kind of commitment and I don't care what you say... you're messed up beyond repair."

You're only two years older and you're marrying Oliver Jackson...

Shut up!

He lets me yell at him for a few more minutes before stepping back in. "Look, Jules, I said I'm sorry and I'm going to fix it, okay? Just go home to Oliver and when I get things in order, I'll call you and we can set it up so Oliver never has to know."

Oliver never has to know.

Rule number three: Keep your secrets safe.

Even if they will hurt someone in the end.

"Fine," I growl before hanging up on him. I'm really in no position to drive but I do anyway—I can't sit here steaming in the school parking lot much longer. I don't have any classes for another two days and that's too much time to dwell on something like this. The entire twenty-minute drive back to Oliver's apartment forces me to think about what I'm going to say to him and how I'm going to break his heart. I have to do it gently; he's still wounded, after all.

I force myself to nod at the security guard as I pass him; he watches the war waging between my head and my heart before I push the elevator button and step inside. I wonder if he can feel the emotions bleeding through my skin as the doors close and I start feeling suffocated. I gasp for air and clutch my chest, trying to breathe, but the panic has now set in and I don't know what the hell I'm going to do. I know what the right thing to do is…but is it really the *only* right thing to do?

The apartment is eerily quiet when I walk inside. I don't hear Oliver talking on the phone doing his business or shuffling around in his bedroom. I do smell something amazing that wafts from the kitchen, so I turn to find out what the source is. Breathing deeply, I follow the invisible ribbons of deliciousness around the corner and my eyes nearly pop out of my skull.

Oliver stands in the kitchen, wearing nothing but a chef's apron, grinning from ear to ear.

"Welcome home, baby." He puts a spatula down and reaches out for me. Still shocked, I trail my gaze down his tall, muscular body and swallow the huge lump in my throat. I push it down into my stomach and let it sit there, ignoring the gnawing feeling that I need to tell him my secret before letting things get too out of hand. "I made chocolate chip pancakes to celebrate your first day of class."

I let my eyelashes touch my cheek when I blush and look at the floor; I know he likes it when he has this particular pull over me. How can I be married to someone else when this godlike creature wants every part of me to be his? Maybe I *can* let Brandon take care of this and never speak of it again…maybe I *can* trust him to keep his word and undo the chaos he's created.

"I only had two classes today—hardly anything to celebrate." I look back at him and smile.

He twirls me around and laughs. "You're a good enough reason for me to celebrate *anything*. I don't care if you just went to the grocery store…I'll *always* be happy to see you walk through the door."

Crap.

He deserves to know.

Oliver's eyes get dark as he licks his lips and moves slowly toward me. I know what he wants—the same thing he wanted in the shower on Saturday morning—but I can't sleep with him when I know what I know…it wouldn't be right.

"I'm so glad you're home." He breathes into my hair once he's captured me and pulled me into his warm, naked body. "I miss you when you're gone."

I smile against his hard chest. "I wasn't gone for more than a few hours. You better figure out something to take up your time besides missing me."

"Oh, baby, I'll never stop missing you. But, funny you should mention that…" His frown finds me as he lifts my chin up to see him. "I actually have to leave town for business in a few days. Will you be okay without me? I want you to come with me, but you just started classes and I knew you'd say no."

"You're right, I *would* say no." I giggle. "Some time apart might be good for us."

His eyebrows rise before he opens his mouth. "You sick of me already?"

Even on my tiptoes, my lips hardly reach his mouth. He leans down the rest of the way to meet me and everything that's happened since I walked into my first class and laid eyes on Heather washes away. It's just me and Oliver again, just the way I like it.

Okay, so there's a looming secret that I have to address too.

"You fail to remember that I'm completely naked beneath this apron, Julie Remington." He winks and smiles at me. "Or the fact that I've already unhooked your bra and unzipped your jeans without you even realizing."

I look down and notice that he's right; my jeans are unfastened and I can feel my bra slipping off my shoulders. He picks me up and sits me on the counter, pressing his naked body between my legs while he kisses and nibbles at my neck. I lose myself in his warm lips against my bare skin and his rough fingers gripping my waist beneath my shirt. He groans into my ear as he nibbles the soft part and I find my hands around the back of his neck, tugging at his hair in pleasure.

"Oliver...the pancakes..." My breath is ragged as he presses harder into my legs. He reaches over and turns off the burner, moving the skillet to the other side of the stovetop. His long, dark eyelashes capture me when he caresses my jawline and leans down to kiss me again. His dark, shaggy hair is tangled between my fingers as he picks me up and fastens my legs around his torso before taking off to the bedroom with my body literally in his hands.

He's already naked, which is unfair by the way, so I reach underneath the apron and grip his hard-on in my hand, gently squeezing to send pings of pleasure up his body. He moans when I touch him, throwing his head back so I can see how defined his chest and shoulders are when he flexes them without even trying.

Oliver is a god.

He has the body of something unreal.

And a heart of gold.

But I'm lying to him and keeping secrets.

I don't let that thought enter my mind again; I make sure to push it far enough down into my brain that I can enjoy this with him and not feel guilty. He's my fiancé after all—it's not like we're strangers.

There I go…justifying everything.

When he can't go on any longer, his hands grip my sides and he lifts me up again. He bends me over the bed and I hear his hitched breathing as he slowly peels my jeans from my body, letting me step out of them before he trails kisses up the roundness of my ass then my spine. He kisses my shoulders and puts his thick lips everywhere imaginable; my body shakes beneath him…I'm ready for him.

I'm ready to let go.

"Julie." He breathes and playfully bites the flesh of my hip. "From the moment I laid eyes on you again, I knew I wouldn't be able to stop myself from wanting you." I feel his thumbs in the band of my panties and he slowly removes them too. "You were made for me, baby. You were created to contain the beast inside of me, and I don't know how to live without you."

Did he say again? Like he's met me before?

I mumble something that even I can't comprehend. His hands tug off my shirt and bra without any real

73

effort. He braids my hair that flows down my back and holds tightly onto it. After he rips open a package, I can feel the rim of his erection playing with my swollen, bare flesh. He breathes in so deeply that it's hard to hear him blow it out, but when he tugs backward on my braid…he pushes inside of me and the whole world explodes.

I don't remember much after that. I'm so lost in the moment and the pleasure that Oliver gives me that it's hard to even open my eyes. His skin is on fire as he slows down and curves my body upward, combining our flesh. His hard chest presses against my back and it's the best sensation I've ever felt. His fingers untangle from my braid and my hair flows down my left side. His teeth gently graze the back of my right shoulder blade and I can feel his broad smile against my bare skin.

"You like it when I do that?" He chuckles and his teeth hit my skin once again. I shiver beneath the pleasure waves and we stand still with him still inside of me. "You taste so fucking good." He growls and clutches onto me a little harder.

I'm not one for dirty talk during sex…Brandon used to try and get me to say dirty things to him when he did what he wanted with me.

Oh, crap.

Julie…don't think about that.

Oliver.

His hard breaths against my ear bring me back to where I want to be. Oliver's small moans are exotic—he can't get enough of me, and that's the biggest turn-on of all. I feel the build inside of me as I arch my back a little so he'll be forced to hold onto my hips. It grows inside of me like nothing I've ever experienced before… nothing comes close to the tingling happiness about to burst from my chest.

Everything is perfect.

I linger in a small moment of unawareness where everything around me just…doesn't exist. I can create any thought I want to and twist it how I want my story to end. My story ends with Oliver: I'm over a thousand percent sure of that. He kisses the back of my neck and thrusts slowly into me, but I can feel his need for me growing thicker by the second. I think he's going to let me explode this way, but inside of my euphoric moment, he pulls out and flips me around to lay me gently back onto the bed. As he kisses my jawline, I feel him enter me again, except this time it's like the shower sex we had a few days ago. He's attentive and caring; he's controlling himself because deep down inside he knows he can't do it forever.

I lock my eyes with his bright emerald balls of fire. Sweat wets his dark hair and it's matted to his forehead, so I reach up and brush it back a little and he slows down to smile. "You are incredibly perfect…do you know that?" His lips find the tip of my nose. My hips arch up to meet his, wanting more.

"I'm not perfect," I whisper and arch my hips more so he'll get the hint.

He laughs, nuzzles against the side of my face, and then gives me what I want while holding my arms down over my head. I break free and claw at his back; it's so hard that it revs him enough for his body to tense and my euphoric moment is shared by the stars in his eyes. I let him catch his breath before releasing mine and my entire body is pulsating so fast that there's a small chance I'm having a heart attack.

"*Fuck*, Julie." Oliver pants so hard that his breath feels like a hot summer's breeze. "I don't know how I'm going to survive you."

Once I'm able to open my dry mouth, I laugh. "I'm sure I don't know what you mean."

His thick, hot lips press against my open mouth and he twists his tongue around mine. I kiss him—*hard*—all of the love and guilt that I have wrapping around his lips and punching through my heart. I can't believe I just made love with this man when I'm married to another man.

What have I become?

To be fair, we slept together before I knew any of this. But now that I *do* know, it makes it worse in my mind.

My situation is unconventional, sure.

But that's not an excuse.

"I love you, sunshine." He kisses my forehead before extracting himself from my body.

Forget Oliver's rules.

I have to tell him my secret before it eats me alive.

EIGHT
BRANDON

THE SOFTNESS of Julie's skin will haunt me forever. Even when she hangs up on me…I'm still completely intoxicated by her. Somewhere, deep down inside, I know that it's not love anymore. No, that love ship has sailed long ago and it's all my fault. I promised her I wouldn't destroy anyone else like I did with her and I intend to keep that promise.

Spending the past few weeks alone with Heather have mended me somehow. Maybe not completely, but enough to see beyond the monster in my eyes. It's hard —and very self-destructive—knowing that other people see you as a destroyer: someone who turns everything they touch into ashes. It's hard to explain the love that I had for Julie when I met her, the best I could ever come up with is exactly what I told her in our impromptu wedding vows…the same ones I forced her into out of paranoia.

Loving you is like a limitless feeling of happiness.

I think that's why I held onto her so tightly. I

wouldn't allow her to take any college classes like I'm doing with Heather; I was always afraid she would meet someone better and leave me for some other guy. With Heather...she's already had someone better and I don't have that fear.

Oliver.

The scowl on my face darkens and I shut the door to my small office.

That prick.

I look at the time on my computer and I have an hour before I have to slip out of here and pick Heather up from the campus. I snicker when I think about her with her purple backpack she only bought as a tribute to our disgust for the purple room. I'll admit...the more time I spend with her, the less it hurts that I don't have Julie anymore.

I check some emails and tap my fingers on my oak desk, annoyed. I wonder if I should reach out to Nate, my best friend. We had a small falling out over my obsession with Julie and he has been shunning me for over a month. I guess I not only have to show Heather that I'm a different person, but there are countless other people who deserve that respect too.

Jesus.

What has happened to me?

It's true what they say, though.

You never know what you have until you've lost it.

There is the problem of finding a time to get divorced from Julie without Oliver knowing. I owe her that much if anything. Even I can't believe I had to get her drunk to force her hand, but that was the old me...the desperate me. I open a few internet browsers on my computer and search for instructions on how to get divorced in Washburn County without a lawyer. There isn't anything we have to divide and it's stipulated so it should be fairly easy. I thought about using a lawyer at the office like I told Julie I would, but if Vernon Trumbull, my ultra-powerful boss, finds out about this…who knows what he'll do.

Especially if he finds out I was screwing his daughter.

Heather texts me a kissing face emoji, and it actually makes me smile. She's nothing like I thought she'd be. I was prepared for hot, steamy nights with tequila and lace panties. There's definitely been a lot of sex, but it's not what I imagined. It's a different feeling than just straight up fucking someone.

It's *sensual*.

I slam my hands down on my desk in frustration. Someone knocks at the door and I frown; I only have twenty minutes to get to the campus. Whoever is on the other side of that door is going to be in the middle of a race they can't win.

"Yeah," I mumble, hoping they don't hear me.

The door slowly opens and Rachel—long, bare legs and all—steps into my office and paints a sexy grin on her puffy lips. "Hey, there."

No. Not right now.

"I'm busy, Rachel. I'm at work." I try to be as cold to her as I can. Rachel never was one for subtle hints…or just flat-out objections, either.

Rachel frowns and her now cotton candy pink hair falls around her cleavage. "No one is around, my dad is out of town, but you know that. I wore a dress you won't have to take off."

I chuckle. "Well, that's no fun, now is it?"

She licks her lips and sways her body closer to me. There isn't an inch of me that doesn't want to grab her and spread her legs apart with my tongue, but I hold my composure and think about Heather. She doesn't deserve someone like that, and I promised her I wouldn't do that to her.

I promised Julie that same thing.

My forehead crinkles. "I really *do* have work to do, so…" I gesture to the open door. "You can see yourself out the same way you came in."

She pouts. "Oh, come on. I know I freaked you out about the whole 'staying the night' thing," she uses her fingers to make air quotes, which equally freaks me out, "but can't we just get past it and sleep together again? I miss you and I miss your huge—"

I clear my throat for her to stop. "I'm seeing someone."

"I thought she broke up with you?"

Heat flashes through my cheeks. "Who the fuck told you that?"

Her laugh isn't pleasant. She's laughing *at* me. "I know people. My dad does business with someone you might know. Oliver Jackson?"

I choke down my scoff. If her father does business with Jackson, that means I'm doing business with him too. "Yeah, I know him. Julie didn't break up with me. She left me." I don't know why I'm being truthful to someone who doesn't matter. "She left me because I couldn't control myself with you and destroyed her life."

"That sounds like your problem, not mine. You're exceptional in bed, so let's focus on *that*." She comes around my desk and stands next to me, rubbing her palm against my dick. I push her away after a few seconds, startling her.

"Get the fuck off of me. I have things to do." I stand up and brush past her, but her legs catch up to me and I feel her hand push the door closed. "Rachel, open the door." I tower over her but she isn't scared. Her body is positioned with her arms outstretched so I can't leave.

She thinks about it for a few seconds. "I just want to talk."

I snort. "No, you want to fuck. I have somewhere to be."

"What does she have that I don't?"

The look on her face nearly makes me feel bad. "What do you mean?"

Her arms fall back to her sides and tears fall slowly down her cheeks. "I mean, why does the girl you're running off to get to have the real you, but all I get is…this?"

"That's all we ever were, Rachel. We were fuck buddies, grow up." My snarl doesn't surprise her and I realize that maybe I *am* treating her too much like a piece of trash. In light of my new outlook on life, I clear my throat and try harder. "You're not worthless, okay? I really *am* seeing someone, and I don't want it to end up like Julie. I can't see you like that anymore."

Her fingers find the tears falling down her cheeks and she wipes them away. "Okay. I get it."

I let her move her body from the door so I can pass her. I think about stopping and maybe giving her a comforting hug but decide that it's probably not a good idea. Rachel very well could be bluffing her sadness and that's okay...but I have to get the hell out of here before I give in and take her on my desk like I have done so many times before.

The drive back to campus seems long because I try to get myself back to normal the entire drive there. I haven't told Heather about the marriage, either. I know I should have, but our time together has been so peaceful and anti-dramatic that I didn't want to let that go.

I *can't* let that go.

I've kept secrets like this before; I can keep this one.

Julie and I can get a secret divorce and never speak of this again.

Shit. I wonder who she's told.

I park in the student parking lot and text Heather where I am. I should've been a good boyfriend and stopped for flowers to celebrate her first day, but there's no time for that now. Her long legs come into view and I smile, putting my phone in the middle of the front seats and stepping outside to greet her. The crisp air feels refreshing as she jumps into my arms and kisses me, fixing all the bullshit that I had to go through today. I'm so happy to fucking see her that it consumes me and I find myself hardly remembering that Rachel just tried to physically take off my pants after telling me her father does business with Oliver Jackson. As if that guy doesn't already haunt my damn life, now he has a hand in some of the business that I do.

"I can't get past the sexiness of dating a college girl." I laugh into her short, black hair. "Not to mention, *my* girl's the hottest one here."

Heather scoffs and pulls herself from me. "Oh, please. I'm like six years older than all of these little girls and they look at me like I'm some sort of exotic animal they have to take pictures of before I scamper away, never to be seen or heard from again."

"Well, you *are* exotic." I growl and nibble at her neck. "And a drama queen. We have time for an early dinner if you want to eat while we're out."

Her eyes perk up. "You read my mind. Can we go back to that barbecue place on Edmond and Roe? Those ribs seriously haunt my brain."

I laugh as she pecks my cheek and lets herself into the passenger side of the car. Being with Heather is easier than I thought; I braced myself for high maintenance and temper tantrums. She's a lot more chill than I could've imagined.

I join her in the car and she waves at three frizzy-haired younger girls as they pass us and squint their eyes at me like they've never seen a grown man before. I laugh and pull the car away, letting Heather settle into her seat while I make the drive downtown to the restaurant.

"So how was your first day?"

She waves me off. "Boring, just a bunch of introductions. Those girls I waved at are part of my work group in my Economics class."

"You're right, they *are* pretty young." I joke with her but she isn't amused. She's annoyed at something and I know it's not my bad jokes. "Are you sure that's all that happened today? Something's bothering you, I can tell."

Her freshly applied red lipstick tantalizes me as her thin lips turn into a smile. "You're implying that you know me. All you know is that I'm beautiful and talented." She winks at me and plays my game right back at me. "So, in respect of our relationship and because I *wholeheartedly* don't believe in keeping secrets from my boyfriends anymore—"

My eyebrow rises in intrigue. "*Boyfriends*? Plural?"

Her breath exits her lungs with force. "You know what I mean. So…Julie is in my Economics class, she came in after me and sat with Lucy…who is *also* in the class."

My throat swells. "Lucy? The girl who moved halfway across the country to stalk you?"

She blushes. "Something like that. They are friends somehow. It's all karma, you know. I have to sit and look at the back of her head for one hour, three times a week. It's going to be brutal."

I park the car near the entrance of Redwood Barbecue and stare at her. "You're going to be fine. It's just one hour and you don't even have many chances to talk to her in that hour, right? Think of the bigger picture here, think of your future and how bright ours is because of the steps forward we're taking."

Now Heather crinkles her nose in amusement. "Did you read that on a fortune cookie?"

I laugh and unbuckle my seat belt. "Something like that."

She never lets me open her door for her and I'm not sure if she does this on purpose or not. Honestly, I think she's just used to doing things on her own. She's a conundrum, really; as dependent as she is on people for certain things…she's equally as independent in other areas of her life.

The hostess sits us at a small booth near the windows overlooking a huge manmade pond. I order a few beers and Heather sticks to fancy wine, but I don't care. A place like this isn't exactly five-star, so I'm sure I can afford a few glasses of overpriced wine. Besides, I want to give her whatever she wants.

Within reason, of course.

Halfway through the meal, something startles her and she wipes her mouth gently. After she excuses herself to the bathroom, I shove more brisket into my mouth and wash it down with the remains of the second beer. I don't order another because I'm driving, and by the time we leave here I want to be sober enough not to need a cab. The waitress brings me an ice water and winks at me before she walks away. I start to get hard as I graze my eyes over her ass.

Jesus, get a grip.

She's just a woman.

You *have* a woman.

She's in the bathroom putting on more lipstick.

That sweet, sinful red lipstick.

I lick my lips and think about joining her when a woman sits down across from me and stares me directly in the eyes. She's in her forties, but she looks like hell frozen over…a dozen times.

"Brandon Whitehouse?" Her scratchy voice says my name. "I won't beat around the bush here. My name is Veronica and my son is Oliver Jackson."

I let out the hot air I'm holding in my lungs. "So, what? His mommy is coming to fight his battles now? Look, I don't know what Julie told you guys, but I said I would fix it...and I'm going to fix it. My girlfriend is coming back soon, can you get the fuck out of here?"

The woman laughs and it makes me sick. "Julie told me everything. How do you plan on fixing it?"

I click my tongue against my teeth, annoyed. "How else do you get a divorce? You go to the courthouse and pay some money and sign some papers, lady. Now, scram."

Her frail fingernails tap against the table. "So, you and Julie are married, are you?"

My stomach sinks into my lap. "Isn't that why you're here?"

"Answering a question with a question, what a stupid boy. I see you're fucking Oliver's trailer trash ex-girlfriend. She scrambled the moment she saw me through the window. I wonder if my boyfriend has her cornered in the bathroom yet."

My legs start to move, but she slams her hand on the table. "Stay right here. You do what I want you to do and she doesn't even have to know he's there."

What the fuck is happening here?

"What do you want?" I growl. The people around me start to stare.

"I want information on Julie...but it looks like you gave me everything I could ever need." Her smile is wicked and cracked; I feel sick knowing that she's going to use this against Julie in some way.

"If you hurt Julie or Heather—"

She snaps her fingers in my face. "Julie isn't your

concern anymore, now is she? Man, my boys have made their lives a tangled mess, haven't they? Oliver Jackson and his ignorance to lower-class problems around him, and his equally as miserable brother. I'm sure your parents are proud of how *you've* turned out, aren't they?"

I don't answer her.

She chuckles. "Okay, thanks for the information, kid. Your girlfriend will be out here, unharmed, after my boyfriend sees *me* leave unharmed. Thanks for your undivided attention." She winks at me and rushes from the restaurant and the people around us go back to eating their dinners as I panic and look around for Heather. Her bouncy black hair comes around the corner, unaware of anything that's just happened. I can't jump up and hug her, thankful she's okay; that will set off an alarm that something *did* happen, and until I figure out what to do about it…she has to stay in the dark.

"Let's finish up and get out of here," I mumble and shove more food into my mouth, trying to act normal. She notices that I'm awkward but she lets me be as she nibbles on a piece of ham. I push the rest of my plate into my mouth and gulp the water down before she even gets halfway through hers. I wait for her to stop nibbling and drink her wine before paying the check and rushing her back to the car.

When we spend half of the drive back home in silence, she knows something is up. "Tell me what's going on or I'm walking home."

I snicker. "I'm not afraid of you walking home, sweetheart."

"Fine. Just tell me what's going on—I *know* something is up with you. When I went to the bathroom you were just fine, and when I came back…you're tense for some reason."

I sigh and pull into the driveway of our place. "If I tell you…you have to promise me two things: that you won't freak out, and that you won't hate me." She doesn't move a muscle when she hears me say this. I already regret starting this conversation, but I don't want to keep things from her. I'm doing the opposite of what I would've done with Julie.

"When you were in the bathroom, some cracked-out woman sat down in your spot and told me she's Oliver's mother," the look in Heather's eyes reeks of fear, "but I think you already know that. She said you saw her through the window and high-tailed it to the bathroom to dodge her."

Heather nods and takes my hand into hers. "I saw a picture of her in Oliver's grandfather's house once, a few years ago. She looked different in it, full of life and less hopeless. At first, I wasn't sure if it was her, but when we locked eyes, I had a strange feeling and wanted to hide."

I reach out to her and brush her hair behind her ear. "I'm not going to let some crazy ass woman hurt you; she just wanted to talk about Julie."

Heather's eyes light up. "What about her?"

I have a weird feeling about how excited she becomes. "She wanted information about her, but I slipped and told her something she shouldn't know. Now I'm afraid Oliver will find out somehow after I promised Julie I'd take care of it and not say anything."

She listens to me and waits for the metaphorical throat punch.

"The second part is going to be the worst."

The silence is so suffocating inside the car that I want to forget the whole thing.

"Julie and I are actually…"

She takes a deep breath.

"Married."

The word echoes inside the space and I wait for her temper tantrum to start. She collects herself and breathes heavily, pushing the anger back down inside of her almost like an organized dance. When her eyes get brave and find mine, there's no rage inside of them; I see tears form at the corners of her eyes instead, and she fights hard not to let them fall.

"Are you upset because I'm married?"

She instantly answers me. "No. I'm upset that you wanted to *lie* to me about it. I'm more upset that you wanted to make it go away without me knowing. I'm *most* upset that you think so *little* of me that you just knew I'd make a disastrous scene about it. I told you I wanted to change and I'm actually trying." I hear the door open and she steps out, not bothering to look back at me. "I'm going inside."

The door slams and shakes the entire car. I let her go inside and have a few minutes alone to cry. I know I've hurt her deeply. I can't help it—it's not like I planned this. I forgot about it because I never wanted to slip and let Julie know. Somewhere in the shuffle I guess I just… forgot it was real.

I never meant to hurt Heather in the process.

When the front door slams shut behind me, the

condo is silent and dark. The sun has started to go down, the natural light that's left in the room mocking me as it fades. I hear her shuffling something around in her old room, which she's turned into a study. The door is open and it makes me smile because I know she wants me to come in and fix this.

"I'm sorry I never told you," I say when I walk through the door. She's sitting at her desk, pretending to have a book open to study. "I made the right decision by telling you, and yes, at first, I wasn't going to tell you at all. But you're right, we're not keeping secrets. So, that's why I told you now."

"You told me because you're in fear of it getting out," she snaps, not looking up.

I don't like the way she's talking to me at all. My body swiftly comes up to hers and I pull her gently out of her chair so she'll look me in the eyes. "Trust me, if I wanted to take care of it and not say anything, I would have. I'm being a better man and taking responsibility —can't you see that?"

The pleading tone in my voice changes her mind—I see it in the shift of her expression. "Okay, so what are you going to do about it? Have you already been to the courthouse?"

I shake my head. "No, I'll go tomorrow. We won't need lawyers or anything since we're not splitting a *real* marriage. I'll go and pay the money, we'll have a hearing sometime soon, and that will be that."

Heather nods. "Okay, I trust you to do it."

I'm glad she trusts that I'll go through with it.

Someone has to believe in it—in *me*—even if I don't.

NINE
OLIVER

THE MORNING SUNLIGHT peeks through the curtains and Julie sleeps so soundly that it fills my chest with satisfaction. The honey blonde strands of hair that've escaped onto her cheek blow gently with her breathing; she's so incredibly goddamn beautiful that it's hard to believe that this is actually my reality. She's still naked underneath the sheets and her body tangles around mine, but I don't mind. I've hardly slept at all because I know she's hiding something from me and it's *killing* me that she won't just give in and tell me what it is. I trust her enough that she'll eventually give in and tell me...but the waiting is eating me alive inside.

She knows I'll help her with whatever she needs, so I'm not sure why she's hiding things from me. I'm not looking forward to leaving her here alone for a few days—especially when I have no one left to keep an eye out for her. I still have Mrs. Atchley, my somewhat pseudo-grandmother, but she's been holed up in her apartment for weeks with the flu. I know Julie can take care of herself, but there's a gnawing feeling in the pit of my stomach just knowing that I have to be away from her.

She softly moans in her sleep and snuggles deeper into my chest. A satisfied sigh slips from her mouth and it makes me pull her as close to me as I can possibly get her. I know I need to get up and make some phone calls to confirm my meetings later this week, but being with her makes it nearly impossible to want to do anything else. The strawberry scent of her hair fills my nose and sends me back into the good dream that I woke up from in the first place.

When she starts to move her body and wake up, it startles me back awake enough to pretend I've still been watching her fondly. Her little body is tucked flush against mine, but she doesn't move after opening her eyes slowly to let the morning light in. I feel her yawn against my chest and smile, making my breath hitch enough for her to be aware I'm awake.

"Good morning, sunshine." I kiss the top of her head and squeeze her body. "How did you sleep?"

Our naked skin is firmly pressed together; this doesn't make it easy to concentrate on anything else. My mind wanders to the empty house that I bought for her. It's going to stay empty until she decides it's the right time to move in. She was supposed to have an answer for me on that too but has yet to deliver. I don't want to push her, and of course, this pisses me off beyond words. I'm controlling—I've learned that about myself recently, but I still want to live in the house that *I* bought.

For her.

My tongue runs across the bottom of my lip and she looks up to catch my eye. It's amazing how bright blue her eyes are when she first wakes up. The weight of her round ass presses against my stomach as she surprisingly hops up to straddle me. Her small palms press against my pecs and she leans down to part my lips with hers. My fingers tangle around her hair as I sit up and face her. The fire in her eyes burns right through me.

"Good morning." She giggles and kisses my cheek. "I slept like the dead."

What the fuck.

I groan. "Julie, you and I are gonna talk about the meaning of 'blue balls' later."

Her laugh is so contagious that I forget what I'm angry about and start laughing too. "When are you leaving town?" she asks.

My teeth grind together so hard that a stabbing pain travels up my jaw to my left eye. I rub my cheek and try to figure out how I'm going to change the subject. "Tonight. I'll be gone for a few days, maybe three."

Her pout is so fucking adorable, it's hard not to nibble on the thick part taunting me. "Well, I'll miss you. I still have my end of the promise to uphold, right? I told you I'd have an answer about when we could move into that house?"

Yes.

A thousand fucking times yes.

"You did." The excitement builds up in my body, but her soft skin is winning the war for where my thoughts are going. She flexes her thigh muscles against my hips and I know she can feel my dick sliding up her ass right about now. She holds her composure so I'm not going to be the asshole and try to seduce her again. No, next time it has to be all Julie.

"Well…" She drags out the last letter for a few seconds. "Maybe when you get back from your business trip, we can go furniture shopping? I'll stop by there tomorrow and take pictures of the rooms so I can have plans, okay?"

My heart fucking *sings*.

The second time since I've met her, I feel fucking *invincible*.

"That sounds like the best idea you've ever had." I can't help but to spread my smile across the fullness of my jaw, but I don't care. She can see the goofiness inside of me and it doesn't bother me one bit. I love the hell out of this woman, and nothing will ever make that change.

"I do tend to have a few good ones." She smiles and pecks my lips. "Now, it's Tuesday. I want to study for my classes and then I want tacos. In that order."

She slips from my grasp before I can catch her. "But…I want to stay in bed all day."

"Go work out or something. You've already broken the 'no sex for six weeks' rule, and you didn't rip too many stitches. Maybe a light workout would be good for you."

Who is *this woman?*

She walks naked out of the room; her ass bounces with each step she takes, making my mouth wet and legs shake.

I want to follow her so bad.

94

"Just do something else," I hiss. My phone flashes on the side table so I stretch my body, letting the sheet fall to expose my stomach. I sift through the notifications and see that Casey has called me three times and he's left three different voicemails. I scoff and delete them before even listening to them. I don't care what he has to say—I want nothing to do with him anymore. He's not the kind of brother I want in my life, that's for damn sure.

There's a few texts from Casey too.

> **CASEY**
>
> Oliver, please. Call me, okay?
>
> Look, I have something important to tell you. Call me.
>
> I just want to apologize to you, please call me.

I shake my head and delete the messages. I want to erase him from everything, but I can't bring myself to delete his actual number from the phone. I hear the shower start and it takes every single ounce of restraint I have not to run into that shower with her.

My phone rings and I start to hit the end call button, but it's someone I've been waiting to hear back from: Casey's father, Rodney Anderson. He took care of my grandfather's books for the most part, so when I told him I wanted to sell off every property and asset my grandfather's company had, he didn't take it well. In fact, he threatened to take me in front of the Board of Directors. When Julie was at lunch with Nora and Staci on Saturday, I used video chat with the group and they all agreed to the sales if I paid back all the investors and severance salaries before pocketing the rest. I saw that as a fair deal, so I agreed and Rodney was more pissed than he was before we started.

"Rodney," I greet him and snicker. "What do you need?"

"You can't do this. You can't give away your grand-father's money."

My long legs swing off the bed and I stand up to stretch, remembering the stitches as a small twinge of pain shoots down my side. My knee has almost completely healed so I don't need my crutches anymore...not that I used them much anyway. I guess having sex in the shower with Julie is the best kind of physical therapy to have. "I'm not *giving away* anything. The Board has decided that I'm right, and as long as I do things the legit way, nothing can stop me. Not even you."

"Oliver, don't you fucking do this," he warns me. "You won't have a virtually endless supply of money anymore. Your life won't even compare to what it is now."

"Money isn't everything, Rodney." I hold the phone with my shoulder and pull on a pair of sweats. "It's people like you who think it is that make money evil. You'll get your severance like everyone else, and then we're done."

I hang up before he can argue any more. I already made my decision; I want to sever my ties with Victor Jackson and his company obligations and make my own path. I'm going to open that bar in Rockford like planned…just not with Casey. I'll let Julie help me design it and maybe I'll name a drink after her too.

Mint Julip.

I smile and pull on a t-shirt, looking at my shaggy face in the mirror. It takes longer than expected, but I'm almost finished shaving by the time Julie steps out of the shower into the steamy bathroom. My eyes look down at the scar on her leg and it pushes a broad smile on my lips.

"Your scar is my all-time favorite story."

She glances down at her wet leg and frowns. "I think it's ugly."

I finish shaving and put the razor playfully in the farthest corner of the sink away from her. She groans and I wrap her body in the towel hanging on the rack. "Nothing about you is ugly, don't say shit like that. I don't like it when you talk bad about yourself."

She shrugs and wraps another towel around her hair. "Well, what's so special about the time I nearly cut my leg off?"

"First off, you didn't almost cut off your leg, woman. The reason it's my all-time favorite story is… it's the first time I knew my feelings for you were actually real."

Her cheeks flush and she looks at the floor. "Oh, I didn't know."

"I know you didn't, don't worry about it. I thought you were going to study?"

"I am." She quickly kisses my cheek and slips out of the bathroom. I clean up my mess and head to the kitchen to soothe my growling stomach. In the midst of our entanglement the night before, we completely forgot about the chocolate chip pancakes I made to celebrate her first day in class. I toss the pancakes and the batter in the trash and load the dishes into the dishwasher just to gain some extra brownie points.

There's a few steaks in the fridge, but I remember that she doesn't eat very much meat, so that won't do. I grab the steaks anyway and start grilling them on the stove while I make a garden salad off to the side. I sprinkle mushrooms into the bowl and am flipping the steaks one last time as she comes into the room, sniffing the air with pleasure.

"Steak for breakfast?"

I point to the digital clock on the microwave. "It's nearly noon, baby."

She frowns and starts to panic. "I've lost so much time! I could have been studying!"

"I'll save you a plate, go ahead." I nod to the living room. "I'll watch TV in the bedroom to give you peace and quiet."

She squeaks and nearly trips as she gathers her things and settles in on the sofa. I don't bother going to the bedroom like I promised her; I eat slowly in the kitchen and watch the wheels turn in her head and the lightbulbs of ideas floating around the room. I listen to her read her textbooks out loud and talk to herself, teaching herself in her own special way. It's like watching someone understand life for the very first time—the peace they find when they're so certain of something for once.

I don't even own a sliver of my own heart anymore.

Julie consumes every single inch of it.

"I hear you back there." She sighs and turns her

head to look at me. "You've been back there for hours. I thought you were going to work out?"

I point my index finger at her. "*You* suggested that I work out. *I* want to watch you."

"You're creeping me out a little." She hesitates to spare my feelings. "I'm trying to concentrate and I hear your loud thinking from back there."

"What am I thinking about, then?" My eyebrows rise.

She clears her throat and cracks a faint smile. "Nothing that doesn't require a rated-R label on it."

I stand up and leave the room, because she's right. This entire time I've been thinking of tasting her skin and how soft and warm it is against mine. How the thickness of her ass feels in my hands or what her hips feel like when I grasp at them. I don't walk away bothering to hide the hardness of my dick because maybe she'll follow me and forget about studying.

Packing for my short trip seems like a good distraction right about now. I throw a few pairs of jeans into a suitcase, along with neatly folded dress shirts and slacks underneath a brand-new pair of black loafers. I want this face-to-face meeting with the Board to go well, and I want them to take me seriously. I may only be twenty-five, but I know what I want in life, and it's *not* to follow in my grandfather's shoes.

I hear her talking from the other room and it soothes me. In the process of trying to figure out where she's moved my extra toothbrush in the bathroom, I open a few drawers and sift through some of the contents. A piece of paper crinkles underneath some of Julie's tampons. It's weird that a folded-up paper would be stuck in between feminine products like this…unless it's something she's hiding from me.

My blood starts to boil and I start to unfold the paper.

No, don't disrespect her privacy like that, Oliver.

Put it back.

Put. It. Back.

"Oliver?" I hear her call for me from the living room. "Do you care if I skip that monstrous piece of steak and eat tacos instead?"

I shove the paper inside my pocket and leap out of the room to see her. "No—do you want me to get you tacos?" I need an excuse to leave the apartment to read this paper. There's something important enough on it for her to hide it from me. I don't want to open it here just in case it's something that will make me so fucking angry that I won't be able to come back from it.

She smiles sweetly. "Would you mind?"

"Not at all, baby. Let me grab the keys." I snag the keys to the rental car from the dresser—making a mental note that I need to buy each of us a new car at some point—and realize that I'm still wearing sweatpants. I change and find my wallet and phone, shoving them into the pocket of my jeans and throwing my boots on. By the time I get back into the living room, she's curled up on the sofa and snoozing. I kiss her forehead and whisper that I'll be back soon, and then I can't get to the car fast enough. It's killing me—I want to know what's on that piece of paper.

I forgot a jacket, but the middle of October chill is refreshing; my skin radiates heat from the intensity of my anger. I'm about to find out what she's hiding from me. My boots scrape against the concrete and I take one last look up at the open curtains of the living room window, squinting my eyes against the sunlight. This isn't a good idea and I know it.

The car starts and I sit inside for a few minutes, enjoying the silence and trying to keep myself from doing something stupid. It's probably nothing. But why would she hide nothing? Was it even hidden? I mean, it could've just fell into the drawer...beneath layers of tampons and woman products she never thought I'd look through.

Fuck.

Am I snooping?

Who fucking cares. Open the damn paper, you idiot.

My fingers shake as I open one of the folds, taking my time because I really don't have a good feeling about this. I let the heater warm me before unfolding the second flap and shutting my eyes like a schoolboy— like shutting the world out will make whatever this paper says go away.

She's going to be my damn wife someday. I can't go around betraying her and sneaking through her things. I'm not a paranoid mess anymore.

She's changed me—she knows the rules.

Fuck. The rules.

I told her to keep her secrets safe.

She's just doing what she's been told.

As I force myself to start reading, my stomach is burning. When I scan the words for the third time, I know my life is about to come crumbling down around me.

This can't fucking be true. She's married to Brandon. She *lied* to me.

She's *keeping* this from me.

What do I do? I can't be pissed—*I'm* the one who told her to keep her secrets safe.

I didn't mean ruin my fucking life in the process, though.

The air in the car suffocates me, making it almost impossible to catch my breath. My chest hurts—my entire damn body hurts. This. Hurts. The world spins and it's not stopping, no matter how hard I try and yell through my dry mouth.

How could she do this?

She said yes to *me*; she's going to be *my* wife.

Not his.

Why hasn't she asked me for help with this?

Does she not trust me?

I can't go out of town knowing something like this.

I'm going to fucking kill Brandon.

I need to calm down.

Stressing out about why Julie didn't tell me about being married to Brandon isn't going to help anything right now. It's not like I blame her—I wouldn't want to make that public knowledge either, but at least I could help her take care of it. It's just another obstacle in the way of our happiness...there's been so fucking many that it's hard to even blink.

Someone pulls up next to me in the parking garage and I can feel their eyes on me. The more they stare, the more my blood starts to boil. I look up to start mouthing off to whoever it is, but my body turns to stone and all I can do is glare.

Casey.

He has the balls to show up *here* after what he's done?

Before I can stop myself, I'm bolting from the car to tear him to pieces. I'm stronger now, and I'm going to kick the shit out of him without any real effort on my part. My hands rip him from the front seat of his car without so much as one word from his mouth. He stares at me with glassy eyes and no expression on his face at all.

I still want to kill Brandon.

But not before I kill Casey first.

TEN
CASEY

I'M IN A DARK PLACE.

A really, *really* dark fucking place.

The loss of Nora left a gaping hole inside of me. Followed by the loss of Julie, which ripped my soul to broken shreds. Now, I've lost Lucy too. A triple loss in just under six months…that's gotta be a record of some kind, even for me.

Hopelessly pathetic.

My own mother didn't even want me.

The thoughts in my mind are getting a little scary. I'm waiting for my biological mother, Veronica, to show up at a small diner a few cities away from Rockford. She contacted me shortly after I tried—and failed—to warn Oliver about her plan for Julie. Since he won't listen to me or answer the phone, the only thing left to do is play along with this woman to keep Julie safe myself. If Oliver won't get over himself to help me…I'll do it alone.

"Son." Her cold voice smacks me in the cheeks

before I even see her pop out from behind the booth seat. She looks worse than before, and she nervously hides her forearms by pulling down her sweater sleeves. She catches me staring and her long, frail fingers snap in front of my eyes. "Casey, snap out of it. What's your answer, boy?"

I swallow down the scream that's building in my throat. "I'm in. Tell me how to get Julie."

Her wicked smile sends shivers down my spine. I don't trust this woman with anything as special to me as Julie is...no matter what she is or isn't to me right now. Even if I had the chance to tell Oliver, he would take the credit for being the hero when he didn't even lift a finger.

Again.

"You're smarter than you look, kid." She snickers and tips the glass of water sitting in front of her to her dry mouth. It looks like she's having trouble swallowing the lukewarm liquid, and that saddens me. I wish I never met this person; my *real* mother is the woman who raised me, and I'm going to make it a point to hug her the next time I see her.

"What exactly do I do?"

Veronica snaps her fingers at the waitress and orders a cheeseburger and fries. When the young girl leaves us alone, her frail body leans closer to me and I feel the chill of death in her breath. "A little birdie told me that Oliver is going out of town tonight and he won't be coming back until Friday at the latest. Some business deal thing, I don't know. Mac had to pull some strings to find out that information."

"Who's Mac?" I take a fry from the plate the waitress brings and Veronica's eyebrows rise. "Is that your boyfriend?"

She nods. "He's outside. He doesn't like boys like you."

I nearly choke on my fry. "*Boys* like me?"

"My sons."

I force the fry down my throat and nearly choke. I hate that she calls me that—I'm nothing to her but someone she's trying to manipulate. Once I get Julie and she sees me as her new knight in shining armor, this woman is history.

I don't care if Julie just wants to be my friend—I need her back in my life. Ever since I lost Oliver, Nora, and Julie—and probably Harley and Victor too—nothing seems right. I'd give anything to go back to that week in the cabin where everything was perfect. Nora was perfect, her laugh was perfect. The way her almond-shaped eyes followed mine was perfect. Her marshmallow lips were perfect.

"Hey, are you actually stupid?" Veronica screeches. "Come back to Earth, boy."

"I'm here, what did you say?"

"I asked if you were aware of her little secret."

My head hurts; I'm thinking way too hard. "Depends on which one you mean."

Veronica's smoky laugh startles me. "She's married to Brandon Whitehouse."

No.

She's a damn liar.

"She's not married; you're grasping at straws." I cross my arms. "Oliver would've mentioned something like that. He's protective of her."

"You'll find out soon enough." She laughs and smacks her lips. She sighs and slaps her hands together, grains of salt falling to the table. "As soon as Oliver leaves for his business trip, visit Julie. Talk to her, beg her to forgive you. Without him in the picture, she's more receptive to giving you the benefit of the doubt. She has to see the good in people, that's how she works."

"She doesn't trust me anymore," I admit, but Veronica shakes her head. "She hates me."

She snorts and stands up, frowning at her untouched cheeseburger. "That girl is incapable of hate. I know girls like her…I used to *be* her. I'll contact you later to see how it went."

I turn toward her. "Promise me that you'll help me." She stops, looking over her shoulder with the wicked smile back on her face. "Promise me that Julie will trust me again."

"I promise," she says, leaving me alone at the table with a half-eaten plate of fries and a crippling feeling that this thing isn't going to go my way. Julie already hates me…

What is my deal with her?

She's right. She's *not* a unicorn.

But she's compassionate and kind. She cares about how other people feel above herself. Her eyes can turn a grown fucking man to stone. I don't know what her lips taste like, but…I'm willing to bet they taste like honey. She's proof that you can have feelings for someone without even knowing them, but I'm excited—or, at least I *was* excited—to keep getting to know her. The surprises of finding out little things about her are what kept me going. I don't know, maybe finding some feelings for Julie was just my way of trying to get over Nora.

These girls aren't the ones breaking my heart: It's me. I'm breaking my own heart over and over.

First things first: I have to get her talking to me again. That starts with Oliver, and the only way to reach him is by just going to his apartment and knocking on the door. We were best friends once, and brothers without even knowing it, and somewhere in that cold, dark heart of his is the truth.

Veronica is long gone, so I stick a twenty on the table and rush out to my car. It's a thirty-minute drive back to Rockford, so I call Oliver once again to try and reason with him before actually going through with this. He doesn't even let the call go through. Sucking in my breath, I dial Julie's number. Her phone shoots back an error message in my ear.

They've blocked me from their lives.

The anger that this presents inside of me shakes the car on the highway. This isn't fair. I'm being punished for telling the truth and trying to avoid doing something stupid. *This* is how they repay me? I held her hand when Oliver was dying, I comforted her and I was there for her. He never even thanked me. But...Julie did. Her blue eyes sparkle when she cries too.

This is ridiculous.

When I reach Oliver's apartment, my luck changes for the better. As soon as I pull into the parking garage, there he is, sitting in the rental car—that *I* provided for him—and he looks like he's crying. After debating whether I should pull up next to him or not, I park on the passenger side and nonchalantly look over to him. His head is in his hands and he wipes his eyes before folding a piece of paper and putting it in the glove box.

That's when he sees me.

The rage that locks our eyes makes his body tear from the car and rip me out of my front seat. "What the fuck are you doing here?" His growl echoes off the concrete of the garage. "I thought Julie was perfectly clear when she said you mean nothing: to her *or* to me."

I swallow to keep him from crushing my windpipe. "I'm here to talk to you about something. Let me go." His weight is now pressing me against the side of the car, and he holds me by the collar of my jacket. "*Dude*, come on. Let me go."

"How can I let you go after what you've done?"

I find the strength to push him off of me, but I think he's weak from crying. I point to his eyes and want to smile, but I know that won't get me anywhere. "What's the matter with you?"

Oliver coughs to try and hide his sadness. "Don't fucking worry about it."

"Fine." I sigh and straighten my jacket. "I have to tell you something." His fists rise and I hold up my hands to stop him from punching my lights out. "No, it's something you need to know, I swear. Veronica came to visit me…*twice*, actually."

"What?" His roar hurts my ears. "What for? To see another bastard son she's abandoned?"

Ouch.

"Not exactly. She wants money. She said she asked you for money and you said no." I make it a point to judge him with my eyes, because if someone was threatening the woman I supposedly loved...they wouldn't live to tell the tale.

"I'm not giving that wretched excuse for a mother anything," he snarls. "And you're fucked in the head if you think I'm falling for your shit this time."

"I'm not fucking around! She found me after the fight at The Tavern and damn near ripped my head off. She's fucked in the head, man, like hardcore way out there. I just want you and Julie back in my life, that's it. Fuck everything else, I miss you guys. Julie has been a good friend to me and the only person who—until now—hadn't left me."

I can literally hear his heart stop beating. The stand-offish man that stood in front of me now cowers and whimpers like a mouse. It's weird seeing firsthand the effect a woman—no, not just *any* woman—has on even the most boastful and self-loving man. I know exactly how he feels, and that's why it makes me know for sure this is the right thing to do.

"She's already left you, Casey," he says, rubbing his jawline because he knows the sting that comes with Julie Remington being disappointed in you. "She doesn't want to talk to you."

He better watch his fucking mouth.

What Oliver doesn't know is that I have information that could end this right here, right now. All it will take is a short conversation with Julie about Lucy, and I can get what I want. But I'm not stupid; I know if I do it like that, she won't just run to me and things won't just be everything I've wanted. She'll run to Nora or someone else and completely forget about me. I have to grit my teeth and pretend like I have everything to lose a little while longer.

"She will if you ask her to," I blurt out, wanting to punch myself.

He shakes his head. "I'm going out of town. I don't have time for your drama." He sighs and rubs the bridge of his nose. "For once, I wish things could be normal and I wasn't fighting to keep her safe from fucking crazy people."

"You don't have to keep her safe from me, Oliver. I don't want to hurt her." I rub my throat where he was choking the life out of me moments before. "I just want to fix things with her so maybe my life can start shifting back to something normal. You know, before all of this crazy shit and psycho bio-mothers. She deserves that from me at the very least."

He snorts. "That's an understatement. Trust me, you didn't know Veronica and you're better off. You're not scarred like I am—at least not because of *her*—and if she'd kept you…who knows where you would've ended up."

He isn't saying anything I haven't already thought of. Trillions of questions and scenarios ran through my mind the instant I even met the woman. Oliver looks like he believes in me again, and somewhere—deep, deep down—I feel guilty about my true plans. I'm going to do everything I possibly can while Oliver is gone to get Julie to want me.

Crazy, I know.

"Julie doesn't want to go with you?" I fish for information. The more I know about where Julie's head is at, the easier it's going to be to win her over.

"No, she doesn't need to be where I'm going. I want to get it over with and come back as soon as possible. Plus, she has classes now and she won't just leave like that." The exhausted breath he exhales almost makes me feel sorry for him. "She'll be safe here."

"You'll look out for her, won't you?" he asks.

There it is.

A small, miniscule amount of trust regained. It's a start.

"I don't know, Oliver. She's not exactly my biggest fan right now."

He snorts and crosses his arms. "You really don't know her at all. She doesn't hate you—she's just hurt. You betrayed her trust, and that's a huge thing for her. But don't worry about her. I'll get her on board. Just be here tonight at eight so I can leave, and keep your hands off of her. Oh, and pack a pillow, because you're staying a few days on the sofa."

This *really* isn't a good idea.

"You trust me enough to do this?"

He nods and walks back to his side of the car. "You're a shithead, but I know you'd never intentionally hurt Julie. Who's better to look after her than someone who loves her? Sounds like a brilliant plan to me."

He's crazy.

"She's not going to go for this," I warn him, like I know her better.

"I'll talk to her. She'll be fine by the time you get here. Eight, Casey. Don't be late." He gets into the car to drive off. I stand to my full height and look at the cold, gray concrete wall for a few minutes. Several things are buzzing around in my mind, and I need to just take a minute and slow it all down.

What the hell just happened?

I don't remember driving back home, and I don't remember falling asleep face down on my bed, either. Lucy's citrus and spice perfume still lingers in my apartment, and it's just enough to make me want more.

Maybe I can curb my Julie appetite with someone else.

Since I wake up sweating from a sexy dream *about* Julie...the chances of that are slim. I don't know what the fuck is wrong with me or why I'm so damn obsessed with her. It's making me bitter, and no matter how much I tell myself that's a disgusting fucking quality, I can't help it. I want her more than I've wanted anything. The feeling destroys my focus and sends my body through millions of twists and turns to the point of nausea.

It's nearly seven and I haven't packed anything, so I jump up and take a quick shower, washing the dream out of my matted hair. I don't know what I'm more anxious about: spending two days with Julie and not letting myself give into temptation, or if she'll ignore me the entire time and it won't be pleasant for my already crushed heart.

I sigh as I leave my apartment, because I know I'm a fucking idiot for doing this. The more I think about it, the more I owe it to Oliver to be there for him when he needs me—just like he was for me when I started all of this. Maybe if I'd just chased Nora a little longer, I would've eventually met Julie and then Oliver wouldn't even be an obstacle and all this drama wouldn't exist.

In a perfect world.

But I live in Casey Anderson World, where everything comes up Oliver Jackson.

The drive to his apartment even angers me: The well-manicured streets and expensive cars remind me that his life was always destined to be better than mine. Jealousy roars its ugly head the farther down the street I drive.

I have questions for my parents, that's for fucking sure. I always knew I was adopted, but how can they keep something like this from me? Oliver came over to our house for Thanksgiving and Christmas every single year...how could they even look at him with a straight face?

Maybe they didn't know who my real parents are.

Time slows down when I park the car, grab my stuff, and make my way into the lobby of the luxury apartment building. Oliver's parking garage code has been the same since he moved in, and I still even have a key to his place on my key ring too. The night guard still eyeballs me like the pathetic piece of shit I am, but he lets me enter the elevator without question.

I hear Julie and Oliver talking loudly when I step in front of his door. Her voice is raised and he's trying to calm her down, but I can hear what they're saying.

"*Please*, baby. I need someone to look after you while I'm gone."

Julie is closer to the door than he is. "I'm not a *child*, Oliver! I can look after myself!"

"Come on, Julie. Just let Casey stay here with you; he's trying to make up for his mistakes. Wasn't it you who said we should forgive people?"

"That was a long time ago, before my outlook on friendship changed. What mattered to me then doesn't matter to me anymore. I don't want him here."

"He loves you, Julie. I don't know if it's as a friend or something else, but he won't let anything bad happen to you, and I need that comfort while I'm away."

There's a long pause and Oliver speaks again. "I love you…I just want to keep you safe. It's just like if I'm here, only it's Casey. I'd feel better knowing someone who cares for you is here for you if I can't be. Is that so wrong?"

Julie moans. "No, I guess not. I just don't need a babysitter."

"He's not here to babysit you—he's here to hang out so you're not totally alone."

She laughs. "I'd actually *prefer* to be alone. I don't know what his problem is."

"I fell in love with you the moment I met you. It just took me a long time to realize it."

"And someday maybe you can elaborate on just what it is that makes you so smitten with me."

Oliver is standing right next to the door now. "Smitten? You're such a dork. Come here."

I step backward and don't listen to them kissing only inches behind a closed door. It's quiet in the hallway, and I lean my head on the wall behind me.

"Whatcha doin' there, boy?" A woman's voice startles me. "You snoopin'?"

I look at the woman and clutch my chest. "Oh, Mrs. Atchley, you scared the shit out of me."

She isn't buying it. "Don't avoid the question."

Oliver's door is opening and he peeks his head out to smile at the old woman. "Mrs. Atchley? Did you want to come in too? Julie is about to order pizza because I let her tacos get cold."

She shakes her head and glares at me. "No, thank you. I'm headed out. Watch this one—he was lurking at your door being a creeper."

Oliver laughs as she hobbles into the elevator and waves back at him. Julie opens the door wider from behind him but clutches the back of his shirt.

She's *afraid* of me.

"I was just saying goodbye to her—come on in," Oliver grunts, stepping back from the door so I can come inside. "Julie, come into the bedroom with me, please."

She hesitates but follows him anyway. I put my stuff down and try to get comfortable. When they return, Oliver sticks out his hand for me to shake. "Thanks for helping me out. I'll be back on Friday at the latest, okay?" He's looking at her now and he winks, releasing my hand.

He's gone before I can even breathe.

It's just Julie and me now.

I guess I better decide what to do before Veronica calls me. Even though Julie's across the room, ignoring me, it's hard to concentrate.

Speak, Casey.

This may be the last time she ever talks to you again.

ELEVEN
HEATHER

I TOLD Brandon that I trust him to take care of his little marriage-to-Julie problem, and even though I'm crawling out of my skin wondering if he's going to go through with it...I have to keep looking forward. Studying actually takes my mind off my relationship problems and averts it to *more* problems, just different kinds. I don't understand a damn thing in this Economics book; it's all about money and how much the rich people have versus the poor people. Okay, maybe that's not *entirely* accurate, but you can't blame me for being bored. I like different things than most women my age, but I'm still into makeup and dressing up and playing the part of a princess. I don't think that'll ever go away.

The aroma of lavender fills the air, drawing me into the living room where Brandon stands silently, holding a bouquet of the plants. We haven't spoken much since I yelled at him when we returned home yesterday—he kept his distance because he knew he was wrong.

"I'm sorry for lying." The boyish grin he paints on his lips is definitely helping his case. "I don't want to lie to you. Can you forgive me?"

I take the flowers and pretend like I'm thinking about it. "I've already forgotten about it."

His arms are around me and he kisses my lips, the heavy scent of whiskey on his breath. "You're such a bad liar," he murmurs. His body heaves with his laughter and takes me with it. "I just want to make sure we're all good...*are* we all good?"

I nod. "All good here."

Accepting my answer, he lets me free and looks around the condo. "Let's go out for dinner tonight."

"We can't eat out every single night—" I notice the mischievous look on his face and blush. "Between the both of us, we should be able to figure something out, right?"

This doesn't sound appealing to him at all. "I just want to take you out and show you off...what's wrong with that?"

"To *who*, exactly? It's not like we have any friends left." He knows I'm speaking the truth, but he's not ready to let me win yet. "I'll go to the grocery store tomorrow and we can eat in, okay? I'll allow you to show me off one last night."

Brandon smiles and claps his hands. "Okay, so... sushi?" I make a grossed-out face and he laughs harder, knowing damn good and well I don't like raw fish. The thought of something slimy running down my throat isn't something I'm going to line up for anywhere. A twisted look stretches across his face and it drowns out my rumbling stomach. "Are you afraid to go out because of Oliver's weird-ass mom?"

My breath is ragged at the sound of him even speaking about her. From the stories that Oliver has told me about her…she's not someone you want to be around for too long, and I intend to stay as *far* away as possible.

"She's harmless—she just wanted information about Julie. I didn't give her any except for the whole marriage thing, so you have nothing to worry about." He tries to comfort me, but he has *no* idea what he's even talking about. Veronica is up to something—and it's not going to be good.

"Maybe we can order takeout tonight?' A lump forms in my throat. "I just want to lay low until she's out of town…just because she isn't a threat to *me* doesn't mean I need to see her in public again. Plus, you think she's not a threat, but *trust* me…she is. I'm not Julie's biggest fan, but I don't want to see her get hurt or something worse because of Oliver's crazy mom."

"What do you want me to do about it?"

I shrug. "I don't know, but Oliver needs to know about it."

He groans. "I thought we were done with Saint Jackson?" He looks down at me, searching for some sort of compromise. After a few minutes of staring each other down, he backs down and takes his phone from his pocket. "Okay, you win. I'll order Thai and then I'll call Oliver—does that make you happy?"

"I knew you'd see it my way." I giggle and wrap my arms around his neck. "See, living with me isn't so bad. You get to make me happy and *I* get to *be* happy. It's a win-win." He groans and kisses my forehead, tugging my arms from around his neck.

The doorbell rings and we both look at each other, freaked out that it might be Veronica. Maybe she followed us home and she's coming to collect information that she really wants. I don't have any pull with Oliver anymore, but it's not like she's going to believe me even if I tried. Brandon clears his throat and shoves his phone into my hand, giving me a knowing look to call the police if I need to. The sensation of fear builds in my stomach as he creeps to the door; the person outside rings the doorbell again the moment he reaches for the handle. I squeeze the phone in my hands, nearly crushing it in suspense as he looks through the peephole and frowns. Puzzled, he looks back at me and shakes his head before opening the door to let the person in.

"Oliver," Brandon says, and my head spins. "What are you doing here? I was about to call you."

"I need to speak to you," Oliver says darkly as he enters the house, seeming not to care about what Brandon just said. "*Alone.*"

Brandon scoffs. "Whatever you need to say, you can say in front of her."

"Fine." Oliver steps into view and waves limply at me. "I need to talk to you about Julie. It seems my mother has been snooping around, and I have a favor to ask."

I whimper behind Brandon, tugging on his shirt. "I saw your mother the other day..." My voice is weird and doesn't even sound like me at all. "She grilled

Brandon for information about Julie…that's what he was going to call you about."

Oliver's eyes fix on me, and it's makes me sad inside. I haven't looked into his eyes in months—maybe even a year, if I'm being honest with myself. So much has changed since he moved me to Rockford to be with him…he's changed to the point where we're complete strangers wanting the same things in life but going different ways to get them. "What did she want to know?"

Brandon shuts the door once Oliver is completely inside the house. He and I both know that he's going to have to break the news to Oliver about the marriage before Julie gets a chance to. I watch him frantically searching his mind for something else instead of the truth, but I know how to play Oliver like a violin and I need to step in to make this right.

"She was just asking questions. She wanted any information we would give her." I nod at Brandon, who thinks for a few seconds before agreeing with me. "Nothing in particular, but she's *very* interested in all things Julie."

Oliver can't bring himself to look into my eyes a second time, and that speaks volumes. He can't stand to even look at me without shoving his hands into his pockets and shifting his weight because he can't stand still. Brandon notices his reservation and clears his throat to ease the tension in the room.

"What is it that you want, Oliver? Didn't you come here to ask for a favor?" Brandon looks puny standing next to Oliver with his broad shoulders and bulging chest muscles. I used to fawn over him until I met Brandon; there's something about his long legs and thin torso that make me jump inside, and whatever else I uncover that I like...well, that's just another plus for me.

I *do* miss having crazy sex in public places with Oliver, though.

"Heather?" Brandon snaps his fingers, annoyed that I'm daydreaming like he knows what I'm thinking about. "Did you hear what I said?"

I shake my head. "No, sorry."

Oliver snickers. "Typical. Look—" He matches Brandon's angry eyes and they glare at each other before Brandon backs down. "—you two are basically the only people in this world I *shouldn't* be asking for help from. But...I have to go out of town on business." Oliver's eyes find the floor and he blushes, because he knows what happens when he leaves on business and the woman he loves doesn't tag along. "And you're not the *only* one my mother has contacted about Julie."

I listen to Oliver's story while Brandon slides his arm around my waist. We know what's coming: Oliver is going to ask for our help to keep Julie safe. I couldn't think of anything less appealing, but we *are* trying to become better people.

Honest people.

"Casey is staying with Julie until I get back, but I don't trust him."

Brandon scoffs. "Then why is he staying with her?"

I think about Casey and how much he reminds me of Oliver. They both have the same broad shoulders and build, but Oliver takes better care of himself and works out, where Casey just skates on his semi-good looks and pathetic charm. They don't share the same emerald green eyes, but they share the same rugged jawline and thick lips, which I always found odd.

"He's there because he has feelings for her and I know he won't let anything happen to her," Oliver says, catching my eye. "He thinks that he's in love with her."

"Jesus." Brandon starts to rub his jaw in frustration. "Is *everyone* in love with her now? So, what you do want me to do?"

"I know you loved her once…maybe you still do." Oliver shoves both hands into his pockets. "But no one will *ever* love her like I love her. Just because I trust that Casey won't let anyone *else* do anything to her doesn't mean he won't do something *himself*."

Brandon nods. "And you want me to look after *him* while he looks after *her*."

Oliver clears his throat. "She barely agreed to let Casey look after her—she'd punch me in the jaw if I told her you were looking out for her too. This has to stay a secret."

"I don't know, man…"

"If you do this for me, I'll overlook all the shit you've pulled since Julie and I met." Oliver's voice is cold and quick, just enough to whip Brandon in the face and make him back down. He looks at me with the same demanding eyes. "You too. I'll forget everything you've done to me."

There's a sour taste in my mouth. "What exactly is that? Okay, so I cheated on you and played some games with people, but this isn't my fight. I'm not in the business of making sure Julie is okay." I storm off and hide in my room, but I can still hear what Brandon and Oliver are talking about right outside the open door.

"Look, I wouldn't ask if I wasn't worried," Oliver says. "My mother doesn't play well with others, and she *never* plays nice. She's after something—she's just using everyone to get what she wants."

Brandon blows out a harsh breath. "Man, what a crazy bitch."

"Yeah." Oliver chuckles. "She's crazy, all right. Look—there's a lot about my mother that Heather knows, but there's a lot that she doesn't. I just found out that Casey is actually my brother, but I don't know much more than that. Life is fucking crazy and I just don't want anything happening to Julie when I'm away."

"And you *have* to go? I mean, come on man, even *Heather* is scared to go outside with your mom in town."

"She is?" Oliver sounds surprised. "Well, she should be. My mother will go through anyone to get what she wants. If she thinks she can scare Heather into helping her, she'll try. Can you just do me this one solid and keep tabs on her?"

"Shouldn't be too hard since Heather and her friend Lucy are in Economics class with Julie tomorrow. I can stick around and watch them go in and out if you want."

Oliver makes a grunting sound. "She failed to mention that." I hear him rubbing his jaw, the same familiar scratching sound it always made before. "It doesn't matter—she doesn't give much thought to anything besides the future now, and Heather isn't our future."

"I know. She's *mine*," Brandon growls. "Let's not get things fucked here. You came to me for help, and despite the argument I'm going to have to go through after you leave, I'm *going* to help you. I care for Julie; she's always going to be a part of me. I'm not going to let someone hurt her if I can help it."

Oliver's laugh is rough and vicious. "You mean more than you already have? Trust me, it's taking every fucking ounce of everything I have not to kick the shit out of you right here. But you're right, I need your help. Call me if anything gets too fucked up and you can't stop it, okay?"

"Okay."

"Brandon, get Heather on board with this. If you two do this for me…" Oliver's voice gets directive, like he's talking right at me from the other side of the wall. "…I'll send you on a week's vacation anywhere you want."

"I have classes, try again," I yell through the open door.

"Her classes are accelerated like Julie's, though, so she'll be out in eight weeks, won't you?" Brandon's voice turns sweet and patronizing. I bite my bottom lip; going on a vacation with Brandon doesn't feel bad…it's just too overwhelming. I want to take it slow, and having a romantic getaway together paid for by my ex-boyfriend is just too weird.

I launch from the room and the two men stand side by side, both glaring at me. Oliver wants me to agree so Brandon will do what he asks, and Brandon wants me to agree because he wants a free vacation paid for by his ex's new boyfriend.

So damn dramatic.

"If I let Brandon do this…" I hold out my hand and Brandon rushes to me to fold it into his. "Then you and Julie have to try and be friends with us."

Brandon takes his hand from mine and Oliver starts to laugh uncontrollably. I frown immediately when Brandon joins in on the laughter, but I take a little comfort in the fact that they finally agree on something. I know it's insane, but there are no rules for our situation.

No rulebook to guide us through our jacked-up lives.

"You're serious?" Oliver's voice cracks and he tries to keep his composure. "Even if I agreed, Julie would never fucking go for that. I already got her to fake-forgive Casey…I can't fix what you two have broken." He sniffles and clears his throat, pushing his laughter back into his stomach. "Why would you even want something like this after what you've done?"

"Hey, she's not the only guilty one here," Brandon chimes in, finally on my side again. "I did some fucked-up shit too. I think she's just trying to seek some sort of redemption and be normal. Julie and I were friends once. You and Heather were too, right? She just wants a chance to be a person you haven't seen before."

My eyebrows are raised so high that it hurts. "He's right. I-I just want a chance to have normal relationships with people, and what's a better way than trying to fix bridges I've broken?"

Oliver is nearly speechless. "I didn't know you were so deep."

The smile spreading across my lips warns me that

Brandon might get jealous. "I'm a different person now, Oliver. Will you just *promise* to think about it? He *will* help you, just think about it."

"I'll think about it," he agrees, glancing at Brandon. "Call me if I need to get back here and if you think Casey is getting too out of hand." A darkness swirls in Oliver's voice as he sticks his hand out for Brandon to shake. "Take care of it for me."

They shake hands and Oliver doesn't say anything before leaving the two of us alone.

The air that I manage to exhale is stale and dry; it fills the distance between Brandon and I, turning his focus from what just happened…back to me. The look in his eyes is scary, the kind of scary when I've done something he *really* doesn't like.

"Are you pissed that I'm helping him?" he rumbles.

My lips feel raw from my tongue rubbing against the insides. "No, I think this will work. Julie doesn't seem like the type to hold a grudge for long. Plus, maybe Oliver will still give us a vacation if something bad happens and we save her."

"Why do you want to be her friend so badly?"

The lump in my throat rises and I can't answer him.

What do I even say?

I never thought about this; I never even dreamed that Julie and I would ever even be friends. Still, the edge of something better hangs in the balance, and I keep reaching out to grab it only to keep being let down each time.

This time, I'm not letting lies and secrets get in my way.

I'm looking forward, and making a clean break from the old version of me seems like a good start.

Brandon looks at me for an answer. "Who said I wanted to be her friend?" I chuckle loudly and put my hands on my hips. "It's not like I have any friends left, but we might like each other, who knows."

"So you *do* want to be friends with her." He laughs and puts his arms around my waist. "I don't know who you think I am, but you're not fooling me. You have a warm, beating heart underneath that soft, sexy skin, Heather Michaels."

I blush. "You have a little something to do with heating things up."

Things are heating up, all right.

They're about to get so hot that someone's gonna get burned.

TWELVE
JULIE

OLIVER JUST LEFT me alone with Casey.

We all know this isn't a good idea.

I look at the clock above the sofa and make note of the time Oliver left.

8:19 p.m.

I already miss him, but my stomach grumbles so loudly that Casey hears it and his ears perk toward me. He has a lot to say to me, but I don't want to hear anything that comes out of his mouth unless they're the words, "I'm leaving." He opens his mouth and closes it again quickly before something ridiculous seeps out and I have to shove it back down into his throat.

"Julie." His voice is strained. "*Please* say something to me."

My foot taps on the floor. "Like what?"

"Like, *anything*." He starts to move toward me, but I hold out my hands for him to stop. "I just can't take the silence between us anymore. I know you don't hate me as much as you think you do."

"Don't tell me how I feel," I growl. "I don't want you here. I let Oliver think he was doing something by asking you to stay, but now I'm telling you to leave."

Casey licks his lips. "Oliver wants me here with you."

"I don't *care* what he wants!" I scream. "He didn't ask me what *I* wanted, did he?"

"What *do* you want?" The terror in his voice makes me self-conscious. I'm not in the business of making other people feel badly, but there's something crawling inside my skin that's warning me to get as *far* away from Casey as I possibly can. "Julie, what *do* you want?" he asks again, and the calmness of his voice spreads over me.

I click my tongue against my teeth. "I want people to stop treating me like I'm a magical creature. I have problems just like everyone else; I have issues that I need to work out too. I can't be that person for everyone...I can't make people's problems go away just by holding their hand. I want you to stop idolizing me and twisting me into someone inside your mind that I'm not."

He blushes. "You were one of my best friends."

"I still am." A rush of hot air leaves my mouth. "I'm just...*really* mad at you right now for how you've been acting. You try to take things from Oliver that don't belong to you, and that's not fair."

"I know."

My chest is on fire now. "You manipulate people into thinking you're some sensitive and fragile guy, but Casey—" I take a step toward him on accident, "—you're *not*. You're a strong person and a good friend when you really want to be. I never really said thank you for what you did for me when Oliver was in the hospital. You were there for me and I didn't show my appreciation."

The light has returned to his eyes now. "So, does that mean we can be friends again?"

I shrug. "Can you keep your hands to yourself and not express any weird feelings for me?"

The smile that spreads across his face is wide and toothy. "I just want you to trust me again, Julie. I can work on the rest."

I nod. "Okay, then. Let's order pizza, because I'm freaking starving." My eyes fix on the unopened bag of cold tacos sitting on the counter. Seeing it makes me smile, because Oliver went out of his way to make sure I got what I wanted. "So, pepperoni and bacon?"

Casey laughs. "Yes, *so* much pepperoni and bacon." He holds up his finger and dials a number on his phone without hardly looking down at the screen. I listen to him order the pizza and for a split second, it actually feels like nothing that happened in the past six months was real. Of course, I still don't completely trust him, and the fact that Oliver thought it was okay to push him on me is gnawing at my insides. I can feel the depth of my annoyance for him rising into my throat, and it takes all I have to push it back down into the place it slithered from.

"Beer?" he asks.

I shake my head. "Uh, no. I won't be drinking alone with you." I should smack my hand over my mouth, but I'm not ashamed of being straightforward with him. We're friends, after all, and friends don't filter what they say around each other. "I mean, it's not a good idea."

"Yeah, you might be right."

I nod. "Oh, I'm right. Let me just be completely honest…" The lump in my throat forms again and it's hard to swallow back down. "Just because I said that we're still friends doesn't mean things are going to go back to normal."

The fire in Casey's hazel eyes flickers. "I never thought they were. I'm just here to hang out with you until Oliver gets back, that's all."

I squint at him like I'm going to squeeze information out of him with just one look. It's time to let everything go and continue obeying my own rules. I'm not going to let someone else dictate how I'm feeling anymore— well, except Oliver, because that's always going to happen no matter how hard I fight it—and I'm certainly not going to let Casey make me feel bad for being upset with him.

But, I can do this.

I can act mature and let the irritation dwindle away on its own.

"Hey, the pizza is downstairs—I'm going to run and grab it," he says and then he's gone. It's lonely here, or at least it really could be if I let the silence drown out my thoughts. So much is running through my mind that it's hard to just focus on one problem at a time. Staci and Nora have already been helping me with the Brandon situation, and there's another elephant in the room that I haven't really discussed with anyone else:

Oliver asking me to marry him.

I'm not that much older than I was when Brandon

started asking me. Granted, I'm more mature and know what direction I want my life to go in now, but that doesn't change the fact that I'm still too young to be someone's wife. It's not that I don't love Oliver or that I don't see myself with him as his wife *eventually*, but he's never been one for perfect timing on anything considering the two of us.

Casey returns with the pizza and it smells more than delicious as he opens the box after putting it onto the counter. He gestures for me to grab a slice, and I don't hesitate because I'm actually fighting hunger pains in the pit of my stomach.

He groans. "So good." His smile is obscured by a glob of pizza sauce on the corner of his lips. I wiggle my finger toward him so he can wipe it away. "What?" he asks, the schoolboy grin smeared across his lips again.

"You've got sauce on your lips." My eyes narrow. "I could've kept it a secret, but that wouldn't be very *friendly*, would it?"

He wipes the sauce away with a napkin from the counter. "Better?"

I nod. "It's gone. I could've just let you walk around like that."

"Well, thanks for being so friendly about it." He rolls his eyes. "Is this how these next few days are going to be? You're nice to me with a *really* annoyed undertone to it?"

I act shocked. "I'm trying my best here."

He puts his half-eaten slice back down in the box. "*Are* you, though?" The crumbs from his fingers fall like dust to the floor. "Listen, regardless of how pissed Oliver is going to be...I think maybe I should leave like

133

you want me to. It might be better for everyone if I just laid low for a while, you know?"

What kind of person am I?

I hold out my hands to stop him from leaving. "Casey, don't go. I'm sorry. I really *am* trying, it's just hard to let go of things right now. I can't eat this entire pizza alone, you know." I wink at him and regret it, but it's too late to take it back now. Something ignites in his smile and his body relaxes; he picks up his slice of pizza and inhales it in one bite.

I'll never admit this to him, but I'm actually *glad* someone is here with me. Since Oliver nearly died, I've found myself writhing in darkness sometimes, and usually it's okay because there's someone nearby to help pull me out. He nearly died and I've still yet to face it. I nearly lost him and all I can think about is how quickly I can push that thought deep down into the pits of my mind.

"Julie?" Casey says. "Hey, is everything okay? I mean, besides my bullshit."

I nod. "Yeah, why?"

"You've been staring into space for five minutes."

I say the first thing that comes to my mind. "How did you find out that you and Oliver are related by blood?"

He gulps. "Our mother told me."

"Yeah." I cross my arms. "Let's talk about your mother." My voice is dark and cold, but I deliberately sound like that so he'll know I mean business. "She's a real piece of work. Did you know she threatened me while Oliver was in the hospital? Not to mention, she was waiting for me in the lobby when I left the first time."

"Stay away from her, Julie," he warns me. "She isn't a good person. You have to promise me that if you see her, you'll go the other way."

"Casey, I'm hardly afraid of her."

He wipes his hands on the napkin and tosses it on the table, inching toward me with a serious look on his face that I've never seen before. I let him put his hands on my shoulders because I feel like I can handle him if he gets too out of hand. The grip he's taking on my arms now, though...it's a little too concerning taken along with the fear in his eyes. "I *mean* it. You stay away from her, do you hear me?"

I nod but don't say another word. The look in his eyes says it all:

Veronica has it out for me.

"I won't let her hurt you," he blurts out when I realize what he's not telling me. "I fucking promise you that I won't let her hurt you."

The room spins and I need to sit down. I find the sofa and collapse onto it, but I'm not afraid as much as I am shocked by the sudden knowledge of a crazy woman gunning for me. I know that she wants money from Oliver, and if he knew about this, then he'd just freak out and do something stupid instead of just giving her what she wants.

My eyes widen. The missing journals.

It *had* to be her.

"Casey, I need to get to Lake Reed," I say, standing up. "I need you to drive me there."

He looks around the apartment. "It's nearly nine

p.m. and you have class tomorrow. You know it's a three-hour drive." He licks his lips when he sees that I'm not joking around. "Julie, what could you *possibly* need from there right now?"

"Journals from Oliver's dad." I blush. "I need them because…" My voice trails off because I'm not sure what to even say. Why do I need them? "I need them because they help me understand Veronica and how to play her game."

He runs his fingers through his shaggy blond hair. "I don't think we *should* even play her game."

Defeated, I plop back down next to him on the sofa. I can hear the wheels turning inside of his head like the insides of a clock, but he doesn't back down. "Tell you what, when you're in class tomorrow, I'll go up to the lake house and get them for you. What do they look like?"

This will have to do.

"Here." I shake the last journal from the bag next to the sofa. "They look like this. There's a whole row of them, but different colors. They're on the fourth shelf from the top of the first bookcase near the door."

His eyebrows rise. "Well, that's descriptive."

I blush. "These mean a lot to me…and Oliver." Before Casey can retort with any kind of horrible comment, I remember something that puts a damper on my plans. "Oh, crap. I forgot that Oliver changed the locks and he's the only one with a key. Madrie—that sweet older lady who works at the Lake Reed Inn—she has a copy for emergencies. I could call her and have her meet us. She won't just hand it to you."

Casey sighs. "Okay, what time do you get out of class?"

"Ten."

He scratches the stubble on his jawline. "Okay, after class I'll pick you up and we can go to the lake house, get your journals, and come straight back home. We don't need to be caught out and about without any protection against Veronica."

He's serious.

He's really, *really* serious.

"Did she say something to you?" I ask, sitting up and looking directly at him. "Did Veronica threaten you or something? Why are you so keen about her not being near me?"

He looks like he's sucking on a lemon. "I've met her before, when Oliver and I were little. She's not a nice person, and yeah, okay…she contacted me after that night at The Tavern and she has delusional plans to get her money, that's for sure."

"Like what?"

He doesn't answer me, so I straighten my body and turn to face him.

"Like *what*, Casey?"

His eyes flicker down to my fingers, and I can tell he wants to hold my hand. I shove them underneath my legs so he can't see them anymore and be distracted. "She just wants money, Julie, and she'll do whatever it takes and talk to whoever she can to get it."

"What do you mean? Who *else* has she talked to?" It's getting scarier now; the woman that was supposed to love and nurture the man I'm in love with…she hardly had the time to even love herself, let alone Oliver or Colin.

Casey hesitates. "Brandon. She's talked to him."

"What!" I can't control the fear in my voice. "What did he tell her?"

Now he *really* wants to change the subject. "I don't know—can we drop it?"

My eyes narrow. "Casey Anderson, you tell me right now—"

"He told her about your little secret, you know...the one about you two being married?"

"Shit," I whisper. "Does Oliver know?"

He shrugs. "I don't know, and I don't care. I'm really not in the mood to talk about what Oliver knows or doesn't know or how he feels. I want to talk about this...I want to talk about how you could keep something like this a secret instead of asking me to help you."

"This isn't your problem, and it's not your place to help me out of it."

He closes his eyes, then opens them slowly. "It's my place if I care about you."

"I *don't* need your help."

He snorts. "Clearly, you do. How are you going to make it go away without Oliver finding out?"

I blush. "Brandon is getting the papers drawn up, and all I have to do is sign them."

"Jesus, Julie, can you *be* any more naïve?"

I really want to punch him in the jaw now. Who does he think he is? I finally got Oliver to slow down on acting so possessive, and *he* actually has a right now. Casey doesn't, not by a million miles. I know Casey cares about me and would protect me if need be, but I believe Brandon is going to do what he says he's going to do. I heard the apology in his voice.

Casey sighs. "Okay, if you say he's taking care of it…then I'll let him take care of it."

Wow.

"But don't think for one second that I'm not going to keep tabs on this. It's one thing to keep it from Oliver, because we know he'll blow his top, but keeping it from *me* isn't an option. Understand?"

I nod. "Yes."

"Good." He stands up and retrieves a few bottles of beer from the fridge. Instead of handing me one, he puts it on the coffee table in front of me to decide if I want to open it or not. After shoving a few more slices into his mouth and chugging his beer, something comes over me and I feel the need to share more information with Casey. I don't know if it's out of vindication or friendship, but it jets out of my mouth before I can stop it.

"Oliver asked me to marry him."

He exhales hard. "Did you say yes?" He shakes his head. "Jesus," he whispers before he can meet my eyes. "I suppose you want me to be happy for you two?"

"I just thought you should know."

He takes the beer intended for me and snaps the cap off before guzzling the liquid. "And now I know."

"I'm sorry, I shouldn't have—"

He waves his hand through the air. "I'm a grown man, Julie. I *am* happy for you, that you've found the kind of love you never want to go away. That's all I can wish for you. I'm not going to cry and kick and scream over this. There's nothing I can do but tell you good luck, okay? I'm trying to be a good friend and be happy for you, no matter how it makes me feel in reality."

I want to know how it makes him feel.

Why?

I have no idea.

"Let's watch a movie." He changes the subject and turns the TV on without looking at me. After flipping through several choices, he lands on a scary movie about a killer clown. I pretend to watch it while the thoughts are swirling around in my head.

Being married to Brandon without knowing it.

Hurting Casey on purpose.

Feeling so much love for Oliver that it sometimes hurts.

You know. Normal things.

THIRTEEN
BRANDON

I'LL DO anything for Julie.

Fact.

I'll also do anything for Heather.

Fact.

For two different reasons, of course.

Julie deserves a better version of me and Heather gets to be with that version.

Even now, as Heather smacks her lips in the mirror behind the sun shade in my car, fluffs her shiny black hair, and winks over at me...I can't help but be a different man. Heather brings out the good inside of me from deep down somewhere I thought I'd never see again. I was a good person once, before my anger soured my soul.

"Okay, so you're going to be out here until we come out of class, right?" Heather looks nervously around and I know she's looking for Oliver's crazy ass mom. "I mean, just in case?"

I take her hand into mine and caress her fingers.

"Nothing is going to happen to either of you."

She chuckles. "I know that you won't let Veronica get to me or Julie; it's just crazy that you even have to secretly babysit her and keep an eye on me, is all."

I know what she means. If I had it my way, Oliver's crazy mother wouldn't even be an issue. Why doesn't he just give her what she wants to make her go away? If it were me—not that I was any better to Julie before—I wouldn't risk her safety for anything.

In another life, perhaps.

"Try and have a good class, okay?" I wink at her and kiss her fingers before she gets out of the car. "I don't want to deal with grumpy Heather all night long."

She pouts. "*Grumpy* Heather? What does that mean?" My eyebrows rise and she understands just where I'm coming from now. "Fine." Her voice is low and she shuts the door behind her. I didn't park that far from the building because I wanted to be in a clear spot so I can see everyone and everything. So far, I haven't seen Oliver's mother, but when Heather disappears into the building, Julie shows up a few minutes later in a car with the guy she left with before Oliver's accident.

That guy is just as annoying as Saint Jackson.

I lower myself down in my seat and watch them as he parks the car a few spaces from mine and hardly even notices anyone around him but Julie. They're to my left, so I can see his face perfectly and he's totally infatuated with her, which makes me laugh. Julie is turned to face him so I can't make out what's happening, but he doesn't like what she's saying to him at all. His face crinkles like he's eating a sour lemon before he notices that I'm staring and it catches her attention.

"Shit." I duck down further in my seat. I wait for a few minutes to make sure she doesn't see me, but I have to make sure she gets into the building safe and sound. I wonder if I should call Oliver and tell him that she's with another man, but I remember he said his friend Casey was also looking out for Julie while he's away, so I keep my phone where it is.

A loud knock on my window startles me.

Julie doesn't look pleased to see me.

I roll down my window and sit straight up. "Yeah?"

"Are you *spying* on me?" I can hear her foot tapping on the concrete.

I scoff. "Uh, Heather is in your class, you know that."

Her eyes narrow. "I know she is. Are you waiting for her?"

I nod and don't answer her. Julie has a way of seeing right through me—

"Is that the only reason you're hanging around here?"

I open the door and slightly move her out of my way as I push my body outside and stand next to her. Casey—is that his name?—gets out of his car and puts his arms on the roof, watching us closely. She nods sweetly toward him to stand down and I chuckle. "I see you have a different guard dog today. Where's Saint Jackson?"

She frowns when she looks back at me. Fuck, that hurts. Why does that guy get the sweet nod and smile and I get a frown? I can't even look into her eyes…I'm that ashamed of myself.

"Oliver is out of town," she tells me, "not that it's

any of your business. How are you coming along with the little problem we have?" She looks around to make sure no one can hear her. "Did you get the papers for the divorce yet?"

Casey is still eyeballing the two of us as I lean into her and whisper, "Why don't you just go to class and let me worry about that, okay? Heather is already inside; you should try and talk to her. You might have more in common than you realize."

When I pull away and finally look into her eyes, she's amused. "What the hell can I possibly have in common with someone like Heather, other than being blindsided by you?"

Ouch.

"Just go to fucking class," I groan as I start to get back into my car. "I don't need you badmouthing my relationship or my girlfriend." The door pushes her farther away from me, and I can tell that I've hit a chord. "I just want to put it all behind us and be a better person, Julie."

She smiles. "You haven't used my actual name in years."

"Well I'm changing, if you haven't noticed. I could've been a total fucking asshole and never told you about this marriage thing and let you find out on your own." I can tell she's thinking about the alternative scenario in her mind, and her nose crinkles in disgust. "Plus, you're reading way too much into yourself if you think I'm here trying to spy on you anymore."

"I saw you outside my house a few days ago." The glare is back. "Don't think you're getting off *that* easy. If

Oliver hadn't just gotten into that wreck, I would've let Randy kick your ass."

I scoff. "Or that other annoying poster boy for men's underwear you've got tagging along this time."

"His name is *Casey*, and you know that. He's a friend of Oliver's...and mine too. Not that I have to explain anything to you. Just...get the paperwork done and text me where to go and sign it so we can get this over with and I don't have to see you ever again."

I slide fully into the car and don't bother looking for her body parts as I slam the door closed. "You know what? You've become a real fucking bitch." I press the window button and close it before she can swing inside and connect her fist with my jaw. I point toward the building and narrow my eyes at her so she'll get the damn hint and go away.

My phone buzzes from the console, so I pick it up and notice an email I've been waiting on from an attorney friend of mine, Rafael. When I look up, Julie's gone. I can breathe freely again as I skim the email and frown. Raf has bad news for me and I don't want to accept it, so I opt for texting him instead of calling and biting his head off.

> Is the paperwork done?

RAF

> Paperwork is done. But like I said, it'll be three months before a judge will see it.

> Why is that? She wants it. I want it. It's not that hard.

These things take time. You have to
wait in line like everyone else. Maybe
your boss can help you out, but I can't
do anything. Sorry, man.

I don't answer him before I slam the phone back
down in the console with anger. I hardly want to bother
Vernon Trumbull, one of the highest-paid lawyers in
New York, with my stupid marital issues. He sees me in
a different light than other people—mainly because he
has no idea that I was sleeping with his college-aged
daughter—and the fact that he does business with
Oliver rubs me the wrong way. That's just asking to get
Oliver involved somehow.

My stomach grumbles and I rummage around for a
granola bar in the glove box before the hour-long class
is over. I don't see Veronica anywhere around and no
one looks suspicious, but that's okay. I don't need any
extra drama right now anyway. After shoving the food
into my mouth and spotting a trash can a few feet from
the car, I step out and head for it so I can discard my
wrapper.

"You there," I hear her scratchy voice. "Babysitting,
are we?"

My shoulders tense before I turn to face her. "What
the fuck are you doing here?"

Veronica smiles and it grosses me out. "You know,
just checking things out. Maybe I want to relive my
youth and try to make something of myself."

I laugh. "Lady, I don't even know you and I know
you're a damn lost cause."

This doesn't make her feel good, but I don't care. I

look nervously at the door where Heather and Julie will be coming out any minute, and Veronica makes a clicking sound with her tongue. "You should take me up on my offer, you little shit. Did I mention that I'm offering up a big payout to whoever helps me get my money?"

Money is a motivator for me—okay, it's a *huge* motivator. Still, I'm not quite sure that even money is going to make me keen on helping her. I made a promise to Oliver to help keep Julie safe, and I made another promise to Heather to try and be a better person. I don't want to stray from that now.

Veronica can tell that I'm thinking about it, so she steps a few feet closer and rubs her index finger and thumb together, making the gesture for money.

"A fat paycheck, kid," she repeats herself. "*No one* can pass that up."

I snort. "*I* can. I don't need your money, and Oliver sure as hell isn't giving you any. Now scram." Julie emerges from the double doors of the building, followed by a redhead who I assume is Lucy. *Jesus*, Lucy looks like a model, but I shake my head because I can't be thinking about that right now. Heather's shifty eyes look around when I see her come through the doors, and she locks eyes with me and then Veronica.

"Ah, my son's old trailer trash." She breathes in as deeply as she can with her damaged lungs. "Maybe I'll talk to her—"

I grab her arm and squeeze tightly. "*Don't* you fucking *dare*. You're not to talk to either one of them, you understand? Now get out of here before I toss you back into the hole you crawled out of." I can feel the heat slicing at my ears, but it doesn't bother me. This is a time for the old Brandon to come out and play, but I'm afraid he'll want to stay out forever and undo everything I've worked for these past few months.

Veronica doesn't look scared. "You'll take your fucking hands off me right now before my boyfriend takes care of you," she snarls. "Julie has too many eyes watching her, anyway." She jerks her head toward a point somewhere behind me, and when I turn, I see Casey walk over to Julie, take her backpack from her, put it over his shoulder, and escort her to another building before she slips inside and vanishes. Heather notices that Veronica is still lurking around, so she walks to me with hesitation, grabbing onto my arm once she reaches us.

"You need to get out of here," she says to Veronica. Her voice is so shaky that it's heartbreaking. I don't like seeing her scared, especially when it has nothing to do with her.

"I'm going," Veronica says with a cough, "but don't think this is the last of me. I'm getting my money—you can relay that to my son. Or don't. Either way, I'm going to get what I want." Heather grips the back of my dress shirt so hard that her nails nearly rip the fabric. We watch Veronica disappear from the parking lot but don't see her get into a car or meet up with anyone.

"Jesus," I whisper. "She's fucking nuts."

Heather moves in front of me and nods. "I know. Are you sure you want to do this? What if she's crazy enough to hurt you?"

I laugh. "She's not after me, beautiful. She's after..." I blink a few times and my stomach starts to hurt when

I think about the reason I'm standing here guarding the parking lot. "Julie." My eyes scan the quad and I spot Julie standing outside a different building with Casey, both of them laughing. Honestly, I thought it would piss me off. It's weird, but I feel more protective over her now than I did when we were together. The heat that flushes my cheeks is noticeable, but I don't give a shit…

…I don't like that she's giggling with someone who isn't Oliver Jackson.

"What the fuck?" I mouth, and Heather doesn't notice. After I clear my throat, she looks where my eyes are focused and frowns. "You're done with classes, right?" My voice is gruff. "Let's get out of here."

"But…Julie still has another class. Maybe we should wait."

I growl. "She has *Casey* to look after her, and they look like they're doing just fine." I nod toward the two of them. Julie waves at him as she disappears inside the building and he parks himself on the steps with his phone in his hands. "I guess Oliver was right: He's got it bad for her."

Heather scoffs. "How can you tell from this far away?"

"Trust me, I know that look. He's fawning over her —she does that to people. It's different with Julie…she's like a butterfly you can't even believe you've caught." I know this isn't what Heather wants to hear, but it's true.

Julie Remington is a diamond in the rough.

"Well, don't consider my feelings or anything," she

snaps, throwing her bag into the car and crossing her arms over her chest. "I'm just your girlfriend, is all."

I find her arm and pull her into my body; she lands against me with a thump and a half-cocked smile on her face because she knows I only have eyes for her. "You know I'm into you—don't act like you don't." I kiss her lips and she opens them for me to fit my tongue inside to slide against her bottom teeth. Before she can latch onto me, I tip her chin up and look into her eyes as deeply as I can manage. "Julie is naïve and tries to see good in people…that's going to be her ultimate downfall. I can't let her fuck up the best relationship she's been in because of some other loser."

"You mean Casey, right?"

I nod. "Yeah, that guy. He's lurking around, wanting things he can't have. I know what you mean about being friends with Oliver and Julie now; it's hard not to like them."

Heather blushes. "See? I want some of Julie's goodness to rub off on me."

I laugh and pull her closer. "Well, don't look now, but Casey is headed over here to have an argument and you can see me be the better man."

Just as I finish this, Casey reaches us and shoves his hands into his pockets while steaming from his ears. "What the *hell* are you two doing here?" he demands. "You're like a stain that just won't go away, aren't you, Heather?"

My fists clench, ready to strike. "You better calm the hell down, man."

Heather lets go of my arm so I can hit him.

But I don't.

Instead, I shove my hands into my pockets too. "Listen…" I shake my head. "Julie and Heather have class together, so don't worry about why we're here. We can be wherever we damn well please."

"Just stay away from Julie." Casey clenches his jaw and turns to walk away. "She doesn't need people like *you* messing up her fucking life again."

"Oh, so she just needs pathetic losers drooling all over her while her boyfriend is out of town?" Heather speaks up, and I give her a hard look. He's not supposed to know anything about that, and here she is, opening her big-ass mouth. She sees the look on my face and frowns.

He spins and looks like he's about to kick my ass. "What the hell did you say?"

Dammit. Now I'm going to have to fight him.

I put my hands up to let him know I'm not willing to fight. He glares at her and takes a step forward. "You don't know anything about it, do you? Julie and I are just friends, nothing more. Not that it's any of your business, but really…I could do without someone like *you* judging me."

"Someone like *me*?" she squeaks. "What does that mean?"

"Call it how you see it, Casey," I warn him. "But just keep in mind that I'm within distance to properly punch your fucking lights out."

He decides to take another step forward. "You two deserve each other. You're both a waste of space, and I really can't speak for *you*—" he darts his eyes toward me, "—since all I know about you is that you like to smack women around."

My fists clench tighter. "Shut the fuck up—I'm warning you."

He doesn't heed my warning. "But you—" he looks at Heather and she starts to tear up, "—I wish Oliver never met you and brought you into our lives. The slime you leave behind after you're done with people stays around *way* too long. You destroyed Nora, and she was your *friend.* I hate you, Oliver hates you...*fuck*, even *Julie* hates you. So maybe it's time you left Rockford and went back to whatever dirty-ass trailer you came from."

My fist hits his jaw so hard that I think I break a few fingers.

"Don't fucking talk to her like that!" My voice rises. "Don't say another *fucking* word!"

Casey spits out blood and rubs his jaw. "You deserve to be sucked in by her bullshit. I hope she ruins your fucking life like she's done to ours."

Dammit.

My fist hits his eye this time, and he falls to the ground. Heather squeals and clutches my arm so I won't continue punching him. I'm thankful she does, because I want to kill this guy right now for the way he's speaking of her. I don't know what comes over me, but no one is going to fucking talk to her like that and live to tell about it.

"Calm down," she whispers, looking down at Casey writhing on the ground and clutching his eye. "He's going to have to explain to Julie why he's got a black eye...you know that, right?"

Casey looks up at us with questions.

"Don't fucking tell her where you got that black eye," I say. "All she needs to know is someone kicked your ass because you deserved it." I nearly spit on him, but he quickly moves from our feet as fast as he can. I didn't see her come out, but Julie is running over to us, fire in her ocean-blue eyes. She helps Casey up and he cowers behind her like a hurt puppy dog. It's pissing Heather off so badly that she's going to slip up and make the wrong move here.

Julie growls. "*What* is going on out here?"

"Your little boyfriend on the side called me some pretty horrible things." Heather puffs up her chest. I know she's not afraid of Julie, but she still dreams about a friendship someday, so she doesn't unleash her attitude in full. "I don't appreciate being called a 'waste of space.'"

Julie laughs. "I'm sorry, he called you that?" Her snickering is more than Heather can bear. I touch her arm to calm her down and keep her head in the game. "You can't be surprised. I mean, you *aren't* the greatest person in the world, Heather."

My teeth grind together. "I stand by what I said before: You've become a real fucking bitch, Julie."

She doesn't care. "Okay, we're leaving. We don't need to be here with you two." She takes Casey's arm and he smiles wickedly at me as she starts to pull him away. "You two should be ashamed of yourselves, you know that? I thought you were starting to be different, better people."

Heather and I look at each other but don't say a word.

We *are* different, better people.

Julie just has no idea what we're doing to be that way.

FOURTEEN
CASEY

JULIE USHERS me away from Brandon and Heather and I'm thankful that they aren't screaming after us, trying to start more drama than there already is. I can't stand either of them, and what was that fucking bullshit about Oliver being out of town? How would they even know that?

She buckles herself into the seat next to me and frowns. "I'm missing the rest of class because you three can't act like adults in a parking lot." The air she exhales fills the car. "Why can't everyone just act like freaking adults around here?"

"I'm sorry, Julie." My eyes meet my lap. "I know that your classes are important to you."

She nods. "They really are. I never got the chance to do this college thing, Casey. You and Oliver did…even Heather did once. I just want it to be a normal experience and yet…here we are." Her long fingers wave around as she looks outside. "I wish Oliver never left."

Ouch.

"I can take care of you," I blurt. "You can count on me."

"I don't *need* you to take care of me." A tear falls down her cheek. "I just need you to take care of your-self and stop being this...*hurtful* person that you're being. Can we just start heading to Lake Reed now? I'll be in and out...let me call the caretaker, Madrie."

I listen to her pleasant phone call with the caretaker of the lake house, and before she hangs up, she's so personal with them that it makes me smile. She asks about the woman's husband, Paul, and how their kids are. She asks how they've been and gives them well wishes with a genuine smile on her face.

Jesus.

There's literally no one in this world I'd rather be here with.

My eye starts to throb as she hangs up the phone and looks around to make sure Brandon and Heather aren't still lingering around.

"They left already," I say and rub my jaw. "I watched Brandon peel out of here."

She doesn't answer me and puts her seat belt on. I know she wants to just leave and get whatever it is that she's wanting from the lake house, but I want to talk to her. I can't drive three hours in silence with her...there's no fucking way.

"Julie?"

I start the car and she looks over at me.

"I can't make this trip with you mad at me. Can we just talk about something...anything?"

She sighs. "Fine. How is your eye?"

I want to smile so badly but I'm trying not to be a

creep. "It fucking hurts." I start to laugh and rub the corner of my eye. "It's going to be a beautiful shiner for sure."

I can feel her smile without looking at her. "Yeah, Brandon can throw a mean right hook. You should've seen Oliver's lip when they scuffled at the lake house a few months ago…it was bruised a little bit for a *long* time."

My stomach turns when she talks about Oliver.

I'm such a loser.

"I'm sorry you missed your class." I try to change the subject quickly. "Is there any way I can make it up to you?"

The car lurches onto the freeway and we start the three-hour drive to our destination. I don't have a bench seat like Oliver did in his Jeep, so there's no hoping that she'll slide over and get closer to me—not that she would, anyway.

"Not really," she says. "I just want to get up there, grab what I need, and then come home. Oliver will be home tomorrow night and things will all go back to normal."

I chuckle. "Whatever normal is for us."

She giggles. "Exactly. Normal for our bunch isn't exactly picture perfect."

I shrug and notice that she's shivering. I find the heat controls and turn them on, directing the soft rush of warm air toward her body without saying a word. She thanks me silently by nodding toward me and snuggling into her seat.

She's fucking adorable.

I shake my head and keep my eyes on the road for

the entire trip, letting her fall asleep and snooze softly next to me. I want to make her feel safe, and if she didn't feel safe with me, she wouldn't have fallen asleep so quickly. It takes so much time to get her out of my brain that when I pull into the long gravel drive of Oliver's Lake Reed house, she stretches and moans and her essence is put directly back into my veins again.

"Oh, I'm sorry. I slept the whole way here!" She covers her mouth as she yawns. "I didn't sleep well last night without Oliver home."

I frown. "I'm sorry about that. But…we're here, and I think that's the caretaker waving at you."

Julie's eyes light up and she smiles. Her legs pull her from the car without even looking at me and she runs toward the woman with open arms, hugging her. The larger, older woman puts her arms around Julie and glares at me…probably because I'm not Oliver. People tend to do that when they see me alone with Julie, like I'm a predator and she's a fragile gazelle that I'm about to devour.

Okay, they're not totally wrong there.

"Casey, this is Madrie." Julie smiles at the woman as I walk up to them. "She's the new caretaker for the lake house. Well, her and her husband, Paul. Where is he?"

Madrie takes Julie's hand and smiles. "Paul had some work to do for another tenant down the road today, so it's just me." The smiles they exchange are oddly comforting to me. "He sends his love and wishes he could see you, but he has a crew of workers that need supervision."

Julie laughs. "I understand. I'm glad you're here! Is the door unlocked?"

Madrie nods. "Yes, Miss Julie. Do you have time for lunch? I can make you some freshly caught salmon and buttered squash."

My stomach growls and Julie notices. "Well, I guess that's a yes, isn't it? Thank you, Madrie. I hope you'll be joining us?"

The woman shakes her head. "No, Miss Julie. Once I make lunch, I should join Paul down the road and offer my help. I won't hear the end of it if I don't." The women laugh as they walk inside the lake house, and I hesitate. I never realized what I would feel like coming back here. The last time I set foot inside this house, Nora was on my arm, giggling and totally infatuated with me.

Where did I go wrong?

I growl and enter the house because I know *exactly* where I went wrong.

I'm a fucking idiot.

"Casey?" I hear Julie call for me from a room on the second floor. "Can you come up here and help me in the library, please?"

I've never run up a flight of stairs so fast in my life.

Since I've never been to the library, it takes me a quick minute to find it. I push the door open the rest of the way and see Julie stretching her small body to reach a few books on a high shelf near the window. Madrie is downstairs making the lunch she promised, so it's just me as I catch Julie before she falls backward and crumples to the floor. I hold her in my arms a little too long, but she doesn't pull from me. She lets me gently set her back on her feet as she blushes.

"I'm trying to get those bound books up there, the

ones with the different colors." Her finger points up high. "I'm not quite tall enough to reach them."

A smile spreads across my face. "I see that. Let me get them for you."

I brush past her without any real effort and reach to the shelf, taking down four of the books she pointed to. When I hand them to her, she smiles and looks at the floor. Our bodies are so close to each other that it'd take nothing for me to whisk her into my arms and devour her mouth.

"Thanks. I'll have to ask Oliver to get a small ladder installed in here."

The heat between us quickly fades when she says his name.

"Yeah." I clear my throat. "I'm sure he'll be happy to do it."

The air between us is awkward now. I know she's fully aware of what I want our relationship to be, and I know she's also aware that I won't make a single move to do anything about it. She's not mine, she's Oliver's, and I have to respect that if I want to keep her in my life.

She glides over to the golden chaise and sits down, packing the books into her bag for safekeeping. Her hand pats the empty spot next to her and I immediately sit down, making sure that our knees are a safe enough distance apart.

"So, how is Lucy?" she asks. "I know I see her in class, but we haven't talked about what happened."

I wave her off. "I haven't spoken to her, really. Your guess is as good as mine."

Lies. You know Oliver cheated with Lucy.

Julie's lips purse. "She seems like a good person, so maybe she'll come around. What happened after Oliver and I left the bar parking lot?"

I don't want to have this conversation with her.

"Do we have to talk about this?"

She blinks a few times and straightens her pale green blouse. "No, I guess not. I just thought since we're friends maybe we could talk about our lives together. Maybe I was wrong…"

"You're not wrong." I look at the fabric of the chaise and run my fingers over it. "I liked Lucy a lot, but she realized that I wasn't fully into it."

"Why not?"

Because I like you. *Are you kidding me?*

"She just noticed that I was trying to get over my crush on you." She blushes and folds her hands across her lap. "But she didn't want to hear my side of it. Now she won't even talk to me and I don't blame her. I mean, I screwed up with Nora, Lucy, *and* you."

Shit.

"Me? How did you screw up with me?"

I can't find another way to say it. "I thought that by showing you what a bad guy Oliver was and what a good guy I am…I don't know. I wanted you, and that's all I could think about."

Instead of changing the subject, she digs deeper. "I still don't know why everyone thinks they are in so much lust over me. It puzzles me sometimes why *Oliver* even loves me." Her gaze meets mine and I can see tears forming in the corners of her endless ocean blue eyes. "This whole thing surprises me…we never actually had a real foundation, you know? I mean, I love

Oliver, don't get me wrong. I love certain things about him that form into one big feeling, but he's never told me why he *specifically* loves me. Not really."

I let her continue and my heart starts beating faster.

"I'm just *me*, you know? I try to be a good person and just fly under the radar sometimes, but I'm still just a normal, regular person. I'm not magical." Her gaze meets mine again and I feel my cheeks flush. "No matter how much people think I'm something special, I'm really not."

I hold up my hand playfully. "Can I be truthful with you without getting my head bit off?"

She nods and laughs. "I guess so. This is a head-biting free zone right now."

"Good." I relax into the chaise and lock my eyes onto hers. "You *are* special, don't ever fucking think you're not. You turn lost and confused men into *warriors*, Julie. I've said this before, but you didn't know Oliver before our first trip up here. He was *not* headed down a good path. I'm surprised he didn't catch some disease from the number of women—"

She holds up her hand. "—Skip that part."

I nod. "Oliver wasn't interested in white picket fences and putting down roots until you came along. Something about the way you love him or how you handle yourself puts people in the mindset that everything is going to be okay. I mean, it's easy to fall for you, it really is. You just make people…*better*."

She wipes away tears and I can't help it, I reach out and flick away the last few drops that linger on her cheek. "You bring out the best in people, Julie."

I want to kiss her so fucking bad right now it's unreal.

161

"Casey," she whispers my name and leans into my touch. "We can't do this."

I can't hold air inside my lungs anymore, so I blow out whatever I have left. "We're not doing anything, we're just talking." I smile, but I know she feels guilty so I pull my hand away. I'm not going to make a move on her—not after Oliver finally trusts me to be around her again.

"We should go downstairs." Her voice is low. "Madrie might have lunch ready."

"You go ahead, I'll be down in a minute," I say. She doesn't waste time before she stands up and leaves me alone in the library, where I collapse into the chaise and put my hand over my chest. My heart is beating so fast it feels like it's going to burst through my ribcage.

I almost kissed her.

I almost took her innocence from her and made her a horrible person.

I'm a damn mess.

After making sure to wait a considerable amount of time so I can compose myself, I head downstairs and into the kitchen, where Julie and Madrie watch me with wary expressions. A glass of iced tea and a full plate of salmon, asparagus, and buttered yellow squash wait for me across from Julie as she sits down with her own plate. Madrie eyes me with annoyance as I join Julie at the table.

"This looks really good, thanks Madrie." I flash a toothy smile at her and try to melt some of the ice around her hard gaze. "I haven't eaten this good in a long time."

Julie giggles. "Madrie, if you need to go...I understand. Thank you so much for the delicious food." She takes a bite and moans, making me nearly drop my fork as I pick it up. "Tell Paul hello for me, and I promise Oliver and I will plan a trip up here when my classes are over in seven more weeks."

Madrie nods and hugs her. "You be safe, Miss Julie."

I dig into the food and hardly notice that Madrie leaves us alone until I'm halfway done. Julie is right; this food *is* delicious.

"Maybe you should breathe a little." Julie laughs and takes a bite of her own salmon; her eyes roll back into her head with pleasure. "This is *so* good!"

Watching her lips around the fork turns me on.

Her eyes closing and opening in pleasure turns me on.

The small giggle she gives me when she notices me watching her turns me on.

"Do you want a beer before we head back? I'm not for drinking and driving, but I can drive back if you want." She stands up and her body brushes past me to get to the fridge. I let her hand me an ice-cold beer, and it takes me no time to open it and chug it down. I need the release; I need her to stop tantalizing me before I do something I'll regret.

She clears her throat when she sits back down. "Do you think we can hit some of the antique stores in town before we head back to Rockford? I want to start looking for items for the new house."

Fuck.

I forgot that he asked her to marry him and bought her a house.

My mood instantly drops and I stand up for another

beer, throwing my bottle away in the process. I don't speak to her as I drink the second one and toss it into the trash can with the first. It's not a secret that I'm having a rough time with all of this.

"Casey? The antique stores?"

I grunt and nod. "Sure."

Anything for you, Julie.

My best friend's girl.

FIFTEEN
VERONICA

IT'S a damn miracle that my sons even know how to walk upright without hurting themselves. The fact that my eldest skipped town and left his precious Julie behind with my *other* son who clearly has a hard-on for her too...well, doesn't make him the brightest bulb in the box, now does it?

I watch Julie and Casey get into a black car and back out of the long gravel driveway. I know the caretaker won't be back soon and I want to take another peek inside. But the last time I set foot in this lake house was only months ago, when the kids left the first time. Mac and I started to run through the place but noticed the security system cameras and bolted. I managed to make it out with a few things, including a few of Colin's journals.

Colin Jackson was one of the best men I've ever known.

The grace he pulled out of me was addicting, I'll admit; it was fucking nice being someone else for a little while even if the darkness at the end of the tunnel dooms you once you reach it. I always went back to Mac, though—the different forms of happiness he provided me were just much more addicting than being a housewife and mother.

I *was* only twenty-two, after all.

I wasn't ready to be a wife to someone. Especially not someone honest and pure like Colin Jackson. I know that people can get married in high school and stay together forever, but a tornado and a tidal wave never mix. *Ever.*

"Hey," Mac's gruff voice jabs through my daydream. "We gonna try and swipe the place again?"

I shake my head. "No, idiot. Remember they have cameras, and I ain't going to jail for you again. I told you that the last time."

Mac snickers. "You told me that the last *three* times."

I lower my eyes to my lap because I'm defeated. "I know that," I say to myself, because he stopped listening once he said his piece. He knows I'll never leave him because I need what he needs—the catch and release that we give each other.

"Well, if we ain't swiping the place, are we followin' those two?" He points where Casey and Julie have passed us and driven off without a care in the world. I find myself desperately wanting to leave Mac in the dust and become the matriarch of this family, but I know both of my sons want nothing to do with me. I've done too much and gone too far for them to forgive me easily.

Mac's large foot nudges my leg. "Hey, you listenin' to me? Don't make me ask you again."

I lick my lips and think for a quick second. "Let's follow them and make sure Casey doesn't fuck shit up for us." The sweat running down my cheeks is from the fear Mac puts inside of me whenever he teeters on the edge of revealing his true self.

It's not the easygoing and fun-loving man I met so many years ago. I'm careful not to let the monster inside of him out.

"Fine," he growls, lurching the van far behind Casey and Julie. I'm sure they'll be too distracted with each other to notice anyone following them and that's fine by me; I'm not in the mood for a fucking confrontation right now. My eyelids flutter and I know it's a long drive back, so I close my eyes and dream of something —anything—better than this.

———

There he is.

I wonder if my hair is doing that awful side curl thing it likes to do. Can I reach up and fix it without being obvious? The fear of being caught staring at their table—the rich kids table—rises in my throat and it makes me want to scream.

All that comes out is silence.

"Hey, Veronica. You might want to get a move on to your table, Mac is watching us," another waitress, Polly, says to me. "You know he doesn't like when we stand around."

My eyes move to the corner that Mac, our day-shift manager, likes to lurk in and watch us. There he is, licking his lips and staring at me. I admit, there may have been a time when I crushed on him. That time has long passed me since Colin Jackson started showing up at Lake Reed. First, he started coming in the summers with his father when we were teenagers, then it became winters too. He never realized I existed until earlier this summer. He was always different from the other boys that would come and go; he never made fun of me in passing or even batted an eyelash at the thought of having a summer fling with the dirt-poor help of the Lake Reed Inn.

We've been secretly seeing each other all summer, and it's bursting inside of me; I want to tell someone so badly that I don't care what his rules are anymore.

Pfft. Rules.

Colin loves his rules.

I think it's a way for him to protect me from his friends.

My mother worked at the Inn when she was a teenager too. She loved the Inn just as much as she loved Everett Lathrop, the son of the richest man on the east coast, Dr. Carlisle Lathrop. Unfortunately, after declaring their undying love for each other when they were seventeen, my mother found out she was pregnant with me and Dr. Lathrop took his son far, far away and never returned.

This didn't deter her from loving me. She made the decision to keep me as her own and we lived at the Lake Reed Inn, down in the basement employee apartments, for six years. I can still smell the mildew caked on the pipes that ran through our ceiling.

Then, she was gone.

Just like that.

I was playing upstairs on a Sunday morning and when I came back downstairs to wake her...she wasn't there. Her things were scattered and mostly gone, a roll of money laid next to a folded-up piece of paper on her bed.

My dearest Veronica,

I have spoken with Madrie and Paul, they will watch over you. I know you can't read this letter, so I can only hope someone will explain to you why I've left.

I'm not meant to live this life.

Please, don't go through life with hate in your heart for me.

I know you're just a child, please forgive me.

Just know, I do love you.

Mommy

That piece of paper sits folded in my small cedar box where I keep my important things. I haven't seen her since the night before she left, but I'm mostly over it now. Madrie and Paul took good care of me even though they were barely twenty years old themselves. I know it's a sad story that I've lived, but it's my story and I'd like to think that's what makes life complicated enough to call it a shitstorm.

"V?" Polly nudges me. "Go!"

My legs work before my brain does. I find myself in front of the rich kids table and they stop their conversation to glare at me with disgust and pity.

"Another minute there, blondie?" One of the guys snickers and smacks hands with another to his left. I don't even bother studying them when I know they don't compare to the dark chocolate hair and cool gray eyes of Colin Jackson. I find them and blush; my insides are raging with adrenaline and fear.

"Hey, don't I know you from somewhere?" Colin jokes and smiles at me. "You look very familiar."

The first guy snickers again. "Yeah, I'm sure she does look familiar to you. You've probably slept with her already, man...let it go."

Colin's eyes lock with his. "I'd rather you didn't talk about her like that."

My heart melts into my chest. "I-I, um...well, is there anything...do you need?"

The two guys and three designer-labeled girls at the table laugh.

Not Colin.

He leans in and the three girls at the table drool all over themselves. When they notice that his eyes are locked on me, their ruby-red lips turn into frowns. "Can you tell my girl-friend that I can't wait until I see her tonight?"

His eyes burn into mine.

I'm going to faint.

He smiles. "Veronica?"

"Yes?" My throat is so dry that it hurts. I know Mac is watching, so I want to stay professional, no matter how bad I want to jump into Colin's lap and smack the other girls in their damn faces. "Yes, Mr. Jackson?"

He blushes. "Please, V. You know you can call me Colin."

Mac's snarl is near my ear as he walks up to the table. "I'm sorry, Mr. Jackson, but I can't."

Colin's lips turn into a wicked smile. "Well, then. You can call me whatever you want." He bites the inside of his *cheek and sucks his bottom lip in. "As long as you're the one saying it."*

"Is there a problem here?" Mac grunts as he reaches us. "I can get you a new waitress if you'd like."

The three girls at the table start to protest, but Colin waves his hand in the air like a magic wand and they go quiet.

"Absolutely not," Colin says, glaring at Mac. "You'll keep our waitress the same, and when I leave her tip on the table, she will get all of it and you won't pocket it anymore, will you, Terrance?"

Mac tenses when he hears his real name. "Who do you think—"

Colin's eyebrows rise. "Do we have an understanding?"

Mac nods and glares at me. "If he touches you, I want to know."

Colin stands and towers over me; his dark hair falls into his eyes and I almost need him to help me stand on my own two feet.

He's gorgeous.

"Veronica," he purrs, "what time does your shift end?"

I let him pull me away from the table and to a secluded part of the dining room. "I took a double shift today, so I won't be off until after midnight."

He plays with the loose strands of my hair. "Then I'll come pick you up at midnight."

"I don't know about this." I can barely breathe. "I'm not going to fall for this, Colin. I want more than this."

"I'm not trying to trick you." He licks his lips and looks like he wants to devour me. "I just find myself wanting to know you more, is that so wrong?"

I'm not going to fall for this.

I'm not going to fall for this.

I'm not—

His eyes glow. "Please?"

I find my voice. "Okay. But if this is a joke or a trick, I'll tell Mac and he'll probably run you over with his ATV." I giggle and crane my neck to see Mac, still seething toward us in his corner. "I'm sure he won't waste a chance to beat you."

Colin laughs and slides his rough hands around my waist. "I couldn't care less about what he wants or doesn't want; I want to kiss you, and that's all I can think about right now."

His lips touch mine and it's like fireworks explode in my body.

———

"HEY!" Mac's harsh whisper jerks me awake. "Wake the fuck up, they're stopping!"

My eyelids flutter and it takes me a few seconds to realize where I am and what I've become. My vision focuses just in time to see Julie and Casey leave the car laughing, walking into a small off-the-road antique store halfway between Lake Reed and Rockford.

"We goin' in?" he asks.

I shake my head. "No, we have to wait for the right time to snatch her."

"When is that?" Mac snarls. "When you've changed your mind and backed out of this?"

He knows.

Dammit, he knows.

"I know you're thinkin' twice about this," he says, and I can feel the heat of his breath on my cheek as he leans closer into me. "But don't you fucking *dare* try and back out of this, you hear me? I *want* that money, we *need* that money. Those boys don't fucking want you, so don't fuck this up."

My hands slam onto the dashboard. "I said I'm doin' it, so I'm doin' it! We can't just go charging into a place we ain't ever been before and kidnap someone! Jesus, Mac…get a damn grip on yourself."

He thinks about what I've said and clicks his tongue. "We can't follow this little bitch forever—I hope you've got a plan. And it better be a good fucking one."

We wait for over an hour before Julie and Casey come back out of the antique store. He holds a few packages and puts them into the trunk before they start to drive away. This time, Casey gets into the driver's seat, and as they pass the van, he looks nervously over and we lock eyes.

"Shit," I say, ducking my head. "I think he saw me."

Mac groans. "Jesus, leave it to you to fuck this up. I'm still followin' them, right?"

"Right," I hiss. "Maybe he won't freak out and draw attention to us."

The rest of the drive is silent between Mac and I, just the constant buzzing of the van's engine as it struggles on its last leg. I wonder how we blew through that last hundred grand so fast without so much as considering the fact that we needed a new car. I mean, we fucking *sleep* in here…the least I should've done was buy an RV.

"They're going back to Oliver's apartment," I say when we get into Rockford and they pull into the parking garage of his apartment building. "They're not going anywhere tonight…let's park and get something to eat."

He snorts. "All you ever do is eat."

I look down at my thin arms and legs. "Then, let's sleep. I'm tired."

Sick and tired, to be honest.

I want a different life. I want the life I was *supposed* to have. It's too late to go back now.

No…I *have* to do this…I have to snatch the girl and get the money. Except now, I'm going to take the money and run.

Without Mac.

SIXTEEN
HEATHER

"WHO DOES SHE THINK SHE IS?" Brandon's deep voice rises in the sealed cab of his car. "If she only fucking knew what we were doing for her, she wouldn't be such a Grade-A bitch!" He blows out a typhoon of air from his lungs and taps the steering wheel impatiently. It's been an hour since Julie blew us off and he's still steaming over it, which can only mean one thing:

He's not over her.

I listen as he rambles on.

"…right? It's not like she's innocent in all of this… she knows what she's doing with that second-rate Saint Jackson…"

I find a package of mini peanut butter cups in my bag and start popping them into my mouth as he trails off and cranes his neck to stare at me while driving.

"And what do you think you're doing?"

I toss another chocolate into my mouth. "Eating candy and not giving a shit about what Julie said to me, that's what."

He scoffs. "You're not pissed? That's surprising."

I shake my head. "I don't care what she says—I know that I'm doing a good thing for once, and that's all that matters. Who cares what she thinks? Oliver knows the truth about how we're trying to be better people. In the end, she'll know too. Just be patient." Brandon's jaw drops and I stick a chocolate inside and smile. "You want people to see you in a better light, then act like it."

"You're right," he says, chewing the candy. "I shouldn't be a dick to her when I haven't told her the worst news yet." He sucks in air through his teeth. "We can't be divorced for like three months…there's a whole process and waiting time we have to adhere to."

I don't act surprised, even though I want to claw his eyes out. "Okay, so we wait three months. I'm not in a hurry to get married, so it makes no difference to me."

"You don't want to get married?"

Oh, no. I struck a chord I didn't mean to.

"Someday, sure. Not anytime soon."

His teeth grind loudly. "I see. I was under the assumption we were working *toward* something like that, and here you are…wanting the opposite."

Shit. I have to fix this before he blows up.

"You didn't listen to me. I said *eventually* I want to get married. We aren't in any rush, are we? I'm not going anywhere…you're not going anywhere. We've only been dating for less than a month. Maybe after a year we can talk about something like that."

The steam in his breath chills. "You're right…again. I don't know what my problem is. I guess Julie got under my skin. It's a fucked-up feeling knowing that someone you once loved is marrying someone else. It makes you crazy and want to rush things."

I hiccup at the sugar overload and he laughs at me, so I shove a candy into his mouth to shut him up. "Let's talk about something else, okay? I'm not Julie's biggest fan right now either, but in her defense, we haven't been angels to her a day in her life…why would she believe we are now?"

Brandon tugs the car into a parking space outside of Rita's Boutique and puts it into park. My insides panic; I haven't told him this is where Lucy works. "What are we doing here?" I squeak. "Are we going into another shop?"

He shakes his head. "No, we're going into Rita's. I know it's not Dolce or Versace like Jackson could give you, but I have a black-tie charity thing next month for work and I need my girlfriend to look fucking more amazing than she already does." He winks and opens his door. "So, shall we?"

I quickly try and think of a reason to get out of it, but he's already opening my door and pulling me out of the car. I don't know where Lucy goes after our class, but hopefully she doesn't work today or this entire transaction is about to be awkward.

Once Brandon opens the boutique door and pushes me inside, I look around frantically for Lucy to pop out from behind the counter. Instead, a small-framed woman with bushy black eyebrows and bottle-cap glasses greets us.

"Hello there, kids. Welcome to Rita's Boutique…I'm Rita." She makes a weird giggle. "What can I help you with today?"

Brandon speaks for me. "I work at Walden and Trumbull—" The woman's eyes grow big and suddenly she's more attentive. "—and my girlfriend needs something spectacular to wear to the children's hospital gala next month."

The woman gasps. "The Gatlin Children's Hospital Gala? Oh, honey, that's *fancy*." Her eyes dart toward me and she looks me up and down. "We have some gowns I've been saving for special occasions like this, what are you…a size four?"

I blush. "Yes."

She doesn't miss a beat. "Okay then, honey, have yourself a seat and I'll run up and grab them for you. Black-tie, yes?" She nods at Brandon, who nods right back to her like this isn't the first time he's done something like this. "Excellent. Help yourselves to the sparkling white wine on the table there."

Brandon pours each of us a flute of wine and sits down on the oversized white sofa. He takes a huge swig of the wine and notices that I'm staring at him when he crosses his legs. The suit he's wearing is charcoal and cut just right for his body; the cool, silky fabric calls to me to snuggle up next to.

"You okay?" He snickers. "It's just a dress, babe."

I swallow whatever feelings were about to burst out of me. "I know that. Are you sure about this? What happens if we go to this charity thing and something happens to Julie?"

He puts the flute down and uncrosses his legs, putting his elbows on his knees as he leans forward to scold me. "Oliver will be back in town by then—this gala is a month from now. I'm not going to let anything happen to her, so just enjoy this, okay? I thought you might need this after the shit day we've had. I've gotta make a few phone calls…you'll be okay in here by yourself for a few minutes, right?"

"Of course I will." I playfully roll my eyes and let him kiss my cheek. "And thank you."

He shakes his head. "No need to thank me; you deserve something like this for the kind of person you're trying to become. I envy you that you've been so cool-headed about everything…it's really *sexy*." His lips turn up into his wicked smile before he steps back outside. I watch him through the front windows as he pulls his phone out and dials someone, looking around before he starts talking.

Don't worry about it.

You can trust him.

The woman returns with several dresses folded over her small arms. "Is your boyfriend on to bigger and better things?" she jokes, hanging the gowns on a rack next to the dressing rooms. "Don't worry about it—men don't usually stick around for this part, anyway. In you go." She takes my hand and shoves me behind one of the purple silk curtains.

Purple.

I chuckle to myself at the irony. The woman reaches into the room and hands me four gowns, each as sparkling and stunning as the next. After the first two, a black floor-length strapless gown and a short, baby pink cocktail dress…I take the third off of the hanger and swoon. The fabric feels like butter against my skin and hugs my hips just right to accentuate whatever curves are there lying dormant. I smooth the ivory satin over my stomach and wiggle my toes because the dress is touching them and tickling them.

"This is it," I whisper, feeling the breeze of the shop door opening and closing. I nearly burst from the dressing room to greet Brandon and show him the dress, but something inside of me tells me to stop and take a minute. I continue looking in the mirror and smiling when I hear Lucy's voice waft through the curtain as she greets the saleswoman and tries to catch her breath.

"Sorry I'm late, Rita," she pants out. "My last class ran late and there was traffic. But I'm here now...what can I do?"

Rita sighs. "Take a breath and slow down—put your things away. I'm going to grab a bite to eat down at Dilaggio's and there's a customer in the dressing room trying on gowns for the Gatlin Children's Gala. Can you handle that?"

"I can handle it," Lucy grumbles. "Bring me back some chocolate cake?"

"You and that chocolate cake," Rita says with a laugh. "Consider it done. Oh, and that man out there is here with the girl in the dressing room, so don't be alarmed when he comes back in."

Lucy scoffs. "I'm not scared of a random guy."

Rita doesn't answer and I feel the door open. I start to panic and reach for my phone to text Brandon when the shop door closes and I hear his voice come into the room.

"Hey...oh, you're Lucy, right?" he says to her. "I'm Brandon...Heather's boyfriend?"

Lucy doesn't answer him.

"Heather Michaels?"

I should get out there before she pisses him off.

"*Oh*, yeah." Her words are drawn out in annoyance. "I guess you are, aren't you? Nice to meet you finally. I've heard a lot about you from Julie."

Brandon sucks air through his teeth. "Well, I wouldn't believe everything you hear. Is Heather still in the dressing room?"

Shit.

I poke my head out and fake a smile. "I'm here."

The color drains from Lucy's face. "Oh! I didn't know it was you in there! *You're* going to the Children's Gala? How did that happen?"

Brandon clears his throat. "She's going with me. Did you find a dress?" I open the curtain the rest of the way and his eyes grow wide. "Jesus, step out of there."

I do what he asks and when I fully emerge, he licks his lips. "What do you think?"

Lucy's jaw drops. "Heather, that dress is gorgeous on you."

Brandon growls at her because I wasn't asking for her opinion. He steps toward me and runs his hands down my arms, leaving goosebumps on my skin. "I think you've found your dress." He clears his throat and eyeballs Lucy, who's still gawking from behind the cash register. "She's going to need shoes and whatever else she wants."

It takes Lucy a few seconds to start moving. "Uh—yeah, I think we have some satin pumps to go with that dress…do you still wear a seven?" She swallows down the air that she's holding in as I look at her with sass. She doesn't wait for me to answer before skating out of the room with us. Brandon looks like he's about to devour my whole body; the hunger in his eyes makes me smile.

"So, *do* you like it? I figured you'd like a floor-length gown so no one could see anything they aren't supposed to."

He grabs my waist and plants his lips on mine; I snake my arms around the back of his neck and let him cradle me how he wants to. I hardly care about Lucy, who walks back into the room and shuffles her feet nervously at the sight of us kissing, because even though she never did anything to me…when she noticed I wasn't the same person I used to be, she didn't see a point in continuing our friendship.

Or whatever we had.

"Oh…" Lucy fakes a small cough and Brandon smiles against my lips. "Did you two need a minute alone? I can see what sort of bags we have to match the dress."

I wave her off. "I don't need a clutch, I have one. We'll take the dress and the shoes, thanks."

Brandon's eyes glow as he looks at me. "You're completely gorgeous," he whispers before pecking my lips again. A wave of heat travels through my body as he grips my hips with force. "Go change, we're going home."

Fire flashes in his eyes.

That can only mean one thing.

I quickly take the dress off and hand it to him through the curtain. I hear Lucy trying to make small talk with him while she rings him up and he pays for everything; I make it a point to take longer than I need to just so I don't have to get caught in an awkward situation. I'm not exactly fully comfortable with him paying for everything yet, but I can't exactly do anything about that right now.

"Babe?" Brandon calls as I zip my jeans back up. "You ready?"

I pull the curtain back and step out. Lucy's face is pale and surprised. "Ready. Thanks, Lucy." I sweetly smile at her and let Brandon escort me out of the store.

"I thought she was your friend?" he asks me once we pull into the driveway of his condo. "Didn't she move here for you or something?"

I shrug. "We had lunch, I spilled about everything that's happened in my life—including Oliver and all of that—and she said we'd meet up again but wouldn't answer my text or anything." I know I sound like a child, but he asked and I'm not in the business of telling lies anymore. "I don't know, maybe I was trying to make something out of nothing. We hadn't seen each other for years and maybe I hoped she'd just come running back to me like nothing ever changed."

He clicks his tongue. "I'm sorry, babe. I know what that's like."

I smile at him and the air thickens around us. The world around us is stopping just for us to take in this moment, and I like it. It's simple…uncomplicated… whatever you want to call it. Even though I'm not fully trusting of him yet, I give him everything I have because…why the hell not? Just because I destroyed my own happiness last time doesn't mean I'll do it again with Brandon.

I'm a better person now.

I know what kind of life I want and I'm going to take it.

Brandon reaches out and holds my hand. "I think I can get used to this."

"Used to what?"

His thumb rubs the inside of my palm. "Things going our way."

I don't say anything—I don't want to jinx it.

I'm *used* to things going my way, but this is different.

Easier.

Better.

Stronger.

Forever.

SEVENTEEN
JULIE

CASEY and I spent over an hour inside of the small off-the-road antique store, and it was actually pleasant enough where I wasn't constantly reminded of his feelings for me. Oliver called a few times, but the service in the hills isn't exactly spot-on, so I texted him that I would call him when I was in an area that I could make a phone call.

He didn't like it, but that's not what's on my mind.

Brandon's text is on my mind.

He told me that we'll have to wait three months to get our problem taken care of.

"What's wrong?" Casey asks as we turn back onto the winding roads that'll lead us into Rockford. "You look like someone just gave you a puppy and then took it right back."

I laugh. "No, it's the marriage thing. Which, by the way, I'm grateful for you not telling Oliver about. I thought I could get it taken care of before he came back, but looks like we have to wait three months for the paperwork to go through."

He sucks in air through his front teeth. "*Ouch*, that's a long time to keep a secret like that."

"Don't remind me." I groan and put my head into my hands. "I'm going to have to tell him…it's not fair to keep a secret like that."

"He keeps secrets from *you*, Julie," Casey warns. "Don't forget that. This isn't a life-or-death situation, and honestly, I don't think he'll care as much as you think. He's going to be pissed at Brandon for…wait a minute. Exactly *how* did this happen?"

I don't want to tell him my intimate details, but other than Staci—who's been hard to reach after our lunch together—and Nora—who's more involved with her new flame than her friends right now—I have no one to talk to about this. Oliver has become my best friend, but I don't want to feel his disappointment when he finds out that I've been keeping this from him.

There's no other way to deal with it than to just tell Casey the truth.

"Brandon got me drunk and then took me to an all-night chapel."

Casey doesn't like it any more than Oliver will. His face turns bright red, but he keeps his cool since he's driving down windy roads. "He *forced* you to marry him? Exactly what kind of loser tricks a woman into marrying him? If someone doesn't love you enough to marry you…"

He looks over at me and stops talking.

I blush. "I love Oliver enough to marry him."

"I know you do."

My gaze fixes on the passing trees outside my window. Realizing I haven't called Oliver like I said I would, I find my phone and push the call button underneath his name. It rings a few times and when he answers, he's out of breath.

"Julie?"

I feel my eyes narrow on accident. "It's me."

"Where are you?" he demands. "When I called you, I could barely hear you."

"I texted you and told you Casey and I came up to Lake Reed so I could grab more journals. We ate lunch, I talked to Madrie, and we stopped at an antique store, and now we're on our way back to Rockford."

He doesn't speak for a long time, but I can hear his breathing in the phone.

"I guess that's okay." His voice is small when he returns. "Is Casey behaving himself?"

"Yes." I smile and keep my gaze focused outside. "You don't have to worry about that. How's California?"

He sighs. "Fucking horrible without you. I miss you, sunshine."

I don't know why, but I look over at Casey before answering him. "I miss you too. When will you be back home?"

"Well, the deals are done and I've signed everything imaginable, so I'm trying to get a flight out tonight, but it looks like it'll be tomorrow morning before I'm able to get home."

I see the sign for Rockford and tap my fingers on the console between us. "Okay, be safe. I'll see you then, okay? We're about to get home and I want to start studying since I missed my second class today."

Oops.

"*What?* Why did you miss it?" His voice rises. "What happened?"

Way to go, Julie.

"Oh, Casey got into it with Brandon and Heather in the campus parking lot. Heather is in my Economics class...I didn't tell you because I didn't want you to try and make me change my schedule around when I worked so hard to get in."

I wait for the fireworks.

"I'm sure Brandon had his reasons for whatever he did to Casey," he says. "Just go home and study and stay out of trouble, okay? I love you."

"I love you too." I hang up before it goes on any longer. Casey looks nervous as he pulls the car into the parking garage of Oliver's apartment building and shuts the engine off. I'm torn between two different emotions: I don't want to make Casey feel awkward when I tell Oliver I love him, but I'm not going to stop just because he doesn't like it.

Casey speaks first. "When is he coming back?"

"Tomorrow morning."

"Oh." I can feel his sadness. "Well, we can order takeout Thai tonight and I can find something to do while you study."

"Don't you work?" I blurt. "I mean, don't you need to go to work sometime?"

He shakes his head. "I haven't found a job since I've graduated. I've been too busy..." The blush in his cheeks is enough to make me uneasy. "...chasing other things." The light dims in his eyes for a few seconds as he rushes around to figure out what his next move is going to be. "Maybe you can help me look for one later?"

His smile warms my skin and it makes me feel weird. "Sure, what did you major in?"

"Education." He blushes. "I wanted to be a teacher years ago."

"A teacher!" I get excited and turn to face him. "That's really awesome—why don't you use that? I think you'd make a great teacher, Casey!"

He scoffs. "You hardly know me."

"That's not true." The swell of my excitement dwindles. "I *know* you."

"Not really, Julie. You know I'm a damn mess, and someone like me should *not* be teaching children right from wrong when I hardly know the difference myself."

I have to change the subject.

Now.

"Oh, hey…" The wheels in my head are turning so fast that steam could billow from my ears any moment. "I forgot about the things we got at the antique store; they're for the new house. Do you mind if we take them over there and I can get some pictures of the rooms? It's a few blocks from my brother's house. Do you remember where that is?"

He nods. "I remember. I thought you wanted to study?"

"This will be *much* more fun." I try and lighten the mood with a huge smile, and it works for a few seconds until the car becomes silent again. I let him drive us toward Randy's house, directing him to the new house as we get closer. When we pull into the driveway, his eyes look like they're about to burst from his skull at the sight of it.

"Jesus, Oliver really outdid himself," he murmurs.

I ignore him and climb out of the car, taking my keys from my pocket and opening the front door. Oliver had given me a spare key to the apartment and the new house before he left because he knew I wanted to come here and look around. My thoughts race back to when he first brought me here; the smile on his face was so genuine and happy that it hurt me to make it disappear. I couldn't move in with him knowing that I could've been pregnant.

I'm so thankful that the results were negative and I wasn't forced to become something I'm not ready to be yet.

Like a mother.

Or a wife.

But I'm already a wife and didn't even know.

A chill runs down my spine and my body shakes. When we step into the foyer part of the house, our voices echo from the lack of furniture occupying the space. He whistles and shuts the door behind us, shoving his hands into his pockets and doing circles around me like a dance.

"This is crazy big." His eyes reach the vaulted ceiling with double-paned skylights above us. "I mean, even for Oliver, this is crazy."

I smile at the thought of how Casey and Oliver might be if their egos hadn't gotten in the way. I'd imagine they'd be rough-and-tumble brothers, always playfully wrestling when no one was looking.

"It's big, sure," I mumble, because I don't like drawing attention to those things. "I don't care how big it is, but I *do* like that he bought it for us."

Casey shakes his head and his sandy blond hair shuffles around his forehead. "And you don't think that's a little crazy? Buying a house for a woman you barely know?"

I should be offended. But Casey is right. It's an absurd thing to do.

But it *feels* right.

"I don't know what it is." I sigh and take my phone out, snapping pictures of the living room as we enter it. "But I know that Oliver will never let me down and he'll always love me. Don't ask me how I know." I see the question in his eyes. "I just do. Oliver and I are meant to be together—the only people who need to believe in that are us, and we do."

I can't get what Oliver said about finding me *again* out of my mind.

"You're right." His gaze fixates on the half-open curtain in the living room window and he frowns. "You can't deny something like that. I can just hope I find that someday." His words are rushed, and he keeps looking out the curtain but I don't care enough to figure out why.

I should've looked.

I really, *really* should've looked.

When I walk up the curved staircase to check out the second floor, I hear several loud bangs where I left him downstairs. "Are you okay?" I yell down the stairs. I hear shuffling before he mutters something about hitting his knee. I wonder if I should help him since he sounded like he's in pain, but the master bedroom door is open, letting me peek just enough inside to reel me in.

The bedroom is almost as big as the entire pool house at Randy's.

My mouth opens and I look at the four walls and then the white crown-vaulted ceiling. I make a mental note to ask Oliver to have a skylight installed in here, like the ones in the foyer, because it would remind me of the pool house even more and I need that feeling of home if I'm going to sleep here.

The walk-in closet beckons me inside and I run my fingertips along the lower solid oak shelves, imagining several shoe boxes full of pictures from years of memories inside the house. I smile when I reach the middle and think about putting a matching golden chaise inside of the closet like the one at the lake house... That's when I hear more shuffling downstairs, and Casey starts to scream.

"No!" I freeze, my heart pounding as more shuffling noises rise up from the lower floor. "Julie! *Run!* Lock the door!"

The panic in his voice settles inside of me quickly and I spring into action, leaping out of the closet and toward the open bedroom door, but it's too late. Two people rush into the room and glare at me with their dark eyes and angry expressions. One of them manages to get behind me and wrap their arms around me tightly so I can't move. Casey appears in the doorway so out of breath that he has to clutch his side so he won't pass out.

"Let her go," he says.

The person in front of me grins.

Veronica.

Oliver's mother.

"Shut the fuck up, boy," she growls at him. "You're not gonna do shit. You're no good just like my other pansy-ass son."

I'm in trouble.

"What do you want?" My lower lip quivers. "Let go of me!" I scream and wiggle inside of the death grip the other person has on me. The man's arms, with tracks and wounds on the inside of his wrists and elbows, are all I can see of him as he squeezes me so hard that I can barely breathe.

"Just let her go—take me instead," Casey pleads with them. "If you hurt her—"

Veronica whirls around to glare at him. "You did your job well, kid, now scram."

Casey's eyes find mine. "You did this to me?" I whisper. "You *knew* about this?"

His head shakes violently. "No, fuck, Julie...all she wanted me to do was earn your trust back. She fucking *played* me to get to you," he growls at Veronica.

I let my body go limp and the man has a hard time keeping a hold on me. While Veronica and Casey are fighting, Casey shifts his eyes to look at me and silently tells me to run.

Run, Julie.

My brain activates some part of superhuman strength and I elbow the man in the stomach to make him loosen his grip further. I wriggle free of his grasp just enough to separate our bodies from each other.

I have to make it downstairs.

I have to run and hide outside.

Casey pushes Veronica out of my way as she leaps toward me, and I hear him make a weird noise and a loud thud echoes through the house as I reach the staircase. I know they're right behind me, so I don't waste time and take the steps two at a time until I trip and fall on my knees at the bottom.

"Need help?" a familiar voice asks.

I need to run.

I look up and gasp.

Mary Callahan, the nurse who took care of Oliver in the hospital.

"Mary?" I hear my voice, but I don't feel my mouth move. "I-I have to run."

Her laugh is sickening, making me feel queasy. "I don't think so. She's down here!" Her voice billows up the staircase and Veronica, followed by the man who was holding me, race down and pick me up off the floor.

"Mary? Why are you with them?"

Veronica snickers. "It wasn't hard to find someone my son has pissed off so much that they would be willing to help take him down."

"What did he do to you?" I scream at her, unaware of the volume of my voice. "What the fuck has Oliver ever done to any of you people?"

Mary scoffs and shrugs. "Oh, me? I'm just a scorned ex-girlfriend that he doesn't remember from years ago who was promised enough money that I can move somewhere far, far away, that's all."

"Enough!" Veronica growls at her. "Don't tell this little bitch anything else! Give me your phone," she

snarls and shoves her hands into my jeans pockets, pulling out my phone and cackling to herself. She throws me back to the man, who tightens his grip on me harder this time. I see Casey out of the corner of my eye crawling to the top of the stairs, holding his leg in pain. He pulls his phone out of his own pocket and his eyes lock with mine, our fear radiating toward each other.

"Let's just call my good-for-nothing spawn and say hello, shall we?" Veronica laughs and shifts her eyes toward the man holding me, making sure he's watching her. In this moment, I'm not afraid of her. She's just like me…trying to hold onto something that's slipping through her fingers.

"Hey, sunshine." We all hear Oliver answer the phone because she's put it on speaker. "Is something wrong? I'm just finishing up some emails, can I call you back?"

Veronica snickers. "I would advise against that if I were you, son."

A long pause fills the room while Oliver struggles to catch up without being able to see anything. "What the fuck are you doing with Julie's phone? Where is she? If you hurt her, I'll fucking end you." He threatens her without taking a single breath.

Veronica clicks her tongue in annoyance. "Watch your mouth, or something's gonna happen to her. I want my money, and I want it in twenty-four hours or you'll never see her again." I watch her go for the end call button, and I know I have to do something.

"Oliver!" I scream as she hits the button and cuts the call off.

"Shut her up!" Veronica hisses. "We don't want to draw any more attention than we already have."

The man takes something from his pocket; I smell something sweet and see his hand wave in front of my face with a white cloth. My heart nearly beats out of my chest.

I get one last look at Casey before the world starts to go dark.

"I'll find you, Julie!" he screams, but he sounds so far away. "I promise that Oliver and I will come for you!"

My head spins and everything vanishes.

Every light goes out and I'm all alone in the darkness.

EIGHTEEN
OLIVER

"OLIVER!" Julie's voice rings in my ears over and over as I stand in my hotel room in shock. My fear is punching holes through my chest, trying to get me to move and *do* something, but I'm hundreds of miles away from her.

I dial Casey's number and he doesn't answer.

"Fuck!" I scream, picking up the phone to call the front lobby.

A chipper-sounding man answers. "Thank you for calling—"

"This is Oliver Jackson in the Harbor Suite, I need a private plane chartered immediately. Is that something you can do? I don't care about money or how much it will cost—I need to get back to New York *now*."

The man clears his throat. "I'll see what I can do, sir."

I hang up on him.

What the fuck is happening?

I call Casey again and it goes straight to voicemail.

My phone starts ringing in my hand and I answer before even looking at who it is. "Casey?" My voice is frantic and I have to sit down because my heart is beating so damn fast.

"It's Brandon. I think something happened."

Panic sets into my bones and I start to scream louder at him. "You're fucking *right* something happened! Where the *fuck* were you? I thought you were supposed to be looking out for Julie, and now my mother fucking *has* her!"

I hear shuffling and Heather's voice comes through now. "Calm down, we're following them. We won't lose her, but we keep losing service."

Okay, that makes me feel a little better…and worse at the same time.

"Call her brother, Randy." I feel myself losing air and I stand up again to allow my lungs more space. "Make sure he knows so he can use whatever resources he can to get her back. I don't want them alone with her too long, do you understand me?"

Heather agrees and the call drops. I dial the number back three times before giving up and calling back downstairs to check on my flight.

"Thank you for—"

"This is Oliver Jackson again. I need that plane."

"I've made a phone call, sir. They are searching for a pilot now. Shall I get a car for you so you can start making your way to the airport?"

"Make it happen," I growl and slam the phone down.

Brandon's number pops back up on the screen of my

phone as I snatch my bags and close the suite door behind me. "Did you get her?" I ask.

The phone goes dead.

I *have* to get back home.

I call Casey again and no answer.

My fingers are sore when I slam the door in the back seat of the car waiting for me. I have called every single person I know—even Julie herself to see if my deranged mother answers—several times in a row. It's almost twenty minutes of straight silence as the driver pulls through the gates and onto the tarmac where my plane is waiting.

My phone rings and I answer before the first ring is over.

"Hello?"

"It's me." I take the phone from my ear to see who it is.

Casey.

"I'm going to fucking kill you." My voice goes dark and the driver steps out to give me privacy. "I swear to fucking god, Casey; when I get Julie back and she's safe, I'll find you and rip out your fucking throat. You can count on that."

"I tried to stop them." He breathes heavily and moans in pain. "I *tried*, Oliver. That fucking Mac guy broke my leg before they left with her so I couldn't follow. The para-medics are about to put me into an ambulance. The cops showed up quick—I called them as they left the house. I'm so fucking *sorry*, Ollie." He starts to sob, and I know how he feels about her so I don't interrupt. "I didn't *want* them to take her. I tried to get her to lock the door while I called the cops, but she wasn't fast enough. As soon as I get my leg fixed, I'm going to help you find her. I swear to fucking god I didn't mean for this to happen."

I hang up on him.

I can't handle that right now.

The flight crew—consisting of a young and tall, lanky guy and a woman in her fifties—nods at me as I approach the open staircase waiting for me. The jet is huge, but I don't give a shit what it costs. I just need to get the hell back home and find Julie.

A balding man with a big nose salutes me and holds out his hand before I can put one foot up on the stairs. "Good afternoon, Mr. Jackson. My name is Peter Grinaldi, and I'll be your personal pilot today. Do you want to tour the plane before we take off, sir?"

I stare him square in the eye. "I need to get back to New York as fast as possible. I'm ready now."

He nods and smacks his lips. "Understood, sir. Lola and Henry will be your in-flight attendants, and they'll see that you get safely inside and I'll get us there." He nods and disappears up the stairs and into the open door of the plane.

I don't remember buckling myself in or the takeoff. My gaze pulsates on the open sky and the small cities we pass as we soar above them. I can't even think about Julie without freaking out right now, and I'm not going to fucking cry in front of people I don't know.

How could I be so fucking reckless with her?

I can't live without her.

I'm such a fucking idiot to think I could even trust Casey again.

Trying to be the bigger man isn't getting me anywhere.

Breaking the rules isn't, either. Come to fucking think of it…neither is *following* the rules.

Julie's right: We need different ones.

I feel a hot glob of sadness roll down my cheek and I command myself to stop feeling like the victim and start figuring out how to get her back. My mother—as fucking pitiful as she is—has stooped to an all-time low. I never figured she would even go through with taking Julie, and I'll regret that every damn day of my life. Julie can never know what I know…or what Casey knows.

Or Brandon or Heather.

"Shit." I sigh loudly and rest my head on the headrest of the comfortable seat. There's no way I can fall asleep—that wouldn't be fair to her. She's with two people who literally have nothing left to lose and I don't know if she's hurt…or worse.

No.

My mother is a monster, but she isn't a murderer.

The pain in my stomach twists harder because I even have to think about that sentence. My life was a goddamn disaster before Julie and somehow, she fixed the parts of me I didn't even know were broken. I can't lose her because I don't want to give my mother what she wants.

I find my phone and look at Lola as she notices my sudden movement and leaps up to help serve me. I wave her back down and try to smile at her, holding the phone up and silently asking her if it's okay that I use it.

She shakes her head and points to the table in front of me, where a red phone sits.

"Okay," I say, finding the number of my lawyer, Vernon Trumbull, and letting it ring a few times before I start to give up.

"This is Vernon." His deep, scratchy voice answers. "Who is this?"

I lick my lips and realize how badly I need water. "Vernon, this is Oliver."

"Oliver Jackson! How are you, son? I heard you sold yourself into an incredibly early retirement." He chuckles loudly and it's hard not to smile. "I guess that's good for both of us in the long run. What can I do for you, kid?"

"I need you to be prepared to get me a large sum of cash."

He laughs and I can hear the moment he realizes I'm not fucking around. "Oh, Oliver. What did you do? How much are we talking about?"

I sigh and take the water that Lola hands me, smiling up at her. "Look, my crazy fucking mother has kidnapped Julie and I know she wants money. I'll need cash for her and I had to charter a private jet to fly back home to find her, so that bill will be coming too."

"Oliver, this isn't my job. I don't handle your finances." His voice shakes. "I don't know what you want me to do here."

"You swore to me that you'd find someone to replace my accountant after I sold everything off. That's why I fired Casey's dad. Are you fucking telling me that my money is sitting in oblivion where no one can touch it? Vernon, you better fucking fix this. It's your job to figure this shit out. You have to screen people and make sure they aren't going to steal from me, remember?"

"I remember, kid."

I hear the growl in my voice. "Then do your fucking job and find me someone. In the meantime, get me access to my money whenever I fucking want. I'll be in touch."

I hang up and gulp the remaining water down before throwing the bottle into the small trash can next to the table. "It's an eight-hour flight back, Mr. Jackson. Do you want a pillow?" Henry asks.

I shake my head. "I won't be able to sleep."

I'm not allowed to sleep. Not until Julie is safe.

Henry hands me a pillow anyway. "Just in case." He has no emotion on his face as he returns to his own seat. My mind races between Julie and my mother so much that before I know it, the pillow has been placed next to me on the oversized double seat and my head snuggles against it before I drift off into an uneasy sleep.

———

THERE'S a thunderstorm outside and it wakes me up in a panic. I don't like it when it rains; it makes the world wet and sad and cold. Mrs. Atchley says that the rain means the angels are crying and healing the world with their tears. I don't believe her.

I don't believe in angels.

They sure don't care about me.

Dad's been gone for a long time this time. I've been at Mrs. Atchley's for forty-nine days so far, and it's getting boring around here. All I do is go to school and come back to *her apartment, do my homework, and watch TV. I don't have friends I can invite over, or would even want to.*

I'm alone.

Mrs. Atchley knocks at my bedroom door and waits a few seconds before she opens it. The light from the hallway bursts into the room and I pretend that I'm asleep, but she knows better.

"Oliver, I know you're awake. You don't sleep when it rains." Her laugh sounds rough and I like it. "Boy, take your head out from under those covers." Her frail fingers grip the blanket above my head and she pulls it down. My smile widens as she comes into view.

She's gotten older since I met her—since she saved me.

"I can't sleep," I say. "Can we do something cool?"

She smiles. "Like what? What's cooler than staying up late and being scared?"

I know what she's trying to do.

"Can I go outside and play in the rain?" I push the blanket back and sit up on my knees. Even for a ten-year-old, I'm smaller than most kids my age. I wish every night that I will grow up to be big and strong like my dad.

"Absolutely not, it's nearly ten o'clock," she scolds me. "You're crazy if you'd think I'd agree to something like that."

"I knew you'd say no." I pout. "I just wanted to do something cool for once."

She stands up and leaves the room without saying anything, so I snuggle back under the blanket and close my eyes. I can't fall asleep; the rain is too loud.

"Get your shoes on," I hear her say, and I sit back up. She's standing in the doorway of my bedroom with umbrellas and raincoats. "Get some warm clothes on and find your shoes and I'll meet you in the living room in two minutes."

I bolt up from the bed and throw on sweatpants and a sweatshirt, then shove a pair of socks onto my feet. I have a big problem with misplacing my shoes, but I manage to find them and cram my feet in them before my time is up. She hands me an umbrella and zips my body into the raincoat before we make our way out of the apartment building and into the pouring rain.

It's amazing.

It feels cold and electrifying against my fingertips.

"Well?" Mrs. Atchley looks at me with amusement. "What are you waiting for?"

I don't waste any time. I take off my raincoat and hand her my umbrella. My clothes are already soaked before I jump in my first puddle. I splash and kick and exert the pent-up energy I've been saving unintentionally. The world washes away around me and I feel so free that it's hard not to pretend I'm someone else…somewhere else.

A prince in England.

A farmer in Kansas.

A magician in Las Vegas.

Anything.

I hardly notice Mrs. Atchley talking to a policeman that's pulled up behind us. I'm so soaked that I weigh more than normal and it's hard to walk to her; my body stops behind hers and I peek around to see the officer and hear what he's saying to her.

"Hey there, son." He smiles and nods at me. He isn't wearing a police hat and his hair looks like the color of the sun. "Having fun out here with your grandmother?"

I look up at Mrs. Atchley. "I'm his caretaker. Oliver, you can run along inside now."

"I don't mean any trouble, ma'am. I was patrolling the

area and thought I'd stop and see if there's anything I could help with. In fact, I'm a pretty good rain dancer myself." He winks at me and Mrs. Atchley grunts. I know she doesn't like police officers much.

"He's fine." She shakes her head. "Thank you and goodbye."

"My name is Oliver Jackson." I step out from behind her and the officer smiles. "What's your name?"

The man holds his hand out of his window for me to shake. It's big and warm and I like the way it feels in mine, like it's making me safe.

"I'm Officer Randy." He smiles again. "Nice to meet you, Oliver Jackson."

Officer Randy is nice.

I see a pair of bright blue eyes peek out from the back seat. It's a girl, and she's huddled beneath a policeman's jacket for warmth. I don't think she knows I see her, but I can smell her strawberry scent through the rain. I don't know what it is, but something tells me that everything is going to be okay when I look at her.

Officer Randy speaks to Mrs. Atchley for a few more minutes before he drives away.

I wonder if I'll ever see her again.

NINETEEN
JULIE

SCREAMS AND LAUGHTER *of children fill the air.*

Where am I?

A movie plays in my head; there are children scattered around a lush, green backyard with a pool and an oversized tree house in an oak tree to my left.

"Mom!" I hear a boy say, but I don't make a point to look for him. I'm sure he'll find his mother before I even find him. "Hey, Mom!"

Someone tugs at my sweater.

I look down and see the brightest emerald green eyes staring back at me.

"Mom? Are you okay?"

I nod, but I don't answer him. He must have me confused with someone else.

"Where's Dad? He promised to play baseball with us, and I can't find him."

I open my mouth to speak, but I stop to look at the boy first.

Emerald green eyes.

Dark chocolate shaggy hair.

Light freckles on his olive-skinned face.

Tall, skinny body.

I gasp, and it startles him.

He looks like a mini-Oliver Jackson.

"Mom?" He cocks his head and stares at me. "Do you need to sit down?"

I shake my head. "N-No." My mouth is dry, so I grab a water from the waiter and start to gulp it down. "I don't know where he is, sorry…"

The boy laughs. "Colin. My name is Colin, Mom. What is wrong with you?"

"Don't talk to your mother that way, she's perfect… there's nothing wrong with her." I hear Oliver's voice come up behind us, and I can feel adrenaline rush through my body. He still makes me feel things that I've never felt before, even without laying eyes on him.

He kisses my cheek and hands me an amber bottle of beer as he comes into my view from the side. "Your mother is absolutely perfect in every way, kid. Don't ever forget that."

The way the two of them smile at me burns my heart.

And my throat.

The stench of motor oil and gasoline fills the air and starts to choke me. The two of them disappear.

———

"Jesus, Mac! Drive like you're *not* holding someone hostage!" Veronica's voice fills my head. I open my eyes and I can't see anything; there's something over my eyes to blind me. My hands are tied behind my back and my feet are tied together so I can't run. They threw me in the back of a van or large vehicle because I roll around with every twist and turn they make. "Don't hit that fucking ditch, Mac!"

"I had to lose that fucking black car that was following us! I don't see 'em...where'd they go?" I can smell the stench of cigarettes alongside the oil and gas.

Veronica groans. "I don't know and I don't care. Let's just get to the boathouse and call Oliver so he can bring us our damn money!"

Oliver.

I wonder where he is right now.

I wonder if he knows that his mother has drugged me and blindfolded me.

All because of money.

And rules.

Let's not forget the rules and why our lives are *really* in this kind of trouble.

"Shit, she's awake," Veronica says, and I feel her shift toward me. "Should I give her more chloroform or just knock her the fuck out?"

Mac laughs. "I don't give a shit. Knock her ass out somehow so she can't see where we are."

"She has a blindfold on, dummy."

"Who cares, knock her out for the fun of it."

I wait for her to connect her fist to my head, but it never happens.

Instead, she leans down to my ear and whispers, "Stay fucking still and do as you're told and you'll go home soon, okay? All we want is money, and unless Oliver comes through, Mac will want to do more horrible things to you than this. Nod if you understand."

I nod.

"Good girl," she says, punching the floor next to my head. "There, she's out."

"You sure?"

"Yes, dammit. Now, drive."

My entire body shakes so hard that I know I'm going to blow the cover that Veronica just provided for me. I'm not quite sure what's going on to begin with, but I'm really confused at why she's helping me after she kidnapped me.

I've been kidnapped.

Holy crap.

"She ain't knocked out, look at her twitching back there," Mac says.

Veronica comes back and hisses in my ear again, "I fucking told you to stay still."

This time, her fist hits my head and things go fuzzy before going dark.

———

I've never paid much attention to the bigger picture of things. I've always just sort of…lived in the moment, and I've never dared to dream. I'm never getting out of my parents' lives, anyway; they'll see that I'm never able to escape them, I'm sure. I'm a meal ticket for them, and they aren't shy about telling me so every chance they get.

Everything changed this summer: I spent it with my brother Randy in New York. He just married Marianna a few days ago, and I got to be the flower girl in the wedding. It was magical and fun, two things that aren't a constant in my life back home with Mom and Dad.

I want to stay here with them, but I know Marianna doesn't want me around that much. She caught me using her makeup and called me bad names. I didn't tell Randy because I don't want to cause trouble. I'm only eight and still too small to understand adult things. At least that's what people tell me every single day.

I begged Randy to let me ride with him one more time in his police car before he sent me back home to the parents neither of us wanted to claim. They aren't good people, even I can see that, but he's still making me go back to them.

I might not ever forgive him for that.

"Julie, I just got my own squad car." Randy winks at Marianna, who pretends that she even cares. "Not to mention it's not safe for you out there."

"I'm not too young," I beg and climb into his lap, because he's twenty-three and much, much taller than a eight-year-old girl is. "You'll protect me. I just want to have some more fun before I go home."

His face darkens. He knows that if he sends me home that he might not ever see me again.

"Okay, get your shoes on." He shakes his head. "I'll get your coat and get the car started, so meet me outside. Hurry up; my shift is almost ready to start."

I bolt up from his lap and he laughs, shrugging at his new wife and leaving us alone in the room. I've been here for a month and he's spoiled me with new clothes, shoes, school supplies, and various other things that I'm going to have to hide from my parents when I get home.

"Well, better not get your new shiny shoes dirty." Marianna smiles and crosses her arms over her chest. "I gave up my honeymoon in Jamaica to stay home and babysit you for a month so you could have those shoes, girly."

I like the way the new shoes fit on my feet. I'm used to shoes being too big or too small. I'm also not used to a warm, cozy bedroom, either.

Or a woman who even pretends to like me.

The look on Marianna's face when I chose to ignore her comment scares me.

"Better go get your one last bit of fun in before I ship you back where you belong." She scoffs and leaves the room.

It's cold in here now.

I sit confused on the soft and comfy bed I don't want to leave.

Why do people treat me like that?

I try to be a nice girl; I try and help people and do what I can to be a productive member of society like my mother always says.

For some reason, I still get thrown out like the trash.

I drag my feet to meet Randy outside, and he can tell that his new wife has put me down once again. He never says anything about it, he just pats me on the back and gives me presents.

But he's the only one who really loves me and looks out for me.

"Okay, kid." He smiles and helps me buckle my seat belt. "It's Officer Randy time."

The rain starts coming down so hard that halfway into our night we have to pull off the road and try to wait it out a bit. He doesn't feel comfortable driving around with a kid in the car during a thunderstorm, but it's okay.

I just like being here.

When I yawn for the third time, he orders me to get into the back seat and cover myself with his police jacket to keep warm. The rain sends me to sleep, but I hear Randy talking to

*a woman through my dreams and it startles me awake. I don't
see the woman, but I do see someone else.*

A boy.

*He's near Randy's window, and his smile is wide and
curious.*

*The boy is with someone else, but I can't move my head
far enough to see them.*

*"My name is Oliver Jackson," I hear the boy say to
Randy. "What's your name?"*

I like his voice. He's scared and alone just like me.

*Randy rolls his window down further and sticks his hand
out for the boy to shake. "I'm Officer Randy. Nice to meet
you, Oliver Jackson."*

———

I WAKE up in time to feel someone carrying me and
quickly toss me down on a semi-soft surface; I still
make a loud thump as my body sinks into it.

"This is what fucking happens when you break the
rules," I hear Mac snarl somewhere near me. A loud
smack echoes in the room and someone whines. "When
you break the rules, you get punished. Your good-for-
nothing son didn't give me what I fucking wanted, and
now look! Look at her!" I hear someone cry out and get
pushed down next to me. "If he doesn't come through,
what the fuck am I going to do with her, huh? I can't
exactly let her live, right?"

I want to scream and kick my legs, but they're still
tied behind my back and I don't want them to know I'm
awake again. My head hurts so badly that it's hard to
concentrate on what Mac's even saying.

"I'm sorry, Mac!" Veronica cries next to me. "He won't let us down, okay? He loves her—he'll give me whatever I want. We just have to be patient!"

Mac roars like a lion. "You better fucking hope that car didn't follow us here, because I swear to God this is the last chance I'm giving your sorry ass!" He stomps out of the room and slams a door behind him, making both of us jump.

Veronica sniffles. "Are you awake?" she whispers.

I nod.

"Don't let him know." Her breath stiffens and she tries her best to return to her hard self. "I'm going to call Oliver, it's been a few hours. He should be halfway home by now, so this will all be over soon." I feel her weight slowly leave the space beside me. "Just hang in there and you can live a long, happy life with my son."

I feel her leave the room.

I think about Oliver and what Mac said about breaking the rules.

Oliver's third rule—keep your secrets safe—has betrayed me once again. If I'd just told him about the marriage to Brandon, he wouldn't have gone out of town and left me alone with Casey.

Casey.

I wonder what happened to him.

And who was following us?

My mind does jumping jacks as I try to piece everything together. A door opens and I don't hear anyone start screaming to be able to tell who it is. The cologne that comes closer is familiar but before I can place it, someone is tugging at my legs and untying the knots at my feet. Without saying a word, the heavy object keeping my feet together drops to the ground and the person gasps and waits a few seconds before pulling me into a sitting position.

"Jules." I hear Brandon's raspy breath in my ear. "I'm keeping your blindfold on just in case I get caught. They won't hurt you if you haven't seen where you are."

"Brandon?" I choke out, but it feels like I'm in a long tunnel. "What are you doing here?"

"Heather and I followed you." His breath quickens and we hear someone coming. "Lie back down…I can't get the knots at your hands untied. I'm going to get under the bed and hide until it's clear again."

I do what he says, and I feel him pull a blanket around my legs to hide them. He shuffles and his body bumps mine, and I know that the surface they've dumped me on is a bed as the springs push up from his body beneath mine.

"Jesus Christ, it's cold out there." Mac enters the room. "Start a fucking fire or something."

Someone shuffles around and after a few minutes, the room starts getting gradually warmer. No one notices that my legs are beneath the blanket, and it gives me a sense of peace as Mac groans and a chair creaks as he sits down in it.

"You call him?" Mac asks.

"I called him," Veronica answers. "He didn't answer."

Mac grunts. "Wasn't he in California? That's almost an eight-hour flight; he's probably in the air. We'll give him another six hours before we do anything rash."

A tear runs down my cheek.

Oliver didn't answer.

"You're *so* generous," Veronica swoons, and I hear sloppy kissing. I forget that Brandon is underneath me until he moves his body when the kissing starts, no doubt to turn away from it because it's not a pretty sight to see. "I'm hungry, let's eat."

Mac laughs. "You and your food." A smacking sound fills the air and Veronica squeals with delight. "I'll get the food…there's a barbecue shack a few miles from here on the outskirts of the city. Don't let this bitch out of your sight, understand me?"

"I got it…I got it."

A door opens and after a few seconds, Brandon rolls out from underneath me and pulls my body upright again, working on the knots around my hands. "Julie, flatten your hands." I do what he asks. After a few minutes, he finally gets the knots free and takes the blindfold from my face. The fear in his eyes is enough for me to throw my arms around him and hug him like I've never hugged him before. "Hey, it's okay. You're okay." He rubs my back and we hear a car door.

"She's coming back." I start to move my legs, but I realize that my left knee isn't allowing me to bend it correctly. "My knee, I think it's twisted or something."

He quickly looks down at it and applies pressure with his hands. I let out a groan full of pain and he stops and rubs his jawline. "Look, I'll stall Oliver's mom. Heather is waiting in my car half a mile down the road in some bushes off the road. Go outside, turn right off of the dirt driveway, and run until she sees you. Hey!" He snaps his fingers in front of my face. "Do you hear me, Jules?"

"I think she hears you," Mac growls from behind us. "Who the fuck do you think you are?" Mac grabs Brandon by his arm.

"Run," Brandon whispers sharply at me.

So I do.

I somehow get on my feet and my heart is pumping so hard that it hurts. Mac swings for me but misses because he's holding onto Brandon too. I hear the thuds of fists against flesh but I don't look behind me.

I know I'm going to feel guilty later.

He told you to run, Julie.

My knee is burning with pain, but I keep going. I see Veronica in the corner of my eye and she leaps toward me but misses and falls to the floor as I open the only door I see and fall onto an old rickety porch before me.

"Get her!" Mac screams at Veronica.

I push myself up, cry out in pain, and see Heather running down the dirt driveway, her black hair matted to her head with something red.

Blood.

"Get away from her!" she screams and points behind me. I turn and see Veronica reaching for me, but I step backward and fall off of the porch and onto the ground; the dust from the interrupted dirt surrounds me in a cloud as we hear Brandon fighting with Mac inside the house. "Brandon!" Heather screams and runs toward me, helping me onto my feet.

"Get those bitches in here!" Mac screams.

Veronica has an odd look on her face. "If you two don't run, he'll kill all three of you." She nods toward the road. "Go. Run as fast as you can."

"I'm not leaving Brandon!" Heather tries to catch her breath. "I'm not doing it!"

"You have to!" Veronica hisses. "I'm trying to fucking help you!"

Heather screams as Mac stumbles from the house and growls when he sees the three of us speaking instead of fighting. "I told you to get them inside!" He kicks Veronica out of the way and lunges for us, but Heather sprays some kind of liquid into his eyes and he screams out in pain.

"You think a little pepper spray is going to save you from this? Tie them up and throw them inside with the other one. He's still breathing but he's a damn mess." He nods at someone behind us.

I can barely turn my head to see who he's talking to because I'm in so much pain.

Mary.

"Sure thing." Mary laughs and sticks a needle into Heather's neck, making her fall asleep almost instantly. "You want them out for six hours, right?"

Mac nods and takes a deep breath, sitting on the front steps with a smile. "At least. I don't need any more trouble from any of them." He looks over at Veronica, who crumples up into a ball and sobs on the front porch.

I feel sorry for her.

I miss Oliver.

The needle that Mary sticks into my neck stings for a few seconds and then everything slips away again.

Darkness.

TWENTY
CASEY

OLIVER IS SO pissed at me I feel it before he even steps off the plane. Luckily, my leg was only fractured from Mac's fists pounding into my calf and I was able to get out of the hospital with a soft cast and crutches in time to meet him at the airport.

I lost the love of his life. He trusted me with her and I fucking lost her.

There he is.

He looks like he's just woken up.

What kind of man sleeps when the love of his life's been kidnapped?

My fists ball up at my sides. "Oliver," I say through gritted teeth. "My car is parked outside in the private entrance."

He nods and snatches my keys. "Thanks," he grumbles. "Bye."

"Hey, what the hell?" I manage to grab some fabric of his shirt before he storms off. He doesn't like that I'm touching him and his eyes confirm the anger he holds for me in seconds. "Get the fuck off of me, Casey," he warns me. "I'm meeting someone. I need to go."

"I'm coming with you," I demand. "I lost her, I'm helping you."

He growls and almost lunges too far at me. He's able to restrain himself at the very last minute. "I'm trying my best here not to choke the life out of you. Please, don't follow me."

"Talk to me, Oliver," I yell, not giving a shit who can hear me. "Tell me why you won't let me help you. I want to hear you say it out loud, man."

His body whips around before I can even finish my sentence. He leaps at me and forces my body against the wall of the hangar we've entered. He puts his arm across my chest and holds me with little effort against the cold metal, and I *want* him to punch me.

"Do it. There's nothing you can do to me that I won't deserve."

He exhales slowly, keeping his grip against me. "You are so fucking dramatic; do you know that? Grow some balls. Own up to what you've done. You'll never be trusted again. Not by me…and sure as fuck not by her. You'll *never* see her fucking face again."

I thought he was going to spit on me, but instead, he lets go and throws my keys at my chest. They fall to the ground and make a clinking sound at our feet. "I have a ride. I'm a rich asshole after all, right? I do no good, I only do evil? Well…just remember that Julie will always choose me over anyone else. Haven't you learned that by now?" I don't know what to say and he knows it. "Like I said, take a fucking hike."

"I'm going to follow you." My mouth moves before

I can even figure out what the hell is going on. "You can't stop me from helping you find her, Oliver. Take my help and then make good on your promise. I'll help you and then go away."

He knows it's a good idea.

Two is better than one.

Well, one and a half since I'm not at full capability.

"I tried to save her, Oliver." My hands rise in the air in a surrendering pose. "I tried to get her away—this is what they did to me before they took her. I tried to save her, I really did."

He waves his hands in front of my face. "I'm done with the excuses. You can help me, but I don't trust you. I'll use you for bait or whatever I want to do with you, get it? After I get her back and the disgusting pricks that took her get what's coming to them...you're gone. Understand?"

I nod. "Understood."

He groans and turns toward the waiting car. I try my best to keep up with him on my crutches, but he has to wait for me to get into the car and that pisses him off even more. He slams the door behind me as I fall in and see Julie's brother, Randy, on the opposite bench seat of the extra-long town car.

"Mr. Anderson." He nods at me and I notice that he looks like Julie, only a few decades older. "Nice of you to join us since you helped get us into this mess."

Oliver clears his throat. "Let's focus on why we're here."

Randy takes in a deep sigh. "I had a tracker on her phone when she was living with me." The glare he gives me makes me realize I'm giving him the same look. "Because of what happened with her stupendous ex, Brandon."

I scoff and try to be a part of the conversation. "Yeah, making her marry him was a low-life thing to do in my book."

The two of them look at me with anger and confusion. The color drains from Oliver's face and Randy's face is so red it looks dangerous.

"What did you say?" Randy seethes. "She's *married*?"

Oliver puts his head in his hands. "How can you even know about that?"

"She told me." I shrug my shoulders, happy to be the only one with a secret nugget of knowledge about Julie. I want to smile but I don't even fucking dare crack a smirk. "I assumed you knew." I look at Oliver and he frowns. "But I'm guessing you *didn't* know."

I *know* he doesn't know.

I'm celebrating inside.

"Of course I didn't know," he snaps at me, and I get the feeling that he's lying. "I would've confronted her about it, don't you think?"

I wait for a few seconds and collect my thoughts. Calling him out isn't going to help me any; he's already made up his mind about never letting me see her again. Rocking the boat now isn't going to get me where I want to be.

I hold up my hands. "Okay, I believe you. But, I'm sorry to be the one to tell you like this."

Oliver glares at me. "You know what, you little—"

"Dammit!" Randy slams his hand down on the seat next to him. "Fucking stop it, you two little immature idiots! Take this seriously or I'm going to do this on my fucking own!"

Oliver and I both cower and the car goes silent.

The sound of Oliver's phone ringing startles all three of us.

"Let me talk to Julie," he demands when he answers it. "I will find you and—"

Silence as he listens to the other person on the phone.

"Where? I don't give a shit about anyone but Julie. …*Now* you're negotiating hostage prices? What kind of monster have you become?"

I realize he's talking to Veronica, and Randy and I both glue our ears to the one-sided conversation.

"How many do you have? *Jesus*. Fine, I want all three of them. If Julie is hurt in any fucking way—" He pauses, and his jaw clenches. "I'll need time to get that kind of money. …Fine. Two hours. Send me the directions. Casey is coming with me. …Fine, no police."

Oliver looks at Randy, and he shakes his head but Oliver doesn't care.

"Casey and I will come alone. I give you the money, you give me the three of them, and we're done. Let me talk to her. Now."

I hear a high-pitched shriek in the background, and Oliver stiffens. *"Julie!"*

He says a few choice words out loud as he drops the phone to the seat beside him.. "Dammit! They let me hear her voice and then hung the damn phone up!"

"I'm going with you, you're not going alone," Randy demands. "Not with someone who can't help protect you. Jesus, Oliver, he's on *crutches*."

"She wants both of us," he says. "I don't give a shit about anything but Julie."

Randy nods in agreement. "How much does she want?"

"Three hundred grand. It's not just for Julie." Oliver looks at me and his eyes are bloodshot with anger. "They have Brandon and Heather too."

"What? Why would they be there?" I scoff. "That doesn't make sense."

"I asked them to look after Julie, just like I asked you to look after her. I knew I couldn't trust you, so Brandon agreed to help me out too. I'm fucking glad they did, because at least she knows someone was trying to save her."

My face flushes with heat. "You're such a dick."

"Enough!" Randy yells. "You're going to get nowhere by doing this shit! Julie is out there and she's in danger and you two are fighting like old women."

Oliver shakes his head. "I'm done with the subject. I asked them for a favor, they agreed. The end. You don't get a say in how I live my life with Julie. Neither of you do." Oliver's gaze turns to Randy and he crosses his right foot and rests it on his left knee. "Since she's going to be *my* wife soon."

Randy looks defeated. "I tried my best to keep her away from men like you. You've proven me wrong over and over again, so I guess this time I'll just let it be."

I want to shake some sense into him.

Is he serious?

"I'll take that as a blessing." Oliver snorts. "They sent me the directions. Casey's car is back at the airport, so we'll have to use the rental car. Is it parked at my apartment still?" I nod. "Good. Let's head there and grab it. I have a phone call to make."

Randy tells the driver where our direction has changed to and I try to listen in on Oliver's call.

"Three hundred grand. ...I don't fucking care, just get it! I only have two hours. Make it happen or you're fired."

He hangs up the phone and I pretend that I'm looking out the window, but he knows better.

"I fired your father from taking care of the company's money," he tells me with a wicked smile. "I gave him a severance and sent him on his way. I haven't replaced him yet, so getting money is difficult right now, apparently."

I glare at him. "My father is better off without you, trust me. Maybe now he won't be a completely stressed mess every night."

He laughs. "Maybe so."

How can he be so calm and collected when he knows Julie is out there?

When we pull into the parking garage at Oliver's apartment, Randy tries to quickly prep us for what we're about to do. We go and hand off the money at the same time Julie, Heather, and Brandon are being handed over. Not that I care about the other two, but I won't let Julie get hurt...that's what I'm here for.

I keep telling myself that I tried and I didn't do anything wrong.

I'm not sure if I'm right, but I have nothing else to hold onto.

"Casey!" Oliver snaps his fingers at me. "Let's go." He climbs out of the car and I try my best to follow him.

Once again he's waiting for me to hobble to the rental car and slam myself inside next to him. I buckle my seat belt and we look back at Randy, who looks more worried than he really should be.

"What's his problem?" I ask as Oliver peels out of the garage.

He shrugs. "He's worried for Julie. Plus, he can get fired for letting us go alone."

I snort. "Not like you care."

"I really fucking don't." His voice has no emotion. "You know what I care about."

His phone rings and his hand jabs into his pocket to find it. "What?" he answers. "Good. I'm going to drive up to your office. Have someone you trust bring it out to me. ...I don't care who the fuck it is, Vernon. Do it yourself for all I care."

He hangs up the phone and sighs. "We have to make a stop for the money."

He says this like it's no big deal.

A round, bald man in his fifties leans into the open window when we pull up to a tall, sleek glass building in downtown Rockford. "Here you go, kid." He lays a bag on my lap. "Three hundred thousand in cash, but you have to explain to Martin, the bank manager, why you're doing this at a later date. For now, I pulled the lawyer card and that only gets us so far."

Oliver nods. "Thanks, Vernon." He speeds off almost before the poor man can get his head out of the open window.

I don't say anything about how easy it is for him to just want that kind of money and he gets it within thirty minutes.

I don't ask questions I don't need to know the answers to.

We drive for forty-five minutes until all of the houses disappear and we're turning down muddy, dirt-packed roads. My leg is killing me, but I put it in the back of my mind and focus on Julie and how to get her back. Who knows who else is with Mac, Veronica, and that other woman now. Oliver and I have no idea what we're walking into, and I haven't mentioned the third person at all.

He doesn't care.

Honestly, I don't either.

"There." Oliver points to a small, broken-down shack off his side of the road. "I think that's it. Are you ready for whatever happens after we get out of this car?"

I rub my hands together. "I'm ready."

He scoffs. "Just let me do all the talking and you help them to the car when they give them to us, okay? Julie sits in front with me, no arguments."

I nod. "Okay."

"Can I count on you this time?"

I growl. "Are you really going to start this with me right now?"

He opens his car door and gets out, not worrying about waiting for me to catch up this time. He stops in his tracks when Veronica comes outside with Heather—her hands are tied behind her and she starts to sob when she sees us.

"Heather, it's gonna be okay," Oliver says, holding out his hands so Veronica can see he's without a weapon. "I brought the money. Come down here and count it so we can get everyone home and you can go live your pathetic life somewhere else."

Veronica laughs. "I brought this one out for good faith. The boy has some injuries and he can't move so well." Oliver clenches his jaw tightly. "This one is the least wounded."

"If Julie is hurt, I'll fucking end both of you," Oliver growls.

"Well, she's a little banged up too." Mac laughs and comes through the door behind Veronica. His face is swollen and bruised; Brandon must've given him a good run for his money before he was subdued. "Don't worry, it's nothin' that can't heal."

"You fuckin—"

I pull back Oliver by his jacket and nearly fall over. Mac laughs as we struggle and Oliver glares at me, but he knows I was right to catch him.

"Here," Veronica says as she pushes Heather off of the small front porch and into the dirt. Heather sobs and finds her balance, standing up and running for Oliver. He opens his arms for her to run into, not even thinking about who she is—or was—but just as someone who needs to feel safe. She finds his shoulder and buries her face into it and I start pulling her away and taking off the gag around her mouth.

"Brandon is bleeding a lot in there." She gasps for air and looks up at me. "Julie's been punched in the face and that guy tried to break her pinky finger."

Oliver growls. "I told you not to fucking hurt her!"

Mac laughs more. "Collateral damage is all. You understand, boy." He eyeballs the bag lying on the ground at my feet. "That my money?"

Oliver scowls. "You're not getting shit until I get Julie in my hands."

"Well, she's still recuperating from being knocked out for the second time, but as soon as she's coherent enough to recognize you, I'll be happy to fetch her," I hear someone's familiar voice say behind us. "Hello again, Mr. Jackson."

Oliver and I both turn; Heather buries herself against *my* shoulder this time.

"Mary?" he gasps. "What the fuck *is* this?"

"She was at the house when they took Julie," I finally tell him. "Do you know her?"

"She's the nurse from the hospital when I got into that wreck. What are *you* doing here? Someone better start explaining what the fuck is going on here."

Mary laughs and I put my arms around Heather instinctively, just in case this crazy bitch tries something. Her wicked laugh makes my stomach hurt and Heather whimpers into my shoulder so badly that her body trembles and it's hard to keep her still.

She's scared out of her fucking mind.

And she should be.

"You *really* don't remember me, Oliver?" Mary scoffs, disgusted. "You took my virginity in high school and told everyone about it...only we *never* had sex. Remember me now?"

Oliver looks confused. "O...kay. So what? That was years ago. Were you that hung up on me that you had to find me years later and help kidnap my fiancée?"

She spits on the ground at our feet. "You *ruined* my life! People never looked at me the same...my own *parents* never looked at me the same!"

229

He holds out his hands for her to back up. "Whoa, look. I'm sorry I did that to you. I was a selfish asshole back then. I can't make it up to you…all I can say is I'm sorry, okay?"

"*Hey!* All we promised you was money, you little bitch! What the fuck did you bring a gun for?" Mac yells at her, but all I can see is the shine of a metal object in her hands. I turn Heather away so she can't see what's about to happen.

There's a loud bang and Heather screams so loud that my ears ring. My hearing doesn't come back until it's too late.

They're gone.

TWENTY-ONE
BRANDON

I FEEL like I have the worst hangover of my damn life.

The sour taste in my mouth is horrible enough to make me want to puke, but there's nothing there. It takes a few minutes to focus and remember where I'm at and what's happening around me.

Shit.

My hands are tied behind my back and my legs are in front of me, bound with two different ropes. Julie is to my right, her body crumpled on the floor because she's still passed out from whatever was injected into her neck that I heard them talking about before I passed out. Heather stirs next to me, and she starts to panic when her own reality starts to set in.

"Hey, I'll get you out of this," I say to her. "Don't panic. Just breathe in and breathe out, okay?"

She nods but doesn't dare open her mouth.

"When we get home, we're taking the longest, hottest shower of our fucking lives." I laugh and cough, hoping that it makes her feel a little better. Her eyes fall on Julie and they open wide, so I make a shushing sound and shake my head. "She's fine; she's still knocked out. Did they stick something in your neck to make you fall asleep?"

She nods.

I try and think of what it could be, but I know nothing about medicine so it's no use. It doesn't matter anyway—Heather woke up from it, so Julie will too.

"Good news, jerk-offs." The man that kicked my ass comes into the room with a smile on his face. "Your savior Lord Oliver Jackson will be arriving soon with my money. We're going to give him this one for good faith and then torture the other two until the money is in our hands." He nods at Oliver's mom, who comes in after him and walks toward Heather, who whimpers and tries to inch her way closer to me.

"Don't you fucking touch her!" I scream, rocking my body so hard that I trip the woman and she falls to her knees on the floor. "I'll rip you to pieces!"

Veronica laughs. "You lot are so damn dramatic. Kids these days have no respect for real life."

"I'll be okay," Heather whispers, letting Veronica pull her up to her feet. "I won't let Oliver leave without you."

"He *won't* leave without him," Julie says in a small voice as she sits up. She isn't blindfolded anymore, but the swelling around her eyes makes it hard to see where she's looking. "Oliver won't leave without *any* of us—don't worry about that." She glances at Veronica. "Don't tell him I'm hurt," she warns her. "He'll freak out and do something stupid."

Veronica laughs harder. "*Both* of my sons are coming, so it could get interesting."

Julie groans. "You just *love* the upper hand, don't you? I hope Oliver takes you down."

Veronica grunts and yanks on Heather's arm. "Let's go, little one." She laughs and tugs her alongside her, through the door, and out of my sight.

I don't fucking like this.

If she hurts her, I *will* destroy anyone in my path to get revenge.

I love her.

Oh, *shit.*

"She'll be okay," Julie says once we're alone. "Oliver won't let them hurt her."

I swallow the lump in my throat. "I know," I say. I want to wipe the tears away that're streaming down my face. "I don't want to lose her."

Julie smiles. Even in a situation like this, she can still focus on the good in someone.

"I'm glad you have her, Brandon." She sniffles. "You deserve someone who can handle you at your worst and make you a better person. I was wrong about what I said in the parking lot at school: You've changed. I mean...you've *really* changed for the better. I like this person you are now."

I smile at her. "This situation is so fucked up, it's unreal."

We both laugh and look into each other's worried eyes. "I hear someone outside," she whispers. "A car just pulled up and two doors just shut...I think it's Oliver!"

We try to stay as silent as we can while we hear Heather start to cry. My body twitches.

"She'll be okay," Julie whispers. "Calm down so we can hear."

I hear Oliver's voice first. "If Julie is hurt, I'll fucking end both of you."

I nod at Julie. "Good, it's Jackson. I feel better about Heather being out there now. Are you still dizzy from the meds they gave you?"

Julie nods. "A little. Why?"

"Because we're getting out of here," I growl before groaning as I stretch to look at the knots around my feet. "If I get in front of you, can you undo my hands?"

Veronica's voice wafts through the open door. "Here," she says. Heather grunts and sobs as she hits the ground. Rage flashes through my body, but I know I can't do a damn thing with my hands and feet tied up. I hurry—despite the searing pain of getting my ass handed to me and the bruises from where Mac jammed his fist into my stomach—to scramble in front of Julie, and since her hands are tied in front of her, she's able to start fiddling with the knots behind my back.

"I told you not to fucking hurt her!" Oliver yells outside.

"*Shit*, he's getting lit up out there. I need you to *hurry*, Jules."

Julie squeaks. "I'm *trying*!"

She's no use to me in a frantic mess, so I lower my voice. "I know, just keep trying. I need to get out there and help Jackson. Just go slow and don't panic."

She fiddles with the knots more and I feel my hands being set free. I somehow manage to bend over and untie the knots at my feet, but it takes so much of my energy that I feel like I'm going to pass out again. Julie shakes me and looks into my eyes—we know this could be the end for us, and it seems like she's okay with me being the last person she ever sees.

She deserves more than that.

She deserves Oliver.

We hear Oliver again outside. "*Mary?* What the fuck *is* this?"

Julie sighs. "So, Mary is still here. Brandon, you gotta hurry—he's going to lose it and something bad is going to happen."

I fumble with the knots a few more times and feel my legs being released from their chains. I turn and burn my fingers on the rope as I untie Julie's hands and feet; it's eerily quiet outside for what's going on.

"Stay here," I tell Julie and stand up, limping to the door so I can peek outside. Heather is in the arms of Casey, which should bother me, but right now it doesn't. I just wanted to know that she's safe. She sobs on his shoulder and I feel bad; I shouldn't have brought her along.

"You *really* don't remember me, Oliver?" Mary scoffs. She's behind Casey and Oliver, creeping up on them like a predator. "You took my virginity in high school and told everyone about it…only we *never* had sex. Remember me now?"

"Jesus," I whisper, covering my mouth.

All of this over money and something that happened years ago?

I shake my head and look at Julie. "Mary is out there behind Oliver and Casey—he's got Heather now.

Mac and Veronica are right outside the door. I have to find another way out. Are you going to be okay here alone?"

She swallows hard and nods. "I'm not scared."

I smile at her. "Yes, you are. You don't fool me."

She sobs silently. "Just get us the hell out of here."

Before I can move, we hear Mary screaming outside. "You *ruined* my life! People never looked at me the same...my own *parents* never looked at me the same!"

Oliver's voice bleeds through the air. "Whoa, look. I'm sorry I did that do you. I was a selfish asshole back then. I can't make it up to you...all I can say is I'm sorry, okay?"

I look at Julie, tears running down her cheeks. "He *has* changed, Jules—even I can tell you that."

Mac starts raising his voice outside now. "*Hey!* All we promised you was money, you little bitch! What the fuck did you bring a gun for?"

I leap toward Julie and we hear a loud bang, followed by Heather's screaming. Mac and Veronica come bursting through the door, nearly knocking me over. Once Mac realizes that I'm not bound anymore, his eyes fill with more fury and he reaches for me.

"What the fuck do you think you're doing?" he growls. "Get back here!"

"Brandon, *run!*" Julie screams. "Just go! Go get Heather!"

I don't know what the fuck to do. Mac stands up and squares his shoulders at me, but I won't let him kick my ass a second time. As I dig my shoes into the wood floor, Veronica stands up and smashes a lamp over Mac's head, sending him to the ground.

"You fucking bitch," he grunts before passing out at her feet.

Veronica and I stare at each other as Heather screams outside and gunshots ring out in the distance.

"Go help my son." She closes her eyes and grabs her shoulder. Blood starts spilling onto her shirt as she tries her best to cover the wound. "That crazy bitch is chasing him through the forest with a damn gun. Don't let her shoot him."

Julie gasps but doesn't say anything.

I open my mouth and close it again. "I'm not leaving you here alone with Julie."

Mac starts to wake up and I shield Julie's body from him. The adrenaline pumping through my veins lessens, and I quickly realize that I'm not in the best condition to be running through the woods looking for a crazy woman with a gun. Mac jumps on me and tackles me to the ground; Julie limps away so she doesn't get crushed by us falling on her.

He punches me in the jaw twice. "You should've listened to her and ran, boy." He puts his hands around my neck to choke me. "Now you're not gonna have another chance."

"Leave him alone!" Heather squeals as she opens the door, racing inside. "Get off of him!"

Veronica catches her and our eyes meet before the air starts getting thicker and harder to breathe. I can hear her screaming something and Veronica shuffles to keep her away from us. Casey bursts through the door next, but his leg gives out from the strain of his injury. His crutches clatter to the floor before he follows them down.

There's no one to help us.

"You can sleep now, boy." Mac grits his teeth and laughs.

I move my gaze toward Julie, but she's gone.

Heather screams my name, but things are going dark. I can't fight back because my entire body feels like it's on fire and he's pinning my arms at my sides. The blows that he's bringing down on my jaw stop hurting after a while and only tingle—that's how I'm know I'm drifting off into nothing.

I feel running footsteps and Mac's eyes come into view.

They're cold and wide open.

"Julie!" Heather screams, falling to her knees.

Mac groans and starts grabbing behind him, trying to catch her.

"Brandon, get up!" Heather calls to me. "Get up!"

I try my best, but I spit out blood and can't see much of anything. Julie stands back with her hands covered in blood and Mac stumbles around the room trying to pull the small kitchen knife from his back that Julie's stabbed him with. He finally knocks it loose enough to grab it and slide it from his skin like a stick of butter.

"Jules." I cough and spit out more blood. "Run."

She looks at me and shakes her head. I can see her take another knife from behind her back and hold it in a defensive stance against the man three times her size.

"You little bitch." Mac coughs and stumbles toward her. "I'm gonna fucking *kill* you."

Julie holds up the knife to stop him. "Don't come any closer. If you leave now, I won't hurt you."

He laughs. "You're not doing a fucking thing. I'm

going to break your neck and then torture every single person that you've ever loved. Starting with that good-for-nothing Colin Jackson look-alike." He looks back at Veronica, cowering on the floor, and snarls. "Go get our fucking money and come right back inside," he demands.

She nods and leaves to do what he says.

I can tell by the look on Julie's face that she pities her.

The air returns to my lungs and I'm able to find some sort of will to stand back up. Mac notices and swings at Julie, knocking the second knife to the floor and grabbing her by her arm. Heather tries to slip outside beside him, but he grabs her too. Casey stands up with his crutches and stares me in the eye; we try to devise a plan without speaking.

"Pick one." Mac laughs. "Pick the one you want to keep."

"What?" I snap, my hand holding my aching side. "What the fuck do you mean?"

He licks his lips and sniffs Julie's hair. My fists tighten into a ball and it makes him laugh even more. He starts to move toward Heather and I think my fingers are going to break each other.

"You have ten seconds, boy," he snarls.

I look at both of the girls; Julie swallows and presses her lips together. Heather narrows her eyes at me because I'm even hesitating to answer him. She knows it should be her, but I can't leave either of them behind. "I want both of them." I take a step forward.

Casey moves silently behind Mac and he doesn't notice.

"I said *pick* one. Three seconds."

I shake my head and Heather scoffs, but she notices that Casey isn't next to her anymore. I watch her catch up to the situation as Julie breathes in deep, ready for what's next.

"I want that one." I point to Heather, and Mac looks at Julie to laugh in her face.

She doesn't show him any fear.

"Guess you're coming with *me*, little girl," he says, releasing Heather and pushing her toward me. I catch her before she hits the ground and stumble under her weight; searing pain shoots down my side when we fall, making it hard to concentrate. I manage to look up just in time to see Casey hit Mac with one of his crutches and he drops Julie to the ground.

I pass out just after I hear Heather scream Julie's name.

"Julie, watch out!"

The pain shakes my body into a deep sleep no matter how hard I fight it.

When I wake up, nothing is going to be the same.

TWENTY-TWO
OLIVER

MY FEET CAN'T RUN any faster than they are right now.

Any faster and smoke would rise up from the ground, but it doesn't matter. I'm running through the thick, wet brush and shrubbery deeper into the woods. My knee still isn't completely healed so I'm slower than normal, but I fucking hustle the best I can. I'm not sure if Mary is still chasing me, so I take a sharp left and start to circle my way back to the shack I left Julie in.

I trip over a hole in the ground and fall on my face because I'm distracted.

I *left* her there.

Mary's running footsteps start to get closer, so I speed up and taper off against the tree line.

"Come out, come out, wherever you are." She laughs and shoots off the gun into the air; the shot echoes around me. "If you don't show yourself, I'm going back there and shooting your little wife." She snorts. "*Oh*, that's right. She's not your wife yet. *Fiancée.*"

My body gets hot, but I don't step away from the thick tree I'm hiding behind. I can't see her, but she sounds close enough to get a good shot.

"What do you want from me?" I holler.

She giggles, and it makes me uneasy. "I want you to suffer like I did."

"How? By *shooting* me?"

She pauses, and it's hard to tell if she's moving or not. "I want you to suffer like I did...I want you to feel the *pain* that I felt. I'm going to enjoy it too, just like you enjoyed watching me get pulled out of school and sent to a boarding school because my parents were so ashamed of something I didn't even *do*. You ruined my *life*, Oliver."

My heartbeat quickens. "I can't say anything except I'm sorry. I told you—"

"—I know, I know. You were an asshole back then. Oh, except you were *still* an asshole when I tried to take care of you in the hospital, right? I tried to put the past behind us, but when you didn't recognize me, it hurt so much that something snapped inside of me. Then you treated me like trash when I tried to call Julie out for not being your real wife."

I snort. "She's as real a wife as any. You're right: I *did* treat you like trash, and I'm sorry for that. I have tunnel vision and it leads straight to Julie."

She says nothing, and I hear the brush around me start to move. Panicked, I start to run back toward the house and hear screaming, but I know she's right behind me. I'm no use to Julie dead. The thorns and sharp branches cut my arms and she shoots off another shot into the air behind me.

"I know these woods, Oliver!" she shouts. "You're not going to be able to hide!"

Boom. Boom. Boom.

That's six shots she's fired since she pulled out the gun.

I don't know much about firearms, but I know she'll need to be reloading soon, so I pick up my steps and the shack comes back into view. I don't see anyone outside, but the bag of money is still sitting in the dirt, so I bolt toward it and tuck it under my arm.

"If you don't give that to me, Mac won't like it," my mother snarls and walks down the steps. She startles me; I don't even realize she's there until she's got a hand on the bag and she's inches away from me. "He'll strangle those girls in there before you can even escape that." She points, and Mary is emerging from the wooded area with the gun aimed at me.

"Why are you fucking doing this to me?" I growl at Veronica. "Why couldn't you just stay away like you've done for twenty years?"

"I tried! Mac pressured me into this—he wanted the money."

I don't fucking believe anything this woman says. I have to figure out what I'm going to do. *Quickly.*

"Move," I say to Veronica, and her diseased body swiftly moves to her right.

"Julie!" I hear Heather scream, and without hesitation, I leap past my wretched mother. I hear a gunshot but don't look back as I scramble up the stairs and burst into the shack.

243

Casey is on the floor in front of me, writhing in pain.

Brandon is lying unconscious across the room.

Heather is crumpled on her knees next to him, her eyes wide with horror. Her gaze meets mine, and she points to the other side of the room, where we see Julie escape Mac's grasp, pick up a small knife from the floor, and start swinging it at him. Mac dodges the first three swipes, but the last time she swings, she's able to stick him in the stomach and he stumbles backward, falling to his knees. Quickly, she sticks him again in the shoulder and he screams in pain.

She looks at me.

She's covered in blood and terrified.

This is *my* fucking fault.

"Julie!" I hiss at her and reach for her arm. She reaches out for me, but Mac isn't going down without a fight. The rage that builds inside of me is bursting from my fingertips as I push her aside and pounce on him, bashing in his face with my fists. I start stomping his arms, his bones breaking under my feet.

"I'm going to kill you for touching her!" I scream into his now-unconscious face. I turn to Casey and point to him. "Call Randy, *now*!"

Casey nods and finds the satellite phone Randy forced us to take with us in his pocket. I hear him talking to someone as my body vibrates and I continue to wail on Mac until I can't see anymore through the blinding rage.

I fall to my knees and take deep breaths.

Julie finds my shoulder and buries herself against it, sobbing into my shirt. I close my arms around her and squeeze her as much as I can, letting her wet my clothes as much as she wants.

"I failed you," I whisper into her hair. "I'm so fucking sorry."

She sniffles and rubs her eyes. "You didn't fail me. This isn't your fault."

I look at Mac and start to cry. "They did this because I refused to give them any money, Julie. If I'd just given them what they wanted—"

"Oliver, that crazy bitch with the gun is still outside." Casey gasps for air after pulling himself back into a standing position. He looks at Julie for a few seconds and then takes his eyes away. He can't look at her either, because he knows he's failed her too.

"Let her kill my mother. Who cares?" I say.

Julie gasps. "Oliver, I think there's more to this than you think. Your mother…I can tell this wasn't her idea. She didn't *want* to do this."

I scoff. "I don't give a shit. I care nothing about her."

"Well, she's been shot, so soon that might not even matter," Casey says, now standing to the side of the doorway. "That crazy Mary bitch is out there with her right now, hovering over her."

I take Julie's hand and lead her to sit next to Heather and Brandon's lifeless body. Heather nods at me and wraps her arms around Julie. As they embrace, a warm feeling touches my insides and I know that once this all settles…things won't ever be the same.

I owe Brandon so much for this.

After joining Casey at the door, I peek out of the side opposite him and we watch the interactions between the two women. Mary waves the gun in the air and Veronica sits in the dirt, pleading with her.

"Don't do this," Veronica cries. "Just take this money and walk away."

Mary laughs. "*You* were the one who told me I could have my revenge."

"Not like this!"

"Why do you even care?"

Veronica rubs her shoulder where several wet spots of blood litter her shirt. "He's my son. They both are. It doesn't matter to me what you think of me or what you do to me. But let them go. *All* of them."

Mary isn't having any of it. "I don't think so. He's going to pay for what he's done to me."

Veronica snickers. "You petty little shit. You've wasted your life if you're hung up on something that happened years ago. Take the money and go live a better life and let it go."

Julie whimpers behind me.

I know what she wants me to do.

I take one last look at her and wink before I push the door back open and step onto the porch. I don't know how the fuck I'm going to get out of this and keep Julie safe, but when Mary sees me come into her view again, the barrel of the gun points at me instead of Veronica.

"Oliver, go back inside!" Veronica coughs and holds her shoulder.

I look at her and she knows I won't be doing that.

"Oh, how sweet. No matter how horrible this woman is to you, you're sticking up for her. Did you forget that she kidnapped your girlfriend—"

I grit my teeth. *"Fiancée."*

"Whatever. She kidnapped her and let her drugged-up boyfriend beat not only her, but your friends too. She tried to extort money from you and you're *defending* her?"

I look down at my pathetic mother lying in her own blood.

That's where she deserves to be. She deserves to be left there.

But that's not what Julie would want me to do.

I'm going to tackle her and fight the gun out of her hands without getting shot.

That's what I'm going to do.

I dig my heel into the ground and make myself ready to jump on her when the brush around us stirs and several police officers emerge, guns up and pointed at Mary.

"Drop it!" Randy yells, heading toward the group. "You have until the count of three and then we fire! One...two—"

"Okay!" she says and drops the gun on the ground. "Fine! Arrest her too! She's the one who set this whole thing up!" Mary cries and kicks her feet as the officers surround her and subdue her, putting her hands behind her back and pushing her to the ground to handcuff her.

There's so much going on that I forget to breathe.

"Take her too." Randy points at my mother on the ground. Two officers pull her up and drag her away, and I don't bother looking at her. There's nothing there for me. "Where's Julie?" Randy asks, and suddenly everything pops into perspective. I don't answer him and run back into the house, where Julie and Heather are tending to Brandon.

"Is he dead?" I breathe out hot air and join them on the floor. "The cops are here. Heather…is he breathing?"

Heather sniffles and nods. "He's alive. I think he just passed out from the pain."

Julie and Heather both take each of Brandon's hands. I get jealous but I can't let Julie know, not after I let someone kidnap her, beat her, and make her bleed.

I don't deserve her.

"Hey." Her voice finds me in the darkness. "This *isn't* your fault. Everyone is okay, everyone is alive. You didn't know this was going to happen."

I can't swallow the lump in my throat fast enough. "I should've known."

It's time to break another rule, because some rules… some rules are meant to be broken.

I hang my head. "I thought by denying them, they'd eventually go away. I didn't believe Casey when he warned me about her, baby…you have to believe me. I didn't think they would do something like this. I'm so fucking sorry."

She doesn't look at me.

I don't blame her.

"Everyone okay in here?" Randy's voice comes through the open door. "Julie?"

Julie nods her head and clears her throat. "I'm fine. I have bumps and bruises—Heather does too—but Brandon…he's unconscious. That guy—" She points down to Mac breathing heavily on the floor at their feet. "—I stabbed him a few times with a knife."

Randy looks impressed and calls for paramedics. He peels Julie away from Heather to hug her. He murmurs something in her ear and she nods, not giving me a second glance before she walks out of the shack. I start to follow her, but Randy snaps his fingers at me to stay put where I am.

"Don't fucking move," he snarls. "You and I need to have a chat."

I scoff. "I don't take orders from anyone."

"You do if you want to see Julie ever again. After what's happened here, don't think for one second she feels safe with you."

I fall to my knees. "She wouldn't leave me."

The room spins and I can't focus on what he's saying to me. I start calling for her and stand up, stumbling outside and watching two paramedics usher her to the back of an ambulance. As fast as my wobbling legs will take me, I catch up to her and they let her sit in the back with her head in her hands.

"Sunshine?" It's hard to find my voice buried beneath all the fear. "I'm riding with you, okay?"

She nods. "Okay."

"Are you okay? Where are you hurt?" I examine her body and she doesn't lean into my touch when my fingers find her cheek. It hurts my heart that her skin feels cold and doesn't give off the warm, electric tingle like usual.

This is most definitely all my fucking fault.

I've fucked up—*again*.

"Julie?"

She licks her dry lips and her eyes meet mine.

They're lifeless and don't sparkle their normal color of ocean blue. "Yeah?"

"I'm sorry, okay? I know I fucked up."

Her eyes fall from mine and it's like I'm being punched in the stomach.

"You didn't do anything, Oliver. It's not your fault Veronica is the way she is…it's all on her. Let's go and get this over with. I'd like to sleep for about a year."

She looks behind me and Casey makes his way toward us on his crutches. Heather is frantically following the paramedics, who've put Brandon on a stretcher and are loading him into the back of another ambulance. Randy eyeballs us and shakes his head at me.

I know.

I'm a Grade-A asshole.

That's me.

Oliver Jackson.

Man who can't stay out of his own fucking way.

TWENTY-THREE
OLIVER

I SAW HER.

I know my mind wasn't playing tricks on me.

There was a girl in the back seat of Officer Randy's police car. I didn't get to talk to her before Mrs. Atchley forced me to come back inside, but I really wanted to.

I saw her, though.

She was pretty.

And a little younger than me, maybe.

She tried to hide back there, but her blue eyes lit up the darkness like a firefly in the summer night.

I hope I see her again someday.

I could feel safe around someone who looked at me the way she did.

She's haunting me every second of every day.

———

"JULIE?" I take her hand and pull it into my lap. "Are you still in a lot of pain?"

She shakes her head and looks down.

She's defeated.

"Not anymore. Those pills helped and I'm lucky to walk away with a few bruises and a bloody nose. Brandon wasn't so lucky."

I look away from her before she sees the tear racing down my cheek. I don't want to make her feel any worse than I already have. "Brandon will pull through. I told them to put him in a private suite—"

"—I don't care about a private suite."

I nod and think of something else to help her cheer up. "Do you want me to call Staci and ask her to bring you some clothes and things to freshen up with?"

Her eyes find mine. "I'll do it," she mumbles and stands up, walking away from me.

Dammit.

I need to fucking fix this.

I know she says it's not my fault—and really, it isn't —but I'm supposed to fix this.

Even Casey has a smug look on his face as he sits across from me in the hospital waiting room. Heather sobs next to him in her hands, and I feel like this could be my chance to redeem myself a little with Julie if she sees me consoling Heather.

"Hey, Heather?" I soften my voice. "Look, I'll make sure Brandon has what he needs."

She sniffs. "I know."

I start to stand up to move closer to her but she runs off, sobbing. Casey starts to chuckle and then holds his side where Mac was able to get a swing in before he went down.

"What the fuck are you laughing at?" I snarl.

He hiccups and groans. "Oh, man. I'm laughing at the fall of the Great Oliver Jackson."

"The what? You better fucking watch it."

His legs are still weak from the fracture and I think seriously about breaking it the rest of the way to shut him up. "Yeah, the rise and fall of the Great Oliver Jackson. You had Julie, you lost her. Then, you had her *again* and you're losing her quick, *brother*."

"Fuck you," I spit. "Watch your mouth. I told you you're no longer to speak to her…what the fuck are you even doing here?"

He laughs harder. "Julie wants me here."

"I doubt that."

Julie comes back into the room and glares at me. "*I* want him here."

I can't help myself. The rage that I'm holding in is starting to seep out of my mouth. "Do you want *me* here?"

Julie looks at Casey and blushes. I run my fingers through my hair and stand up to leave the room. I can't sit here and take this anymore, especially not from her…the one person that's supposed to be by my side no matter what.

Same goes for you, dumbass.

My fist hits the soda vending machine once I'm clear from both of them, and it sounds like an empty metal drum.

"All these fucking rules," I whisper, laying my head against the cool surface. "Where did it get me?"

Someone clears their throat behind me, but I don't bother looking.

"Oliver?" Julie says quietly. "Can we talk?"

Oh, no.

Fuck no.

We're not *doing this here.*

"We can talk when we get home. I don't want to lose you here," I say, burying my face into my hands. I can't look her in the eye right now, let alone have the conversation that I know is coming. I saw it in her eyes the moment she realized I put her in danger. She fears me, or maybe she just doesn't trust me. Either way, this shit isn't going to end well, and I want to hold onto her for as long as I possibly can.

She puts her hand on my shoulder and my insides melt.

"Don't." I try so hard to hold back the tears that it tenses my muscles. "Don't do this."

She tugs at my jacket and I give up; I let her pull me around and wrap her arms around my neck to snuggle her body into mine. Confused, I wrap my arms around her and squeeze tightly, but I don't care as long as she's not running from me.

"Don't leave me," I whisper into her hair.

She doesn't say anything; she just hangs onto me in silence.

"Guys?" Staci's voice fills the air. "What the hell happened here?"

Julie unhooks herself from me and flings herself at Staci, sobbing into her red leather jacket. Staci looks at me for answers, but I shake my head and say nothing.

What the fuck am I going to say? "I put your best friend in danger and now she's trying to end things"?

My stomach hurts. My entire *body* hurts.

Love Hurts.

"Julie? Hey, why don't you take this bag into the bathroom there and get changed? I'll come in and help you in a minute. Let me talk to Oliver for a sec."

Julie sniffles and takes the bag from her friend. She disappears into the bathroom without looking back at me. I know what she thinks of me right now, and she's right.

I really don't fucking deserve her.

"Okay, spill." Staci smacks her lips and crosses her arms over her chest. "What the hell happened?"

I take a deep breath.

"My crazy fucking mother wanted money and I said no. I had to go to California for business and I asked Casey to stay with her so he could gain some of her trust back, because she loves Casey and I didn't want her to lose him as a friend because of my fucked-up drama with him. Then I asked Brandon and Heather to keep an eye on both of them because I don't trust Casey and then—"

Staci's eyes are glassy and nearly popping from her skull.

"My mother kidnapped her with her drug-dealer boyfriend, and the rest is...well. Here we are." I hold my hands up and wave them around the space. "And now Julie is going to fucking leave me because she doesn't trust me anymore, and why would she? I've created this entire thing because I was too paranoid about Casey taking her from me, and now look what I've done."

I don't know why I'm spilling my heart out to her since she hates me, but I can't stop.

"I can't handle it if she leaves me, Staci." I sniff, but

she knows I'm crying. "I won't be able to fucking function without her."

She waits for her turn to start talking. "I don't know what to say."

"You can say that it's all my fault, because it is."

Her foot taps against the floor. "You really want to know what I think?"

I nod. "You're not going to say anything to me I don't already think about myself."

She groans. "Oh, god. Grow up. Grow a pair of balls, Oliver. Quit acting like Julie is this fragile little flower that you have to protect all of the time. She's a grown woman—she can take care of herself. If you treat her like she's going to break all the time…*she's going to fucking break*."

"Not if I can help it," I growl.

She snaps her fingers in the air. "See, there you go. You don't have to be the president of all that is Julie, you know? You're *smothering* her, Oliver. You need to give her room to breathe."

"I can't!" I snap at her. "I fucking love her more than my own life! There's things no one knows, things Julie doesn't even know that make me want her so fucking bad!"

A security guard peeks his head around the corner to assess the situation. I groan and rub my jawline, pacing back and forth in the narrow hallway. "I don't know how to be with her without keeping her protected and safe. I can't live without her and—"

"—You're starting to act like Brandon." Staci says, her face emotionless. *"Controlling."*

"I'm not controlling, and I'm nothing like him."

"Just because you don't see it, doesn't mean it's not there." Staci smacks her lips at me. "I'm telling you, as an outsider, that you *are* starting to control her. Or trying to, whatever. Next thing you know, you'll be tricking her into marrying you too!"

She slaps her hand over her mouth and I pretend like I didn't catch what she said.

I don't want anyone to know that I know about that.

I think about Lucy—the girl I took home from the bar and the girl that Casey brought back into our lives —and frown.

Julie can't know about that for fucking sure.

I sigh. "Help me fix this."

Staci shrugs. "I don't know how. I can't change you and I don't think Julie wants you to change, anyway. You're just going to have to find a way to love her and not lose her because of your ego." She shakes her head and goes into the bathroom to check on Julie.

Maybe Julie is better off without me. I mean, since we've physically met…all I do is hurt her. But I can't make my legs move to leave.

This is bullshit.

Oliver, you are such a—

The bathroom door opens and Julie follows Staci back into the hallway. Her face is washed, and her cheeks aren't tear-stained anymore. I can see her electrifying blue eyes clearly as she looks at me. She isn't smiling, but she doesn't turn away, either.

"Can we check on Brandon? I want to see if there's any progress."

I nod. "Of course we can." I look at Staci and my eyes narrow. "Are you coming?"

She shakes her head. "Nope. I don't like that prick, and I couldn't care less if he's awake. Julie, I'll wait for you in the lobby whenever you're ready."

My insides melt. "You're leaving me, aren't you?"

Staci walks away to give us some privacy.

"I'm not leaving you." Julie clears her throat. "I just want to stay with Staci for a few days. Is that okay?"

Take it, Oliver. Take the chance to show her you're not like Brandon.

"You don't need to ask my permission, baby. I've told you that."

She flashes a small, quick smile. "I just don't think you should be alone. Maybe if Casey stays with you—"

I take her hand in mine and pull her against my body. "I don't need anyone but you. If you want to stay with Staci for a few days, you do that. I'll be waiting for you to come home when you're ready."

She wraps her arms around my waist. "Thank you."

I feel her breathe a sigh of relief.

There you go, Oliver.

Be a fucking man without being a *bad* man.

"Hey…" I part from her and use my thumbs to wipe her tears away. "Tell you what: Why don't we check on Brandon, and if he's awake and he's okay…I can drive you to Staci's myself and we can stop at Mara Bello's on the way there."

"I think I just want to get some rest." She pats my hand and pulls away from me. "Raincheck?"

"Sure," I say, watching her let go of my hand and walk down the hallway away from me.

Her grace and simplicity.

Her sunshine-colored hair.

Her bright, ocean blue eyes.
Her laugh.
The way her full lips redden as she smiles.
She knows how to handle me at my worst.
She takes my rules and tries to follow them.
I need to fucking change those rules.
Rule number four: There *are* no rules anymore.

TWENTY-FOUR
JULIE

I'VE ALWAYS accepted Oliver for his faults—he's nowhere near perfect.

But he's perfect for *me*.

That's...not enough anymore.

His emerald green eyes are wet with tears that he keeps trying to wipe away before I see him crying. I've been watching him tear up for the last two hours, off and on, and it's more endearing than anything else. We sit outside Brandon's room and wait to see him, and I try my best to clear the smoke inside my head and focus on one thing at a time.

How can I trust Oliver after what he's kept from me?

I'm not the same person I was six months ago; Brandon unfortunately had the luxury of me coming back time after time, but Oliver isn't going to get that courtesy.

I didn't expect much from Brandon, but I expected *everything* from Oliver.

Maybe that isn't fair.

I have my own secrets that will come out eventually.

"Baby?" Oliver's sad voice brushes against my ear. "Are you sure you're okay? If you're in pain—"

I shake my head. "I'm fine." I reach up and touch my nose and it still hurts a little, but for the most part I'm just banged up. "My nose still hurts a little, but nothing a few nights of good sleep won't cure." I fake a smile at him, and it's like I've given him a puppy on Christmas.

False hope.

I'm still completely in love with him.

There's nothing about this man that doesn't excite me.

I just don't know how else I feel about him right now.

"I love you, sunshine," he whispers and tries to see if Casey, who's sitting across from us, heard.

I can't just *not* say it back; it would crush him if I rejected his feelings so openly.

"I love you too." I lean my head on his shoulder to give him a little taste of ease. I needed this too; there's something about the woodsy scent of Oliver Jackson that completely drives me into another universe. I inhale and he smiles into my hair, and this is exactly how it should be.

Minus the hospital.

And the crazy mother.

"Guys?" Heather peeks her head from inside Brandon's private suite. "He's awake."

I stand up and Oliver follows closely behind me; Casey trails after us because he's still walking on his crutches and has new wounds on his arms that make it hard to use them. Brandon moves his motorized bed up to look at us as we enter; he smiles at me once I pass Heather. I want to run over to him and give him a hug, but several people might take offense to that. I'm glad he's okay; I wouldn't forgive myself if something happened to him. Heather doesn't deserve to lose the person she loves any more than I do.

Oliver squeezes my side and leans down to my ear. "Go ahead. Go to him."

Okay, some of the ice is melting around my heart again.

I glide ahead of the group and Brandon's toothy smile greets me when I reach him. "Hey there, Jules. Are you okay? You aren't too hurt, are you?"

My eyes well with tears. "No, I'll be okay. Are *you* okay?" My eyes follow the length of the bed, but his legs are covered with a white blanket. I don't see any blood and that makes me relax a little. He wiggles his toes beneath the blanket and laughs.

"Ah, I'll be okay. Don't worry about me. I just passed out from too much pain, that's it. I'll be ready to go home in the morning."

My eyebrows rise in suspicion. Who *is* this person? He's not acting like himself and honestly, I can't tell if it's an act or a genuine person he's grown into.

"Hey, man." Brandon holds up his hand and Oliver puts his inside of it next to me. I gasp and close my mouth because I don't want to ruin the moment.

Dammit, Oliver. I'm supposed to be furious with you.

"Hey, thanks for the room. I appreciate it. Maybe I can buy you a beer when I'm better and return the favor?" Brandon lets go of Oliver's hand and smiles, nodding at him.

Oliver doesn't miss a beat. "Yeah, of course. Maybe Julie and Heather can tag along and we can make it into a dinner, yeah?"

I look back at Heather and none of this is fazing her at all.

Something's going on here.

My eyes narrow when I look back at Oliver and Brandon. "What's going on here?"

Brandon laughs. "I'm just grateful for the room, Jules. Oliver's a good guy after all. Who would've known?" The two of them laugh and Oliver crosses his arms over his chest; the look he gives me isn't pleasing because I can read him like a book.

He's uncomfortable.

And *hungry*.

Hungry for me.

I blink a few times to focus my eyes on something other than Oliver's lips. "I—uh, well…whatever you say, you're the injured person here. Look, I just wanted to apologize and make sure you're okay before I head over to Staci's house." Oliver's eyes darken and I know he thought he'd be able to coerce me into coming home with him. "She's waiting for me so…I'm going to go."

Brandon nods. "Promise that we can keep in touch, okay?"

This is crazy and weird. I nod and back out of the room, Oliver nipping at my heels once I get back into the waiting room. I whirl around and he has to catch me by the shoulders so I don't topple over. "Whoa, baby." He laughs and kisses my forehead. "Are you *sure* you're okay?"

I throw my hands into the air. "Stop asking me

that!" My voice rises. "God, for once will someone just tell me the truth around here? I'm so tired of people treating me like a glass figurine! You say you love me but you don't treat me with respect!"

He licks his lips and doesn't back down. "I respect you."

"No, you don't. If you did, you would've told me about your mother trying to get money from you before you left. You would've warned me so I could be on guard. You wouldn't have fashioned me *three fucking* babysitters."

There's a low growl deep in his throat and fire burns in his eyes. "I didn't—they weren't *babysitters*, Julie. They're people I trust to take care of the single most important thing in my life." He's inches from me now, and his fingers find the side of my cheek. He runs his index finger down my jawline and across my lips, taunting me. "You are the absolute most valuable thing that belongs to me." I open my mouth to protest, but he quickly presses his warm lips against mine to stall me for a few seconds. "You know what I mean. I'm yours. I've always been yours."

I scoff. "You sound so literal."

A storm brews in his bright green eyes. "You have no idea how long I've waited for you. I don't know how to act around you. I've loved you before I even knew what that meant."

I put my hand on his chest and place distance between us. "You're scaring me."

He instantly releases me. "I'm sorry. I don't mean to. Can I take you somewhere?"

I shake my head. "No, I told you: I'm going with Staci, and I mean it."

"*Please*, Julie. Let me take you somewhere and I promise I'll drive you wherever you want to go. Hell, you can even drop me off in an alley and take the car with you. I don't give a fuck, I just want to open your eyes and maybe you won't think twice about staying with me."

"Oliver—" I take a deep breath and exhale slowly. "What happened isn't going to go away. You can't rely on love to resolve this. We have to face the fact that we're actually hurting each other."

"You're not hurting me."

I close my eyes. "I am. I'm hurting you by resenting you. I don't like that."

"Just come with me."

Staci comes into view behind Oliver and she nods at me, telling me to go. "Okay, I'll go with you. One place and then you have to take me where I want to go."

His eyes clear and he smiles. "Cross my heart. Let's go."

His large hand wraps around mine and he pulls me all the way to the parking lot and places me in the front seat of the rental car. "I'm going to have to get a new Jeep; I can't keep driving this soccer mom car around." He laughs and winks at me and I can't help but smirk while I put my seat belt on. I can't click myself in before he's halfway down the road from the hospital, the lights fading in the distance.

"Where are we going?" I ask, my body shivering from the nip of the October night air.

He notices and smiles. "Are you cold?"

I hide my smile behind my sleeve and nod, knowing what he's doing. He's remembering our first ride to Lake Reed together and the first moment I knew there was more than meets the eye with him. He clicks on the heater and takes my hand, putting it into his lap with his. I don't take it back because I want him to hold my hand; I want to be this way right now.

"So, where are we going?" I ask again.

He sighs. "To the place where we first met."

"Oliver, I don't have time to drive up to the lake right now. I have to go to class tomorrow and Staci is waiting on me."

"As much as I love you for not wanting to skip class…" He lets go of my hand and rubs his jawline— something he does when he's frustrated and sad. "That's *not* where we're going."

We pull into a parking lot as the sun finally goes down. We find a few empty spots of the apartment building lot and he double parks the car. He unbuckles himself and then sets my body free, moving his seat back and pulling me onto his lap facing him within seconds.

"What are you doing?" I look down at him. "We can't have sex here."

He laughs. "I just want to touch you, not have sex. Now that we're alone, I have to feel you. I nearly fucking *lost* you, baby. Did you think it wasn't tearing me up inside to think about that?" He leans up and buries himself in my chest, holding me tightly against him. "I can't fucking lose you again. Just remember that when I drop you off later, okay?"

I run my fingers through his hair and pull his head

back to face me. "I'm not leaving you...why do you think that?"

He shakes his head. "Because I don't deserve you."

"Look, we have to talk about some things, sure. I'm not ready to forgive you, but I know that we have to actually try and work it out for it to actually work out. I'm not stupid; I'm not naïve. I just don't want to talk about it right now."

He nods. "I get it. Let me show you what I wanted to show you and we'll leave."

He puts me back down in my seat and kisses my fingers, stepping out of the car and jogging around to pull me out into the chilly air. His arms lift me up and he carries me down the lot a little and stops to place me down next to a large light pole.

"Okay, I'm confused." I chuckle and look at the light. "Like, *really* confused."

He shoves his hands into his pockets. "I met you here, fifteen years ago."

I snort. "Fifteen years ago? Are you sure you're okay?" I think about what my life was like when I was eight years old. I remember living in California with my parents and not having enough money to eat most weeks. That summer I turned eight, I came to visit Randy and his new wife, Marianna. Clyde wasn't even an idea yet and life was much, much simpler.

"Just *think* about it. It was a thunderstorm and you were in the back seat of your brother's police car late at night. You were snuggled up under his jacket but I saw you...and you saw me."

His eyes aren't lying.

The dream I had was real.

"Are you sure? I remember something about that night, but I thought it was just a dream or something I made up in my mind. Why didn't you say anything until now?"

"I just remembered a few weeks ago myself. Your eyes have haunted me since that day, Julie. I never knew what I needed until I saw you again. You captivated me like I knew you would. I told you that you were made for me…I'm not lying."

I breathe slowly; I have to think and he's not making it easy with his agenda about something that happened almost two decades ago.

How can he possibly remember something like that?

"I-I don't know what to say, Oliver." He swoops me up and cradles me against his chest. "This doesn't change anything that happened, but I'm glad you told me."

I know this isn't what he wants to hear.

I don't know what else to say to him.

I can't think.

I can't even speak.

"I just wanted to try and show you how deep my love runs for you. I can't explain it, but I always knew you'd come back to me, ever since that day. Your eyes, they were in my dreams for years until I buried the memory so it wouldn't hurt anymore."

I run my fingers up his chest and grip his t-shirt between my fingers.

I know what he means.

No matter what he does, it feels like we're meant to be together.

His fingers tangle in my hair and he breathes in

deep. My body moves with his chest, up and down, until he can't stand it anymore.

"Let's just go home," I softly say. "I'll go with you."

He pulls from me and shakes his head. "No, you need some time apart. I know you do. Go stay with Staci and I'll come for you in a few days. You deserve everything I can possibly give you—I've told you that before. I can give you space, so take it."

"Are you sure?"

He nods. "I don't like it, but I love you. Come on."

Rain starts to fall down on us before we make it back to the car. The steam with his breath sizzles against the cool rain and when we reach the car, he looks down at me with his wet, dark hair matted to his forehead and a wicked smile on his face.

"Just a minute." He growls and sweeps me into his grasp, his rough hands squeezing my sides. My body presses against the side of the car and his hips press into mine, making it hard to resist tipping my head up and meeting his lips. He kisses me with hunger and passion, two things I know are dangerous when it comes to the two of us. I feel his tongue glide against mine and he bites down on my bottom lip, sending shivers up my spine. "I have to stop." He clears his throat and kisses my forehead. The rain is soaking our skin but I don't care.

I want more.

More Oliver Jackson.

I tug at his hair and pull his lips back down on mine and he smiles. "Baby, we have to stop. You're going to catch a cold out here in this rain."

"I don't care," I grumble and keep kissing him. "Just kiss me."

I don't have to tell him twice.

He opens the back door of the car and pushes me gently inside. Somehow, our lips are never more than an inch apart the entire time he lays me down and slides his lips from mine down toward my collarbone. "I can't fucking get enough of you," he breathes against my skin. "I don't want to take advantage of you...we shouldn't be doing this."

I hook my arms around his neck. "Don't you dare move."

He laughs and grazes his warm lips against my cold, wet skin. "You are the most amazing...*surprising*... intoxicating person I've ever met," he says in between his light kisses trailing down my chest. His fingers unbutton my shirt and I open my legs for him to rest in between but he stops and buttons my shirt just as fast as he can.

"We need to go," he mutters and sits up to run his fingers through his hair. "I can't do this, not right now. I'll take you to Staci's."

What the hell just happened?

I'm so offended that I don't speak to him as he slides back out of the car and pulls me out with him, opening my door for me and letting me get back inside.

"I know you're confused," he says when he turns the car on. "I just think we have things to talk about before we go down that road again."

I scoff. "What road? The sex road?"

He nods. "Yeah, the sex road. Don't get pissed off— it's not like I don't want you. You know how much I want you; *everyone* knows how much I want you. I just can't *be* with you when we have all this tension and all these secrets between us. Which way do I turn?" He waves his hand in the air.

"I want to go back to the hospital and check on Brandon," I say. "Heather shouldn't be alone right now; I've already texted Staci and told her."

He nods and directs the car back toward the hospital. He repeats over and over how much he wants me but can't have me right now.

"What secrets are you talking about? Do you have more than what I already know?"

He puts the car in park outside of the hospital entrance doors. "I don't want to talk about it in a car. I want you to go inside and do what you do best. That's what I want."

"What about what *I* want?"

He takes my hand in his and kisses my fingers. "Please, baby. I promise you and I will talk and there'll be a time where we can share secrets, but now isn't the time. You're still spinning from what happened, you're still angry at me for putting you in danger, and I know you need time. I know you, Julie. Just take a few days and think about things…think about what you want to say to me."

"I know what I want—"

"Julie." The way he says my name startles me. "Take the days away from me. I want you to clear your mind and get your head straight, because when you come back to me…it's forever. No more bullshit, no more secrets…"

The light in his eyes fires up.

"…no more rules."

I gasp. "What? I thought you lived and breathed by rules?"

He smiles. "I know you said we needed new ones… so here we go. Rule Number Four: There *are* no more rules."

No more rules.

Now that's something that I *do* have to think about.

TWENTY-FIVE
HEATHER

BRANDON SLEEPS like nothing just happened.

Like we didn't get ourselves into trouble and he didn't get injured.

The constant beeping of the machines around him is pissing me off with each sound they make. They're reminding me that I nearly lost the one person on this planet that gets me.

He's not upset with Oliver…and neither am I, really. It's not Oliver's fault he is the way he is.

Stubborn.

Willful.

Aware.

Overbearing.

I know what Julie's going through. I know the power he holds over someone and the little things that just keep you coming back for more. I'm not going to run to her and warn her to stay away from him, because they're not going to end up like Oliver and I did. There's something there that they just can't escape from;

I saw it the very moment she stormed off from him at the lake house months ago.

She tests his patience and it excites him.

Brandon's long eyelashes float with each soft exhale of breath from his mouth. It's crazy how people can just *find* each other in the most awkward, messed-up situations and make something out of nothing. Some people need very little in a relationship and some need so much that it's difficult to maintain one. I always thought as long as a man loved me enough to make me feel it, I wouldn't need much else. I don't know what changed with Oliver, but Brandon is my next chapter.

I can feel his love for me even when he sleeps.

His fingers move around the bed next to him—he's searching for my hand. Once he finds me, he's covering my hand with his and smiling in his sleep. It's endearing to see this side of him, the side that he was so scared to show me at first. Maybe Julie is right…there's some form of good in everyone.

There's a small knock at the door before it opens, letting some of the hallway light into the room.

So that's why people think she's an angel.

Light billows in around Julie's body and illuminates her golden hair flowing around her. Her eyes scan the room and she sees me, then Brandon and looks back at me again with tears in her eyes.

"Do you want some company?" she whispers.

I nod and gesture for her to come inside. She enters the room and quietly shuts the door behind her, pulling up a chair beside me and glancing at Brandon one more time.

"How is he?" she asks.

"He's better, just sleeping. They gave him some pain meds and the X-rays didn't show any extensive damage, so he's going home in the morning. He just got his ass kicked pretty good, but it was for a good cause."

She takes my hand and it startles me. "You should get some sleep, then."

I let her hold my hand because it feels nice to have a friend. "Julie, there's something you should know about Oliver."

She shakes her head. "I've learned enough for one night, thanks."

"No." I turn and face her, giving her back her hand. "I have to say this. When Oliver and I were together—" She flinches, but I keep going. "—we didn't have the dynamic that you two have. We didn't have the type of relationship you have. I always knew he was searching for something more, something that maybe I wasn't giving him. It's my fault for breaking his heart, but it's *your* fault for putting it back together. Only…you fixed him, somehow. Like that empty hole inside his heart that was plain as day for everyone to notice just…*vanished*."

She looks impressed. "I didn't know you were so deep, Heather."

I snort. "I just want to get my point across. Oliver did what he did to protect you…the only way he knows how. He's not a bad guy, he's really not. He just does stupid, idiotic—"

Julie giggles. "I see your point. People tell me all the time what they think our relationship is or why we fit so well together. At first, I didn't see it. But now, it's hard to explain. Funny how that happens."

I smile at her and for the first time, she smiles back. "I'm sorry for everything I've put you through."

"Don't worry about it."

"No, really." I wipe the tears that form in my eyes. "I'm a changed person too. Brandon and I...we've changed each other into the people we should've been. The people we wanted to be."

She moves her chair closer to me and takes my hand again. "I'm happy for you two."

"That actually means a lot."

Julie thinks for a few moments and pulls her phone out of her pocket. "Oliver brought me back here for a minute, he's waiting downstairs. I'm supposed to go to Staci's house, but I have a better idea. Why don't we go shopping?"

I cock my head in confusion. "There aren't any shops open right now."

She pulls me up from the chair and grins from ear to ear. "I know that. But late-night cafeteria is open and we have phones, right? And I'm sure Oliver won't hesitate to give me a credit card."

I want to shake her and hug her at the same time. "I can't leave Brandon."

She puts the phone to her ear. "Hey, can you come up here? No, everything's okay...I just want to take Heather to the cafeteria for some coffee and a breather. She doesn't want to leave him alone. Okay, thanks." She hangs up the phone and puts it back into her pocket. "He'll be here in a few minutes."

"He just instantly does what you ask him, doesn't he?"

She shrugs her shoulders. "I don't ask for much, so when I do, he jumps on the chance."

I don't know Oliver that way. I asked for everything and he eventually just gave me open access to anything I wanted.

"Heather, do you want a few minutes alone with Brandon before we go?"

I nod and she lets go of my hand to leave the room. I can hear her talking to Oliver outside the door; their voices are low and calm and I know they will be okay. There isn't anything Oliver won't do for her…I can tell by the way he follows her around like a lost puppy dog that it's different for him now.

He can't live without her.

I bend over and kiss Brandon on the cheek. "I'll be downstairs, but Oliver will be in here if you wake up," I whisper into his ear. "I'm not sure how you'll feel about that, but at least you won't be alone. Things are finally starting to go our way for once…except this whole hospital thing. I won't be gone long…I just want to get something to eat and breathe a little."

The door opens and they walk into the room. Oliver doesn't look annoyed like I thought he would. He walks to me and embraces me in a long hug, wrapping his arms around me and squeezing tight.

"You should go with Julie—I'll look after him," he says when we part.

I don't know what to say.

"Are you okay?"

I nod. "Y-Yeah, I'm okay. Just not used to all of this." I chuckle and wiggle my fingers around. "It's kinda weird how something like this brought people like us together."

He shrugs. "Life is fucking crazy, and if Julie wants me to give you two a chance, then I will."

I look at Julie and she's smiling behind Oliver, her hands on her cheeks in amazement. She's intoxicated with him and it's so sweet that it makes my teeth hurt.

Julie yawns. "I need coffee. Should we go?"

"Okay, I'll go." The twinkle in their eyes is a little too much for me right now. I thought I wanted to be fast friends with her, but what if she hates me once I show her the real me? "Let me say goodbye." I bend back over and kiss Brandon on the cheek, pulling his blanket around his chest and tucking it in at his sides in case he gets cold.

Oliver snickers. "Trust me, from experience...when you're knocked out like this, you don't feel a thing." He glances at Julie and she looks sick; he must realize that wasn't the right thing to say out loud. "Uh, I mean...he isn't going to be cold."

I roll my eyes. "Let's go, Julie." I snort and brush past Oliver to the door.

I don't look back and watch their goodbye because I know it'll make me feel guilty for leaving Brandon's side at his time of need. Will he wake up and be upset with me for not being there?

The elevator ride is silent. The walk to the cafeteria was a little better, as she made small talk and inserted comfort into the air around us. She genuinely wants to know things about me and not just because it's something she's been asked to do.

"So..." She grabs a tray and waves at a few of the

late-night food workers. "What are we in the mood for? I, for one, want a big, fat, greasy cheeseburger."

I laugh. "You *would* eat that this late at night. How are you not bursting from your clothes?"

She shrugs. "I don't eat like that *all* the time...sometimes I eat a salad."

We look at each other and start to laugh louder. She fills her tray with french fries, two cheeseburgers, and tons of fruit, and I fill mine with pizza and cheesecake for our dessert. It's like we're having a slumber party in the cafeteria of a hospital with the gobbling of junk food and gossip we spread across the table for over an hour.

She snorts. "Oh, God. Sometimes I just want to shake Oliver and scream at him to wake up!"

I cover my mouth to keep the bite of cheeseburger I'd just taken inside. "I'm so glad I don't have to listen to the snoring anymore! The worst Brandon does is fling his arm over and hit me in the nose in the middle of the night! I swear I thought he broke it one day!"

Julie nearly chokes and giggles through her swallow. "Oh, I knew he'd be down here soon." She nods and sees Oliver gliding over to our table, his eyebrows raised.

"You two having fun?" He smirks and looks down at the table full of food. I never let Oliver see me eat more than a chicken breast, and even now with all this food in front of us, I cower and blush. Julie doesn't care and she takes another huge bite of her cheeseburger. "I was starving, so we got anything we could get our hands on. Do you want me to grab you something?"

He nods. "Sure, baby. Thanks."

She gets up and we watch her flitter through the line

again, picking up items and putting them into a paper bag for him to take back upstairs.

"She's a nice person," I say to him as he watches her.

He nods. "Yeah, she is."

"You deserve her."

He looks at me and frowns. "Don't say shit like that. You have no idea."

"Okay…" I look down at my plate. "No, it's *not* okay. You're an asshole."

He laughs. "I know that."

"Well, stop it. Quit acting like you're the only person who can get close to her. She isn't going anywhere, Oliver."

He growls at me. "I *said* don't say shit like that."

"Shut the hell up and listen to me!" I hiss. "I'm *trying* to give you advice."

He sighs and looks back at Julie as she pays for the bag of food. "Fine. What?"

"I just think you need to loosen the reins a little, you know? Share her with the world. I see how she makes you feel about yourself, like you have a sense of purpose again. I just don't want you to overdo things and push her away."

He nods at me, silently telling me he's heard what I'm saying as Julie walks back up to us and hands him the bag of food. She reaches up and plants her lips on his cheek without worrying about who's around to see, and he reaches up to touch her cheek, kissing her on the forehead.

"Roast beef and Swiss. French fries. Chocolate chip ice cream." She blushes.

He laughs. "Three of my favorite things. Four, if you count yourself."

Okay, it's getting a little awkward here.

"Okay…" He crumples the bag in his hands and winks at her. "Don't stay down here too long. You still want to make it to Staci's, don't you?"

Julie shrugs. "When I make it there, I'll make it there."

"Okay, then. See you two later. I love you." He looks directly at her.

She doesn't say it back right away, but she knows Oliver and I are both waiting for her to return the gesture. "I love you too," she says quickly, and he walks back out of the cafeteria as she sits back down in her chair, looking at a fry on her plate.

"Something wrong?" I ask.

She shakes her head. "No, just a lot to think about, and I'm not sure I want to."

I close my mouth. I know it's not my place to comment on their relationship; it's awkward enough just late-night snacking with her and pretending that we didn't have the most horrible introduction of all time. If things had started differently, who knows if they'd be better or worse.

Her eyes get big and she glances up from her fry and back down again.

She *wants* me to talk to her. I'm fighting it the best I can; what if the advice I try to give her comes out wrong or makes her angry?

Here we go.

"Julie, do you want to talk about it?" I inject a soothing tone into my voice.

She doesn't look angry. Okay, that's good. *Good job, Heather…you said the right thing.*

"Are you sure that's okay? Wouldn't it be weird?"

This is your chance.

I shake my head. "No way. After what we've all just been through, you and I are basically best friends now."

Shit. I didn't mean to say that.

I watch her think about it and she bites the inside of her cheek. "I don't know about that, but I definitely don't find you as horrible as before." She laughs and shoves the lonely fry into her mouth. "I think maybe someday we can be friends."

I slowly blow out the air I've been holding in. "Okay, so what's wrong?"

She carefully thinks of what words to use and takes a few long seconds to answer me. She breathes in deep and lets it loose. "Things are different between Oliver and me now. I can't really explain it—it's just different. I know it's hard to listen to someone who's bitching about nothing, but I can't put my finger on it. I mean… what else is going to happen?"

She looks at me for an answer, but she answers herself.

"I mean, honestly *anything* could happen. He chose to consult babysitters—no offense—to take care of me when he knew he should've warned me Veronica was in town. Or at the very least, he should've warned me so I could stay with Randy or something. Am I wrong?"

I shake my head slowly. "No, you're not wrong. But, in his defense—"

She snorts. "In his defense? Really? What did he really offer you to do this?"

She puts her elbows on the table and leans closer, waiting for me to tell her the truth.

"I wanted to be friends with you. I wanted you, Oliver, Brandon, and I to be friends."

She doesn't say anything. Her fingernail taps on the table as she leans back and crosses her arms over her chest, staring at me.

"Why me?"

I nearly choke. "Why you, what?"

"Why do you want to be friends with me so badly?"

I shrug. "I don't know. I don't fucking dare tell you you're a magical being, though."

She laughs so hard that I think her soda is going to come out of her nose. "Oh, so you heard about that, did you? The part where I yelled at Casey and told him I'm not a fucking unicorn?"

I cover my mouth but my laughter erupts anyway. "I heard. And I've never heard you swear like that before, so *that's* hilarious." We snort and throw fries at each other while the cafeteria workers glare at us for making a mess on their floors.

"I don't know, Julie. You're just a good person. Plus, I think I felt guilty about how I treated you when we met, and I had so much bad karma stacked against me that it was time to start making it right. Brandon and I have been trying really hard to erase the horrible qualities in our old selves."

She nods. "I've seen that. You're good for him."

I wave my finger in the air, side to side. "You're not getting off that easily. This isn't about me and Brandon…it's about you and Oliver. How do you feel about him?"

She cocks her head to the side. "What do you mean? I love him."

"But, why?"

"I'm not sure I'm following." She lowers her gaze back to her plate.

"Yes, you are. You know what I mean."

She clicks her tongue and smiles, looking back at me. "I've never loved anyone more in my entire life, and that includes Brandon. Have you ever felt that each person comes into your life at the exact moment they're supposed to? He saved me from becoming someone I didn't want to be. It wasn't me who's changed all these years—it's been the people around me. I just found out that Oliver and I first saw each other fifteen years ago without actually meeting, and he's been pining for me ever since. That's what I love the most about him…the love that runs so deep in his soul that even *he* doesn't understand it."

I wipe a tear from my eye. "That's gorgeous."

She giggles. "I'm sure I read it on a fortune cookie somewhere."

I laugh through my tears and we go back to stuffing our faces with the delicious spread of food surrounding us. I don't want to keep pushing her until she gets annoyed with me and shuts me out completely.

"Oh, I never asked you…how do you know Lucy?"

I freeze. "Oh…I, uh…we grew up together."

"You did? That's awesome!"

I laugh nervously. "Yeah, we had lunch after she moved to town, but she never spoke to me after that. I'm not sure what that's about."

She waves me off. "I'm sure she's just busy. I don't see her as being petty like that."

"How do you know her?" I ask.

"Oh, she was dating Casey for a short period of time but broke it off with him. I met her through him but I haven't really hung out with her other than class."

I snort. "She broke up with him because he's in love with you too?"

Her cheeks flush. "Something like that." She looks at the clock on the wall next to us. "Oh, I better finish up and grab Oliver. Staci won't like that I've made her wait so long to start our girls' night. We're detoxing ourselves from men."

I laugh. "Sounds brutal."

We collect our trash and clean up our table before waving at the cafeteria workers as we leave the room. The ride back up to Brandon's room is awkward again, like we're going full circle on the openness we just had minutes before.

Brandon and Oliver both look like they're up to something when we enter the room.

"Hey, girls." Brandon chuckles. "Did you bring any more ice cream?"

"How long have you been awake?" I ignore his question. "I would've come sooner."

He waves me off. "Jackson's been keeping me company. He shared his food because he's a good man."

Oliver chuckles. "Something like that." He looks at Julie and reaches for her hand. "You ready to get going? It's getting late."

She nods. "Ready."

I watch them say their goodbyes and when the door closes behind them, I get a bad feeling.

"What's wrong?" Brandon asks.

I shake my head. "I don't know; something isn't right. He's hiding something."

He groans. "Don't get into that. It's none of our business."

"He's *hiding* something," I say again, glaring at him. "Something bad."

And I'm going to find out what it is.

TWENTY-SIX
BRANDON

MY MOUTH FEELS like I've been eating moist sandpaper when I wake up. The room is dimly lit and I expect to see Heather curled in the chair next to me, sleeping soundly. Instead it's Oliver, and he's scrolling through his phone, not paying attention to me shuffling around in the bed. I push the button to sit up so I can be at eye level with him and he finally notices, putting his phone away and clearing his throat so the awkward conversations can begin.

"Hey...how you feelin'?" He tries his best to make small talk, but we both know it's going to take more than something like this to get us to see eye to eye. "I, uh...Heather and Julie went down to get something to eat." He shakes a brown bag at me. "You ready for a cheeseburger?"

I groan. "Anything is better than the shit they serve the patients here."

He hands the bag to me and I start to inhale the fries before unwrapping the burger. The smell of the greasy goodness in front of me makes my stomach grumble and he laughs, standing up to grab me some water and turn the overhead lights on. I take the water from him and put it beside me before shoving the food in my mouth so we won't have to have a conversation.

He goes back to looking at his phone like I don't even exist.

"So, you got stuck babysitting me, huh?" I smash the wrapper of the cheeseburger between my hands. I put the bag on the table next to me and pick up the glass of water.

He nods. "Something like that. Heather didn't want to leave you alone and Julie insisted on Heather getting something to eat, so...here I am." He holds his hands in the air.

"Well, thanks."

He snickers and crosses his arms over his chest. "Don't thank me yet. Don't get this twisted—I still fucking can't stand you for what you've done to Julie. Saving her from those crazy fucking good-for-nothing drug addicts was decent enough—even for you—but that doesn't erase all the bad shit you've done to her. Heather wants to be friends with us, fine. But you better watch it and tread lightly."

I take a drink of the water and put the glass back down. "So you're going to ruin it for everyone because you can't get over something you weren't even a part of?"

He growls. "You smacked her around, manipulated her...made her think that she was nothing...and forced her into marrying you. I'm not ruining shit for anyone."

I'm suddenly finding it hard to breathe. "You know about that?"

He nods. "I know about that."

"Why haven't you said anything until now?"

He clears his throat. "Because I don't find it necessary to remind Julie that someone can be that malicious and scary. I want her to trust me; I don't need to give her a constant reminder that she can't fully be mine until she breaks free from your mistake. She deserves better than that."

I nod. "Yeah, but she also deserves to be told the truth."

He laughs. "Right? She really does." He glares at me and then sighs loudly. "Look, the way Julie is, I'm sure her and Heather are best friends by now. Which means —no matter how fucked up it is—we'll be seeing *a lot* of each other. I'm going to keep this to myself until I feel like it's the right time to tell her, and you'll do the same, yeah? Your only job is to get it taken care of."

"I'm getting it taken care of."

"Good." He nods and checks his phone. "They're on their way back. Let's paint some smiles on our faces and pretend for our girls, okay?"

"Fine," I growl. "But this isn't over."

He blows out air. "It's over."

The door opens, and Heather and Julie float into the room with us. They're laughing and have smiles on their faces, which makes me jealous that Oliver can't get over himself and just let things be. They stop and look at the two of us, shaking their heads.

I have to make this believable. *Quickly.*

"Hey, girls." I chuckle. "Did you bring any more ice cream?"

"How long have you been awake?" Heather ignores my question. "I would've come sooner."

I wave her off. "Jackson's been keeping me company. He shared his food because he's a good man." I nearly choke on my words and Oliver shakes his head in annoyance, but no one notices but me.

He fakes a chuckle. "Something like that." He looks at Julie and reaches for her hand. "You ready to get going? It's getting late."

She nods. "Ready."

They say their goodbyes, and when the door closes behind them, Heather gets a sour look on her face.

"What's wrong?" I ask.

She shakes her head. "I don't know; something isn't right. He's hiding something."

I groan. "Don't get into that. It's none of our business."

"He's hiding something," she says again, glaring at me. "Something bad."

"I said leave it alone." My voice lowers. "Just let them be. Worry about *us*—not them."

Her eyes narrow. "You *know* something."

"I don't know anything."

She sits in the chair Oliver was in and shakes my arm. "Tell me."

"He knows about the marriage," I blurt out. "He knows."

She gasps and the air in the room gets stagnant. I don't know what's worse: having Oliver know how I treated Julie, or him knowing I had to trick her into marrying me when all he had to do was ask once. I'll admit, that part pisses me off a bit. Things just seem to *happen* for him; everything I've seen since we crossed paths validates the fact that things just come easy for him…for *everything*.

It's hard not to be jealous of a guy like that.

"Well, is he going to tell Julie he knows?" She narrows her eyes at me again. "You two looked pretty chummy when we walked in just now…did you tell him to shut his mouth and let it get taken care of?"

I nod. "Something like that. He's not going to let her know he knows. He told me that much."

She exhales softly. "Good. Julie and I had a good time in the cafeteria—we were laughing and it felt like we were headed in a good direction. I don't want Oliver to screw that up because he can't let anyone else near her."

I laugh. "Let's just worry about us for a minute, okay?" Worry fills her eyes and I know I've said the wrong thing. "What's wrong?"

I take her hand in mine and pull her to the bed with me. I'm just bruised and fractured, nothing really major, so it doesn't hurt as much as I think it will when she snuggles in beside me. She carefully puts her arm over my stomach and breathes in deep, something she does when she's satisfied and sleepy. I smile and kiss the top of her head, feeling her grip the side of my gown.

"Nothing is wrong," I say. "I just don't want to lose focus on us when we're trying to win over our new friends. Oliver is going to be a bigger challenge, but Julie will take care of that, I'm sure. I'm glad you two had fun down there."

Heather smiles against the fabric of the gown. "We did. It was nice not having to try so hard for once." She sits up and stares into my eyes, a serious look on her face. "Do you think we'll ever get married?"

I nearly choke. "Why are you asking that?"

She shrugs. "Just wondering. I mean, I'm definitely not ready right *now*, and we made that pact to be together for a year, but…I don't know. Sometimes I fantasize."

"You do?"

"Well, yeah. Of course I do. Don't you?"

I want to say the right thing here, but I'm not going to lie to her.

Do it, Brandon. Say what she wants to hear.

"I—uh, yeah, maybe sometimes."

Her laugh fills the room and she snuggles back into her place on my stomach. "You're such a bad liar. I can see right through you. It's okay if you're not there yet. I'm not angry."

"You're not?"

"No." Her voice gets low and she yawns. "There's a lifetime of things I can get mad at you for. If I pouted my lips and threw a fit every time I don't like what you have to say, well…there's really no point in being together, because how can we be happy?"

Jesus. This woman knows how to tug at my heartstrings.

"I love you," I whisper, and my eyes pop open so wide the air stings them.

She lifts her head slowly and looks at me. "What?"

Oh, shit.

I clear my throat. "I—uh, well…I love you."

I wait for something to happen.

She starts to cry but wipes her tears before they fall down her cheeks. "I love you too."

Well. There it is.

What are the rules of love again? I lost my way with Julie. I broke all the rules of making her happy.

It's not going to happen again.

TWENTY-SEVEN
OLIVER

THE HEADLIGHTS SHINE on the front of Staci's townhouse as she opens the door and waves Julie inside. I can feel Julie's hesitation just by sitting next to her; I know she just wants to forget everything and move on with our lives.

I can't do that.

I love her more than myself.

I can't be with her right now.

Not when I'm lying to her and she's lying to me.

My head hurts so bad from thinking about it that I hardly hear her voice when she turns to face me and takes my hand into hers, intertwining our fingers together. "Did you hear me?"

I clear my throat. "No, sorry."

She giggles. "I asked when you'd be back for me."

I want to wrap her in my arms and never let her go.

"Whenever you're ready," I tell her. "You just call me and I'll be here."

She climbs into my lap with little effort and I hold

her against me as tightly as I can manage. Staci notices and shuts the door to give us some privacy. My fingers run through her hair and I know I have to let her go, but I can't make myself release the grip I have on her.

"Do you hate me for this?"

Oh, Jesus.

How can she even ask me that?

My lips find hers and I smash them together, tugging at the ends of her hair. She eases into me, tears running down her cheeks and making our lips salty as they glide against each other.

"There's nothing—" I kiss her lips and she giggles, making my dick harden underneath her weight. "—that you can ever do—" Her thighs grip the sides of my legs and I run my hands down her back, stopping at the roundness of her ass and cupping it inside my hands. "—to make me hate you."

Her laugh sets it off for me.

"Take me home," she breathes into my ear. "We can deal with this shit later."

I try so hard to let her go, I really do.

"That's the problem: We always put our shit on the back burner until it's too late. Let's just take a few days to get our heads straight and have dinner to talk about everything. I'm not going anywhere, baby."

"Me, either." She pouts. "But if you want me to go, I'll go."

I stop her from sliding off of me. "Don't get it twisted. I want you every single way I can have you."

Her laugh makes my dick harder.

"I know that." She winks. "But you're right. We're always so stupid with things, we need to slow down and do it right. Because when I marry you..." She presses her lips to mine again and moans lightly into my mouth. "It's going to be the best day of my life."

My heart stops beating.

"I can't believe I found you again. I can't believe you're real," I whisper, brushing her hair from her face. "You have no idea how badly I can't lose you again."

Staci flashes the porch light for Julie to hurry up and come inside. "She's waiting for you. Go have your girl time and do girl things. Get ready for what's to come."

She laughs again and slides off of me, rubbing her thighs against my already-hard dick as she passes. I try to think about something else to make it go away.

"And what's that?"

I clear my throat and roll down the window, letting in the much-needed chilly October air. "We're laying it all out on the table, all our secrets. We're moving into the new house and we're going to start planning our wedding. In that order."

She makes a sexy agreeing noise. "Yes, sir."

I have to get her out of here before I change my mind.

"Oh, one more thing before I go." She finds my eyes in the darkness. "I want you to go visit your mother at the jail."

I have to stop myself from laughing at her. "You can't be serious."

"She needs you...you didn't see her at that cabin, Oliver. She wants out of that life, she just doesn't know how."

I shake my head. "No fucking way. She's not coming anywhere near you."

"Please? For me? Just go talk to her. Just you and her."

Her eyes are full of wonder and hope, so it's hard to tell her no. "Okay."

She puts her hand on the door to step out, but before she does, her eyes meet mine again and a fire burns in them. "Promise?"

I nod. "I promise. I'll go in the morning."

"Thank you. I love you." She kisses my cheek and gets out of the car before I can change my mind.

Anything for you, Julie.

She waves at me from the doorway and Staci gives me the finger before she closes the door behind them. I think about how we came to all of this all night, and as I drive to the police station and park in the visitor lot the next day.

Casey begged me to be his wingman to capture Nora.

I picked Julie up and felt something for her; I didn't know then that she's the girl with the electric eyes from my past.

Julie cut her leg and I whisked her to the hospital, where I realized I was in love with her.

She left me and then came back to me.

She told me she loves me.

She found out she might be pregnant and I almost died rushing to her after a fight.

My mother tried to extort money from me by getting to Julie…

There we go.

There's the hatred I have for that wretched woman.

Even as I sit in a small room with a large two-way

mirror behind me, the hate I have for her radiates into the room and makes it warm.

"Son," I hear her faint voice say as the door opens. "What are you doing here?"

Here we go.

"I promised Julie I would come." I watch her fragile body walk around the table in handcuffs, and the orange jumpsuit is three sizes too big for her. "She sees something in you that I know isn't there."

Veronica cries. "I know she does. She's a good girl."

Well, this is unexpected.

"She is. I promised her I would come, but I don't know what she wants me to do. She thinks that you have regrets, that you were forced into kidnapping her for money. You and I both know that's a fucking lie."

She doesn't look surprised. "It's not a full lie. I do regret it. I regret letting Mac pull me into something like this for the millionth time."

"You've done this before?"

She shakes her head, her brittle once-blonde hair falling in her face. "Not something like this. I'm really fucking sorry, kid. I'm a real messed-up mom, huh?"

I cringe. "Don't call yourself that. You're not a mother."

"Right, that woman who raised you is your mother, yeah? Marva? You know she isn't who she says she is, don'tcha?"

I clasp my hands together to keep from slamming them in anger on the table. "I know who she is—I know she's my grandmother. You don't have any ammunition to use against me, you know that, right? I know about your drug habits, I know Casey is my half-brother, I know Vic had an affair with Mrs. Atchley that produced my father. I know it all."

She snickers. "It seems that you do. Does *Julie* know it all, though?"

My teeth grind together. "*Don't* fucking say her name."

"Grow up," she snaps. "Do you think I *want* to be in here? Do you think I *want* to be this way? I started out just like Julie: young and naïve and in love with a Jackson boy. I never claimed to be a perfect mother or even a good person…but I'm *done* living this way."

I crack my knuckles. "As far as I'm concerned, you can rot in here."

In place of a tantrum, she inserts a knowing nod between us and finally looks me directly in the eye. "I know I've lost my chance at being a mother, but maybe you can help me be a human?"

"What do you mean?"

Her gaze fixes on the glass window behind me. "Send me to rehab, help me get away from Mac. I'm finally at a point where I want to break free. Julie is right: I *didn't* want to kidnap her. Mac forced me into thinking it was the only way. I found Casey, I talked to him. He declined my offer. I needed someone who hated you enough to help me, and Mary just sort of popped out of nowhere while you were in the hospital. I overheard her talking to someone about you and it clicked."

I growl. "You're *not* helping your case."

Her bony fingers rise in the air. "Let me finish. I'm absolutely disgusted with myself and I'm ready to follow the rules now. I'm ready to follow *your* rules, whatever you set them to be for me."

I laugh. "I'm not responsible for you."

"Maybe you should be. I *need* you, son."

This isn't happening.

"You can't be serious. You *actually* think I'd do this?"

Her cough is deep and rough. "I want to be some kind of mother, Ollie Bear."

My muscles tense. "*Don't* call me that." Her gaze meets mine and I know she wants an answer. "I have to talk to Julie about it. We're going to need to think about it."

For a long, long fucking time.

BEFORE YOU GO...

If you enjoyed my book please take a second to leave a short review. These reviews help me as an author be found by other amazing readers like you.

Thank you so much! :)

ABOUT THE AUTHOR

I live in Kansas City with my husband and our son, Ryker. I have been writing for over a decade, I started out writing songs and music and then realized that those stories were too short for the tales I wanted to tell, so I switched to writing books and articles, which then blossomed into writing contemporary romance and fantasy novels. I am in indecisive person at heart, I love coffee more than a Gilmore girl and my most favorite time to write and create is during a rainstorm (with coffee!).

I love hearing from those who read my stories, I love to hear how much people relate to each character and how they are rooting for their favorites to succeed! I don't only create stories, I create entirely new worlds and people that come to life!

Wattpad
https://www.wattpad.com/user/NBenson